THE 2ND COMING
OF ORLANDO ROCK

THE 2ND COMING OF ORLANDO ROCK

BY

WILLIAM KAUFMANN

ACKNOWLEDGMENTS

WRITING A BOOK IS NO small project. There were many people who contributed by listening and encouraging me through the emotional challenges of completing this work. I'd especially like to thank Tanya Brooking and Claire Isenthal, my writing group partners, for their patience, samurai eyes, and many helpful suggestions. I love you guys. And thanks to my readers, Peter Arnstein and Larry Rodich, for their time and thoughtful insights. Thanks to the many teachers at the Literary Loft in Minneapolis, particularly Peter Geye, teacher extraordinaire and Minnesota Book Award winner, for his inspiring classes. My heartfelt appreciation goes to Noah Kaufmann for his illustrious book cover design. I can't leave out Sarah from Mirador Publishing, who held my hand through the whole process of bringing this work to print, and thoroughly answered so many emails. Such a pleasure to work with. Most of all, I thank Cynthia Mosedale, my wife and partner in life and the studio, for listening to the many versions of this story and for her forthright comments.

"There is no greater agony than bearing an untold story inside you." — Maya Angelou. I stand on the shoulders of all those writers who felt that agony and found the persistence and courage to write what was inside them.

CHAPTER 1

THEY FLY SOUTH TO FALL IN LOVE

I WAS AT THE COUNTER buying dark roast coffee for both of us when the cops arrested her. I met Madison at the Save-the-Geese protest and by chance we met again at Love's, a bohemian coffee shop, after police broke up the gathering. From across the crowded room, I watched a broad-shouldered woman wearing a white shirt with a silver badge pinned to the pocket step behind her. Two officers approached on either side. Madison turned, and an argument ensued. The roar of protesters chattering and baristas shouting orders made it impossible to hear their conversation. The big woman jerked her off the stool, cuffed her, and efficiently led Madison curbside. She glanced over at me—eyes forlorn. Customers in the packed shop booed. I pushed my way onto the street, but by the time I got there, they had shoved her into the back seat. With hands fastened behind her, she gave me a desperate smile as I looked through the window, then mouthed the words, 'the note.' I tapped my pocket. It was still there. The bulky female officer warned me to stay back or be arrested. She slid into the driver's seat. The other two got in back, one on each side of their captive. The crowd was restless, and considering everything that had happened at the protest, the police turned on their flashers, most likely as a warning, and sped away. I stood on the sidewalk, shocked and breathless.

Madison had literally run into me at the rally that Sunday morning in a park close to the Uptown area of Minneapolis. Sounds of guitars mixed with drumming and an occasional 'leave them alone' chant floated over the crowd. It was a merry affair. I laid on my thin blanket, sun shining, eyelids drooping, cotton ball clouds drifting in the cerulean sky, when a foot connected with my leg. Wham! A woman toppled on me, her body landing square on my chest. My eyes jolted open. She pushed herself up on her hands, clothing hanging like a rag from her shoulders. A rosy scent wafted about her and long, wavy, auburn hair swished over my face. I bent my neck up and found myself staring down her threadbare sweatshirt, a naked view between her breasts all the way to her mid-section. When I looked up, intense turquoise eyes gazed into mine.

"It's not the Grand Canyon," she said.

"Never been there," I retorted, "but I'm reconsidering." She smiled and rolled off, sitting cross-legged on my blanket.

"Do you know why geese fly south?"

"Hey. Didn't you just trip over me?"

She collected the bottle of wine that had fallen from her grip. After a swig, she offered the bottle and said, "Friends?"

I took the bottle. "If that's an apology, I accept. Friends."

Her spicy cinnamon lip balm greased the rim, the wine dark and sweet. The magic and curiosity of her eyes danced over me, her smile endearing. She wore paint-splattered baggy pants and ragged sneakers. Not urban hippie, not vagabond, definitely artist. Red lettering on her shirt read, 'You can't save yourself… by yourself.'

"So, why do geese fly south?" I wiped off my burning lips.

"It's not what you think."

"I'm thinking genetic." I laughed.

"Do you really want to know?" Her smile tilted in a mischievous line; eyebrows raised in a dare.

"By all means, enlighten me." I took another swig and handed the bottle back to her.

She leaned over and whispered in my ear—something I would remember for the rest of my life. "They fly south… to fall in love." Then she bit my ear. My heart caught fire.

"Ouch!"

"You said, by all means."

As I turned, our noses almost touched. Her wine laced breath fruity, eyes clear, lips wet and seductive. My stomach floated as gravity seemed to let go its binding force. At the same time, drums beat in unison, cops' whistles blew and an agitated crowd jumped up, dumping their snacks, leaving half-eaten sandwiches on the ground.

No one expected the line of troopers that marched over the hill. They came full force, helmets and face shields, batons raised, shoulder to shoulder, tromping over blankets and forcing everyone to move back. Park rangers followed with their nets in hand. We sprang to our feet. Geese ran wild, honking with the force of air horns. The assembly moved like a slippery mud slide and I reached out to take her hand, but the surging crowd drew her downstream in a different direction from me.

"What's your name?" I stood on tiptoes, shouting above the chanting crowd.

She waved. "Wanna go with me?"

"Where?" I cried out.

"Follow the geese," she yelled back; her voice barely audible over chaos.

The river of bodies swallowed her up and dragged her away. I fought my way through the mass, then circled around, but didn't find her. I let out an exasperated 'argh!' How could the world turn so suddenly from the outside in, to a place I'd kept in waiting, a place I had been ignoring? At that point, I didn't know her name. Yes, I'll fly south with you… and the geese.

Rangers netted birds while troopers arrested scores of protestors. A block away, I stopped, out of breath and ready to give up the search. My ear stung. When I touched it, a drop of blood colored my fingertip. Not sure what direction to head, a leafleteer wearing a duck hat thrust a flyer into my hand. Love's, a nearby coffee shop, offered a special cinnamon drink.

A riotous atmosphere saturated the place as protesters poured in. Raised garage doors opened the front, tables spread inside and out onto the sidewalk. People crammed five and six together, talking excitedly about the police intrusion while cups clanked, and the hiss of espresso machines charged the air. A long line at the counter overwhelmed baristas. The throng was as loud as the honking geese, and I was about to leave when a hand shot in the air. "Over here," a voice yelled. It was her.

She sat at a table against the wall just inside the garage door. From her paint-splattered outfit and long legs to the holes in her sneakers, everything about her fascinated me. My heart thumped as she pulled her bag off an empty stool.

"I almost had to kill someone saving that seat," she said. "I was afraid you wouldn't come." She flipped dangling wavy hair over her shoulder and slid a cup in my direction. "I bought you a coffee."

I swung onto the stool. "Thanks. Dark roast, black. Good guess."

"You're a potter, aren't you?"

I raised my eyebrows. "How did you know? Have we met before... at a show or somewhere else?"

"Art shows? Never. The dry mud hanging from your forearm isn't paint, and the white stuff under your fingernails isn't dirt. It's clay. What's your name?"

"Willi," I answered.

"William, Wilhelm, or Wilhelmina? Birth name, nickname, or made-up name?"

"William August Moses Steuben if you want the full name. And yours?"

"Madison." She extended her pinky, and we shook. "Your name is a mouthful."

"Yeah," I touched my ear. "Speaking of mouthful, I was thinking about a rabies shot."

She laughed. "Should I even it out and do the other one too?" When I mockingly turned my head, she placed her hand on my knee, leaned forward, and kissed my cheek, a kiss that lingered long enough for her coffee breath to filter into my nose and her tongue to wet my unshaven face. Then she bit the other ear.

"Ow!" My hand jerked upwards. "Hmm… no blood."

That side-armed smile appeared on her face. "Should I give it another try?"

"Your cup is almost empty. How about another coffee and a scone instead?"

"I'd like that… but scones are sold out."

"There was a fresh tray in the display cabinet when I came in. I'll get one."

She suppressed a smile, reached into her bag, extracted a sketch pad, and flipped it open. She'd drawn a detail of our table, including the pattern made by wood grain, a crack in the brick wall, and the painting hanging behind us of a farmhand picking coffee beans on a mountain slope. The drawing included a plate with a croissant and my pullover hat next to it. There was no way she could've drawn this in such a short time or known I'd wear that hat.

"That's amazing!" What I wanted to say was impossible.

"It's an almond croissant. Scones sold out."

"When did you draw this?"

"My secret… for now. Better go before croissants sell out too."

I slid off the stool.

"Willi, wait a minute." She took out a pencil and wrote furiously on a notepad, then ripped the page out and stuffed it into my shirt pocket. "Don't read it till tonight."

With a short laugh, I headed for the counter and ordered a coffee and a scone, then stepped aside to wait. That's when the police had moved in and arrested her. What I saw was more like a kidnapping.

AS I WATCHED THE SQUAD car race away, a short stocky man approached me.

"You look like you just had your wallet heisted." He wore baggy pants and a suit coat that looked as though it once belonged to a skid row junkie.

"Name's Jimmy." He put out his hand. "I saw everything that happened. I'm a lawyer and those cops made mistakes. Big mistakes. No Miranda, cuffs cutting her wrists, arresting officer's badge was from out of town, no jurisdiction. I think I can help."

"Yeah, sure." I didn't know what to say. "Any help would be appreciated."

He gave me his card. "Tell your girlfriend to call me."

The man didn't look like he could dress himself, much less be a lawyer. He walked away, and I stuffed the card into my pocket.

Back at the table, Madison's sketchbook still lay open. The barista had delivered a croissant, placing it next to my hat, exactly like the picture she'd drawn. Astounding! I flipped the page. What I saw was mind-bendingly impossible. The portrait was of a customer I met at an outdoor art fair in Oklahoma the week before. The man had taken refuge in my booth, totally drenched from a wicked storm that ruined the show. It was photo perfect, something that would've taken weeks to finish, but there was no indication when or why she drew it. His name was Orlando Rock, a cowboy who came out of nowhere, pointed at the most expensive piece in my booth and said, I'll take it, without looking at the nine-hundred-dollar price. That one sale miraculously covered trip expenses. The drawing included water dripping from his wide rim hat. That Madison would know him was improbable, that she would know it was raining, impossible.

I stared at the drawing and gasped. What the hell? No way she could have seen or met him at a show six hundred miles away. My stomach floated for a moment, as though riding on a looped roller coaster. Both drawings were astonishing!

I grabbed the pad, my hat, and the croissant and headed out. As I passed the checkout counter, the barista waved. "Hey, sorry, we were out of scones." I gave her a brief smile, then walked back to the park.

Rangers had already penned hundreds of birds in wire enclosures. A maintenance crew gathered trampled blankets filling large plastic trash bags. I sat on a bench, mind spinning, and nibbled on the almond-flavored pastry while sparrows feasted on the crumbs. She was truly remarkable, and just thinking about her tickled my insides. When a mosquito bit my ear, I smiled—thrice bitten. I loved the lightness of her being, the playfulness in her eyes, and my stinging earlobe, all remained as impressions, like a thumbprint in clay. I took the note out of my pocket. On top of the wrinkled paper, a remarkably good sketch of a goose flew above the words, 'North side, Lake of the Isles, 4 pm. Thursday. Bring wine. Do you remember why geese fly south?'

That was the day I fell in love.

CHAPTER 2

THE ART EXPERIMENT

SUNDAY TO THURSDAY WAS FOUR days of torture. I had no address, no phone, no last name. Madison had told me she was a painter and part-time instructor at the Art Institute. I thought about calling the school but decided against. I buried myself in studio work, preparing for an upcoming art fair in Chicago. While living in Japan, I had come under the spell of a curmudgeonly old teacher who passed his passion for clay to me. Perhaps I was lucky. At an early age, I fell into what would become my life and my vocation. So, I worked and tried not to think too far ahead. When Thursday rolled around, I bought a bottle of sweet Redblend and headed back to the park. It was a warm, lazy afternoon, strangely silent, with all the geese gone. Madison was there, waiting on an oak shaded bench. A simple tie held waves of auburn hair back, a blue sweatshirt with Picasso in small print over her right breast. She looked different.

I had thought about her all week and was nervous, but glad she was there.

"Hey. Been here long?"

"Long enough to see two good luck white squirrels." She took a deep breath. "I suppose you want an explanation?"

I sat next to her and stretched out my legs. "You mean your black and white taxi service from the coffee shop? Only when you're ready to talk about it. A lawyer gave me his card, said he could help." I gave her Jimmy's card.

"I could use a lawyer." She glanced at the card and put it in her bag. "I think I'll hire him."

"By the way, you left this." I handed her the sketchbook. "The drawing of the cowboy... amazing."

"Oh, thanks for picking that up. It's important."

"He was my best customer at a show in Oklahoma." I didn't want to sound like an interrogator, but I was more than curious about the drawing.

"Hmm. That explains it."

"Explains what?"

"Why I drew him."

"You've met him?"

"Never saw him before, but he's supposed to be part of this."

"Part of what?" My forehead furled.

"Part of what's coming."

I raised my eyebrows. "Toward you or me?"

"Both."

"Ha! So, you can foretell the future?"

"The future's a big place, Willi. Some of us can see the pieces."

"Okay. How did you draw a picture of a man I met, and you've never seen?"

"He's a sizeable piece of what's coming."

"Oh, and how do you know this?"

She held back a smile, eyes dazzling, and kissed me on the cheek. "My secret."

"So... am I a part of this future?"

"Most Certainly. A big part, I hope." She touched my ear. "All healed. What did you bring?"

I showed her the wine.

"I love Redblend." Her face glowed. She pulled out little triangles of individually wrapped Brie and a loaf of freshly baked French bread. "Let's walk a little and then eat."

A three-mile tarred path followed the shoreline of a man-made lake with two small islands in the middle. On a park bench under giant oaks, we passed time and the bottle of wine, snacking on cheese, pulling chunks of bread from the hard-crusted loaf. We shared our histories and work as artists, but she said nothing about her arrest or how she knew the cowboy. Couples on paddle boards glided by, leaving velvet ripples across the lake's surface. A few bikers speed-pedaled on the bike path. She wanted to know more about my apprenticeship in Japan. I wanted to know more about her time in Paris. When she laughed, she'd bump against me, and I took her hand. Her fingers willingly interlaced with mine. Our common thread was art and laughter. She was easy to be with, like a good throwing clay. It felt like we had known each other for a long time. By the end of our walk, we were into advanced chemistry, the kind that creates deep friendships... and love affairs.

As the sun set and tree shadows stretched into elongated alien figures, we returned to the same bench we met at. The evening was just beginning and neither of us wanted it to end.

She turned to me and said, "How about an art experiment?"

"Sounds interesting. What kind of art experiment?"

"It's something I've been working on."

"Here?"

"Let's go to my studio and find out what art is."

"Ha! And what is art?"

"It's never what you think. But I promise, it will be memorable and maybe... we'll discover something about each other."

Sparks jumped between our eyes. "Can you give me a hint what this experiment is about?"

"It's about stepping into unknown territory, Willi. For both of us." Her hand fell into mine, fingers intertwined and pressed together, a touch that radiated with affection. We finished the wine and walked to her car. My heart pounded and my palms sweat. I didn't know what I was getting into.

•

WE DROVE TO THE FORD building, an old, converted warehouse for artists a few blocks west of downtown Minneapolis. Her studio was on the third floor via a freight elevator with a slated wooden gate. The long, wide hallway floor creaked, oil fumes permeated the air. Lights hung by chains from a high ceiling, barely illuminating our way. Various studios had signs by their doors, 'Twister Glass,' 'Photography by Pin Hole,' 'The Un-art Art Studio,' and many more. Her door, made of corrugated metal, slid open on an overhead rail, a simple sign with a crossed out twenty-nine tacked to the surface.

"Why the line through twenty-nine?" I asked.

"Worst year of my life," she answered. "And don't ask. At least not now."

Inside, ten-foot windows faced the city incinerator across the street, providing painterly light. Oil-stained wooden planks made up the floor, knicks and scratches embedded in a yellowed poly coating. The tang of acrylic paint saturated the air. Large canvases, mostly abstract montages suggesting human-like forms, hung on the walls. Paint cans of all sizes and partially squeezed tubes of different colors, along with many kinds of brushes, filled a tall stand-alone shelf. A large drawing table placed next to the windows had two extended arm lights attached, and a paint-splattered laundry sink set in the corner. She worked standing, sitting, and on the floor. When I asked her about a trapeze hanging from two massive wooden pillars, she said painting was like sex—it afforded all positions. Magnificent human figure drawings filled her sketchbook. She could draw any pose. Explosions of color and form defined her exploratory and unconventional style, displaying the power released from every brush stroke. I stood overwhelmed and awed.

As I wandered around the large room, she picked out a dry brush and drew it up her arm. "You ever work naked?"

"Sure. On a hot day without a shirt, but never like... all naked. How about you?"

"I often work with no clothes on. It's liberating. I've been experimenting with something new." She ushered me to a canvas splotched with paint.

"You laid on the canvas?"

"I attempted to paint my body, but as you can see, it didn't work. The colors blotched. I needed a model... or a volunteer." Her eyebrows raised. "Wanna try it?"

"What, you mean now?"

"You wanted to know what art is, right? Now's the moment."

"If I say yes, what am I getting into?"

"To start, take off your clothes." She had a mischievous smile on her face.

"What?"

"You'll be a perfect subject, Willi. Good body type."

"You've never seen my whole body."

"You'd be surprised what a painter sees. Take off your clothes."

And so it began, a spontaneous decision and... I didn't know what. While I undressed, she laid a plastic tarp on the floor and rolled a seven-foot-tall board backed canvas onto it. "Stand in front of the canvas," she instructed.

"Aren't you taking off your clothes?" I raised my eyebrows. "You know, that primal thing."

"This isn't about sex or some fantasy, it's deeper. Much deeper. You'll get used to being naked. If you get chilled while I set up, there's a robe over there." She pointed.

"You sound experienced."

"I also model for an advanced drawing class. After a few minutes I'm hardly in the room." She tramped over to a standup locker, kicked off her Sketchers, slipped out of hip-hugger jeans, and peeled off her sweatshirt. The line from her hips to her neck resembled the curve of a Persian vase. She slipped on loose cotton pants and a paint-splattered white shirt, no shoes.

She approached, taking in my whole body, her eyes like searchlights.

"Naked can be embarrassing at the start," she said. "You won't be naked for long. You'll see."

My body tingled as she circled the tarp. She placed a light on a pullup stand so its beam angled from the right side, then gathered a sketch pad, brushes and three buckets of paint—blue, yellow, and red.

"Put your left hand on your hip. Fingers down. Now the other arm... loosen it, let it hang free by your side. Okay. Good. Really good. Don't move."

She sat cross-legged on the floor with the sketch pad and began drawing. "Not overly muscular, but fit. Nice smooth stomach, not much hair, no fat. I like the curve of your shoulders. You're well-proportioned. Swimmer's legs, a bit more than half your body height. Knees not too knobby. You should model." Her pencil never stopped moving. "Now, flip that long hair back over the left shoulder. Perfect." Ten minutes later, she announced, "Done! You're not a practiced model, but you held still enough to get the essentials."

"Can I see it?"

"No. We'll lose momentum. You can see it later." She put the pad aside and picked up a long carpenter's pencil. "Let's get to work."

She started by dividing my body in half with a line of blue tape that stretched from my forehead to the base of my penis. Then she gently backed me up until my butt touched the canvas behind me. "Be still," she said. I could feel her body heat close to mine as a long, cold pencil ran up my side. Pulling a step stool next to me, she rested one hand on my shoulder, traced my head, noting where my ears set, made marks indicating eye position, then continued down my right arm. Her touch was electric, my forehead sweat, and armpits dampened.

"I like your scent." She stepped off the stool. "Orbis, isn't it?"

She was so right, it made me smile. "And yours is rosy, a subtle fragrance, perhaps Giorgio Rose?"

She laughed. "Peking Rose, my deodorant." Fingers slid gently to my chest, pressing slightly as the pencil ran down my side. Her palm was warm, not sweaty. Touch gentle and stimulating. Her hand slid to my stomach as she traced down my hip to the outside of my leg. The lead came back vertically on the inside of my right thigh. She pushed up my testicles to complete the turn at the crotch. A bolt of energy shot through my solar plexus, and I took a deep breath.

"It's really cheap deodorant." She looked up; a faint smile crossed her lips. "Made in Indonesia." She released my testicles and continued down my inside left thigh, traveling to the foot. When she finished, she stared directly into my eyes. I had never seen such an intense blue.

"Let's begin," she commanded.

Grabbing a wide horsehair brush, she plunged it into the yellow bucket, pulled it out dripping. "Close your eyes." Starting from my forehead, she stroked down the left side of my face, carefully wiping paint from my eyelid and inner lip with her little finger. My whole body shook from the shock of cold yellow paint. More paint, then more long strokes down my neck and the left side of my chest, brush hairs against chest hairs sent chisels down my side. She moved deftly to the left of the belly button, continuing downward to my groin, skirting my genitals.

"Don't worry… I'll get back to the boys," then continued down my left leg. Side muscles reacted reflexively to the prickly brush, making them contract.

"You're ticklish, aren't you?" The yellow brush passed quickly over my twitching side. "I like ticklish." Each pore vibrated as she unhurriedly dragged the bristles across my body. I watched her fill in the spaces, using my body as her canvas. The brush became an extension of her hand. My skin shivered under her touch.

Madison looked up. "How're you doing?"

"Nirvana."

She smiled, turned me around, and did the left backside in the same manner, using long downward strokes in slippery yellow paint. She carefully ran the brush down the groove between the buttocks. Not only was I her canvas, but she explored my contours.

Blue and red brushes were sable and silky smooth. Starting with indigo, she painted my left arm, then faced me forward. With a brush in each hand, she dabbed over the yellow with quick thrusts of different colors. Her whole body swayed with the strokes, arms slashed downward and to the side, on the angle and perpendicular, sometimes in long flowing movement, other times in short bursts. Paint flew in all directions, but never on my right side. Blues transformed yellow into streaked shades of green with different values, red crossed blue creating deep purple and luscious lavenders. She made hundreds of quick strokes, then lifted her arms like a conductor merging with the score, baton raised, movement unrestrained, sliced downward on a beat only she could hear. Her eyes were devilish, her drive feverish, and at some point, she took off her shirt, breasts swaying with her motion. On long strokes she took in a deep breath, on short ones she puffed out. Velvety brushes moved paint like whipped cream, energy burst within her movements. She painted as naturally as light passing through a prism, releasing color unencumbered and free with no effort.

Stopping suddenly, she turned inward and painted a red stripe from her neck down between her breasts to her belly button, then splashed two yellow lines across her cheeks. She turned me around and went at my backside with the same fierceness, which made me quiver. Hundreds of quick smacks slashed my left side, under my arm, over my hip, slapping the buttocks, and down to my foot. The energy of the bristles extracted an electrifying sensation from deep within my body.

With hands on her hips and paint dripping down her pants, her fury receded. Turning me around, she inspected her work. The hint of a smile crossed her face, then spontaneous lunges added more color. She painted her one breast with straight yellow strokes, the other in blue circles.

She folded her arms and stared. After a long contemplation, she said, "Okay, this may hurt a bit." She stripped the tape off my body. Leaving the brushes on the tarp, she dragged a cheap six-foot mirror in front of me.

Half my body was a montage of integrated colors. The other half, untouched. My bisected body shivered. I stood dumbfounded, looking at the transformation. "Who is that person?"

"That's you, Willi. The part you haven't connected with yet, the part you don't know about, yet."

"Oh? And you see this?"

"I do. Your cowboy customer saw it too."

"Ha! I love that." I thought it was a joke. What wasn't a joke was my reflection in the mirror. I could hardly believe so much was inside me. "So, are you finished?"

"Should I be?" She added black lines under her eyes.

"How do you know when you're finished?"

"You don't 'know'. I listen to my fingers, my eyes, ears, all my senses. They tell me when to stop. But finished? That's a different connection."

She opened a new can of white paint and placed it on the tarp. Using a narrow brush with an angled flat edge, she began with my genitals, swishing the loaded brush from side to side.

"Did you know that true white reflects ninety-six percent of all sunlight colors?" She ignored the stimulation and continued upwards with a steady one-inch stripe to my belly button, stroking up my chest, over the neck, to the chin and across my mouth. Wetting her little finger, she again wiped my inner lip, then continued over my nose and up the middle of my forehead to the hairline. Never had I experienced an intimacy that reveled in such sensualness and freedom. My nakedness transformed into textures imprinted by brush bristles; vitality expressed in her spontaneous thrusts. Lowering her arms, she circled, using impulsive bursts to add accents to my already colorful left side. Adding white stripes to her face and sides transformed her into a warrior painter.

Using a smaller brush, she decorated my fingers in rainbow colors. When I ran them over her long auburn hair, she responded by dipping her hand into the paint can, streaking her hair white, then plunged her fingers into blue, stepped on the stool, and stroked down the left side of my long blondish hair.

Hand and brush had become united, revealing the raw energy of life she saw within me…. It was exposure like Eve in the garden, realizing there was more to that apple than she thought. Artist and object became one. Shivers rocketed through my body.

"It's alright, Willi. I'm having the same feeling. You're truly beautiful." Madison read my mind.

"Can I move yet?" I asked.

"Not yet!"

Wiping her hands on her pants, she rolled a tripod with a camera in front of me.

"I'll need pictures to finish the canvas."

"Ya, but no posts on social media!"

"Why not?" She was serious, but it made me laugh.

She took her time snapping photos, getting close-ups and different angles. She turned me around, examining her work. "I didn't expect this to be so fun."

I was floating, as though I had entered a different universe. Her universe. The exchange was deeply personal, artist and subject revealed in a strange and mystifying dance, delving into the unknown, delighting in the said and unsaid.

After photos and more inspection, she stood back. "Done—for now, anyway. Let's clean up."

She slid a metal washtub from under the sink. A hose snaked up the wall, slumping over a circular frame, one end connected to the faucet.

"It's much easier to get this paint off while wet. I've learned from experience. Don't worry about splash, we'll mop up later."

Taking my hand, she led me across the room. About halfway, I twirled her into my arms and squished our bodies together. Like accepting an invitation to dance, she put her arms around me and pulled in tight, imprinting her body on mine. The paint squirted from between us. She caught globs in her fingers and ran them down our sides and painted my face. Slowly releasing her arms, she slid her body across mine, dragging wet slimy paint, colors smearing and streaking, then pulled away. With the right side of her body mopped with color, she drew her fingers across herself horizontally, making stripes. She handed me a towel.

"Wipe your hands. I need a few pictures of this." She slid out of her pants, fingerpainted her legs, then posed in front of the camera. She wanted shots from all angles. When she was satisfied with the photo shoot, we laid the canvas on the floor. She laid the front side down next to the outline of my body.

"I want you to press my body into the canvas," she instructed. Like a printer inking the press, I pressed her body into the hard surface, leaving my handprints all over her backside and down her legs. With a helping hand, she peeled herself off.

"Okay, now your turn."

I laid supine over my outline. She lowered the trapeze for support, swung over my body, left a footprint by my side, then stepped on my stomach. Muscles tensed as she walked up and down my torso and legs, pressing me into the surface, leaving toe prints on my painted front side. Satisfied that my imprint was secure, she used the trapeze to swing off the canvas. When I started to get up, she shouted, "Wait!" Lowering the trapeze, I grabbed the handle and pulled myself up. She slid the canvas out from under me then walked across it leaving her colored footprints. We stood the painting vertical, the imprinted figures were next to each other. With an oversized sumi-e brush, she painted a black line on one side of her impression, giving it curvature, then cleaned up the white line dividing my body in half. Her head bobbed in satisfaction as she stood back and absorbed the painting.

"It's amaz…"

"Shhh… this is only the beginning." Using a smaller brush and quick simple strokes, the blurry outline of male and female figures emerged as if pulled into life by the color within them.

She grabbed my hand and dragged it across her paint smeared stomach and added random handprints on the canvas.

We stood next to each other, looking at the collage of abstract human forms and color. She moved left, then right, folded her arms against her painted splattered chest and stared.

"What are you thinking?" I asked.

"Nothing."

"Nothing?"

"Looking without thinking is called seeing. It also allows me to listen."

"Listen to what?"

"To what the eyes cannot see and the ears cannot hear."

"I don't get it."

"Exactly."

With a smaller brush, she painted in the musculature of her leg, brought out the imprint of her right breast and added form to her head. Deft strokes defined my colorful left side, and an outline completed my right side. With the placement of a few simple lines, something different emerged. Two human forms related by the energy within them. She stepped back.

"Finished for now." She laid the brushes down on the plastic tarp.

"What happens next?"

She laughed. "We're a mess, aren't we?"

When I went to dab the picture with my fingers, she grabbed my wrist. "One cook."

We walked to the washtub, and she pulled a clear plastic curtain to a semi-circle, making for a crude shower. She turned on the faucet. I stepped in. Warm water cascaded over my head and down my shoulders. With a cloth, she wiped paint off my body. The watery mixture ran down my legs looking like rivulets of mix colored blood. She sponged paint away from my eyes, made me raise my arms and took extra time to get paint out of my armpits. After washing, she lathered me with shampoo and gave me a complete cleaning, front and back. I stepped out of the tub, scrubbed clean, and went for the towel.

"Not yet." She stepped into the tub, handing me the washcloth. "My turn."

With a wet towel and a stream of warm water from the hose, I wiped down her arms, across her chest. For a moment she squished my hands against her breasts, then let me wash them. I continued to her stomach and down her legs.

"Why the chain and key around your waist?"

"My secret," she answered.

"Hmm. How many secrets do you have?"

"A few." Her smile compressed.

I continued down to her feet. Her hair hung forward like a dripping mop, eyes closed, a nirvanic smile on her face. She was muscular, and soft, and ticklish. After the paint was mostly off, I used soap, lathering her up, then rinsed her down. There was a slight lavender aroma when she stepped out. Her body glistened, and water droplets ran down her chest and stomach like water runs off a freshly waxed car. I handed her a towel, but she gave it back to me. I toweled her dry. When finished, she toweled me dry. We stood facing each other, naked in a way that went beyond body. She had touched me in an unanticipated and beautiful manner. A visceral way, which revealed something about myself I had never seen before.

"Did I answer your question?" she asked, scrubbing her hair dry.

"What question?"

She smiled. "Perfect answer."

"Are you hungry?"

"I'm starving," she said. "Let's eat."

"How about Chinese takeout at my place?" I suggested.

She pulled a comb through long, wet hair. "I'd love that."

We finished dressing and cleaned up the studio. I called for delivery to my basement apartment.

•

I LIVE IN A ONE-BEDROOM flat, simply decorated. A planter with a large philodendron grew to the ceiling, potted dieffenbachias hung from ceiling hooks. We sat at my two-chair table in a small kitchen and ate with chopsticks. A single light above made us look like an Edward Hopper painting. Auburn hair cascaded over the Picasso sweatshirt offset on her shoulder. She sat with one leg crossed up on the chair, relaxed.

"Madison… I'm like… I'm still floating. It was so amazing. I think it was… I mean, the total experience was…" words stuck in my throat.

"Shhh," she put a finger to my lips. "No words, just be in it, Willi. It's a vibration. Believe me, I feel it too. But say nothing, at least not right now. It's fragile. Too many words chase it away."

The experience had tenderized both of us. My heart sizzled and she gave searing glances as we talked about the difficulties of being artists and the struggle to make a living. After dinner, I opened a bottle of homemade plum wine. Madison settled and got quiet. She took a sip and a deep breath. "I'm ready to talk…"

"About the arrest?"

She tapped the table with her fingernails. "No… something else. Something I've told no one. It has to do with the cowboy and you."

"Okay." I leaned back in the chair, sweet plum wine penetrating my mental capacity. "I'm listening."

She took a sketchpad from her large bag and laid it on the table. After flipping through a few pages, she turned it toward me.

A detailed drawing of my face, down to my uneven eyebrows, lay before me. So detailed it looked like a photograph.

"What the… you did this from memory?"

"I drew this before I met you."

"You saw me somewhere and sketched me?"

"A week before the rally, a voice woke me in the middle of the night and said, 'get up.' The voice was velvety, a woman's voice whispering. My feet moved almost mechanically from my bed to my drawing table. Your image appeared in my mind's eye, like a desert mirage. The more I drew, the more detailed your image became. After I drew you, I drew your cowboy customer."

"You mean like a dream?"

"No, Willi. Different. Very different. A real voice. It's happened before. I think I was supposed to meet you."

"Are you saying… you hear voices?" I couldn't cover the incredulity in my tone. "Like an imaginary voice in your head? And that's how you drew the cowboy? That's a bit crazy, isn't it?"

Her face flushed, chest deflated. "I've said too much."

"Do you see ghosts too?" It was a stupid thing to say.

Her stare washed over me, as though she could see every doubting micro-muscle movement in my face. She pushed back from the table. "I should go. I've got to teach class in the morning." Her gaze turned away and she wouldn't look into my eyes.

"You think I'm crazy, don't you?"

"No, Madison, wait, it's not that at all." I looked at the picture. "It's… it's so impossible."

"I… I made a mistake. I should have left this alone."

I jumped up, but she was already putting on her jacket. "Madison, stay. I want you to stay… please." My heart was bleeding.

"A part of me wants to, Willi, but…" She let out a long sigh and tilted her head up. That feeling of lost gravity came back. Our lips touched lightly, then pressed together, tasting of sweet plum wine. She drew tight against my body, like she was trying to pull herself inside me. The kiss extinguished my breath, its soft texture and underlying tenderness heart-melding. She pushed against my mouth without rushing, her fingers caressing my hair. Longing and hunger remained, our sticky plum wine lips parted, foreheads touching, we shared breaths and the drumming of rapid hearts.

"I… I shouldn't have said anything, but I didn't expect to…"

"Expect to what?"

"To fall in love," she whispered.

"Then… Madison, let's follow the geese."

"I am. I mean… I will. But… the voice…" She pulled back and looked away. "It told me not to stay. Something extraordinary is about to happen."

"To who?"

"To you, Willi."

CHAPTER 3

CHICAGO

THE DOOR CLICKED CLOSE BEHIND her. I sat at the kitchen table under a yellow light bulb that turned dull whites to shadow grey. A buzzing refrigerator and the remains of Chinese take-out left the final moments of the evening empty. I yelled at myself. Sometimes my mouth is so big and my brain so small. She was extraordinary and trusted me with a monumental secret. I had run over it. I cleaned up spilled sweet and sour sauce, which seemed a metaphor for the evening. I did have multiple tasks to complete. The kiln needed unloading, the van packed with work, and a dozen other details before leaving for my next show. I mulled over her mysterious voice. She was a brilliant artist, not crazy like van Gogh cutting off his ear, but the experiment was extraordinary and my body quivered just thinking about it. It revealed volumes about her and me. I wasn't sure what to make of the clairvoyance. I could hear her saying, 'let it be, Willi.' So, for the time being I got on with my life. But circumstance would soon prove she was right.

THE ART FAIR TOOK PLACE early spring in Schaumberg, a suburb west of downtown Chicago. Art fairs always have a high risk of failure but the disastrous show in OKC and low money reserves gave me no choice. Even though it was an inside show, weather could keep people home. Many artists like myself had traveled hundreds of miles hoping to put a little oomph into skinny checkbooks. Exorbitant booth fees and expensive Chicago hotel rooms raised the stakes proportionally. On the show circuit, artists have only two seasons; winter, when cash is short, and summer, when they're catching up from the winter before.

After an eight-hour drive down Interstate 94, the one hour wait to get in the exhibit hall entrance was annoying. The venue held three hundred booths; each exhibitor crammed into ten-by-ten-foot spaces, which had to include a display, a sales area, checkout, and room for storage. I hauled one ton of materials and artwork from the receiving docks to my assigned space using a handcart.

Kim, a painter who lived in Chicago, was my booth neighbor. I knew her from times we crossed at art fairs, and it was good to see a familiar face. She greeted me with, "We have a problem, Willi, no electricity." For the next thirty minutes I hunted down the artist coordinator who said the electrician would fix it by morning. During set up, I ate a soggy tuna sandwich and drank bitter coffee provided by the show. Two hours later I popped into Kim's booth. She hung work done in a mélange of color swirled into abstract forms and dark shadows.

"Wow, this is challenging. What's going on?"

"I've decided to let more of myself out."

"Darkside coming through?"

"It's the dark side that teaches, Willi."

One painting, quite large, suggested a woman giving birth. The three by four-foot image was chilling as blood poured over a child halfway born out of darkness.

I stood back. "I'll have to think on that one."

"Please, don't 'think' at all. Let it be what it is."

I wondered if she knew Madison, who would say the same thing. A wide smile crossed Kim's face.

"By the way, where you staying?" Her eyes flitted upwards.

"Spotlight Inn, some place I found on the internet."

"Ha! You know that's a red-light hotel?"

"What? Chicago has whore houses? All I want is a pillow and shower."

She laughed. "Well, if the walls vibrate, you'll know why."

THE SPOTLIGHT INN WAS MORE than a total dump. The counter clerk asked how many hours I wanted my room for. When I said all night, he raised his eyebrows. By that time, I didn't care where I slept. Exhaustion had set in. My head hit the pillow like a lug of clay hits the potter's wheel. Up early the next morning, I ate a bland hotel breakfast of plastic wrapped muffins and coffee with powdered creamer. Thirty minutes later, I pulled into the convention center parking lot.

When I arrived at my booth, the electrical was still out. Madison had left a message on my cell. "Miss you, Willi. Good luck today." Definitely heartwarming.

FRIDAY SALES WERE HOPEFUL. THE weather held. I made expenses, a little over a thousand bucks.

Kim wandered in at the end of the day. "Hey, Willi, how'd it go?"

"Made expenses." I moved pots from front shelving to inside the booth.

"Lucky you," she responded. "Does that include paid time at shows?"

"Ha, good one, Kim."

She pursed her lips. "Road time is always a benevolent donation, isn't it?"

"Shows are fun, right? Why charge yourself for fun time?"

"They get me out of the studio," she sat down on my counter stool. "Otherwise, I'd go crazy."

"Right," I said. "Who pays themselves for therapeutic show time?"

"Not me." She laughed.

This exclusion of work-time built the art fair circuit.

"By the way, how'd it go at the Whore House Inn?" Her eyes danced across mine.

"Ha! Rhythmic vibrations and low moans lulled me to sleep. So lucky."

She laughed again. "I don't live far from here. You could stay with me." She tilted her head in a manner that seemed to make it more than an offer of a bed.

"Thanks, but I'm settled in there."

She slung her bag over her shoulder. Her eyes giving a crispy smile. "Your choice. See ya tomorrow, Willi."

ON SATURDAY, USUALLY THE BIG day for any show, a cold rain set in. Sales nose-dived. I sat in an almost empty hall with a couple hundred other artists milling about wondering where all the people were. In frustration, I sauntered into Kimberly's booth.

"So much for Saturday paying the bills. I need a break. Have you seen any booth sitters?"

She looked up from a magazine. "They took the day off."

"Isn't Saturday supposed to be the big day?"

"Ya, it's been a tough show, Willi. I haven't even made expenses."

"Ouch," I replied.

"Wanna help drown my sorrows later on?" she asked. "A bunch of us are going to Raison d'être downtown." Kim wore tight jeans and a safari shirt cinched with a belt and dirty blonde hair that had grown out a bit. An outdoorsy look. It was common to go out with artists after the show, and I knew of the place, loud music, good food, a whiskey bar, but waking with a hangover wasn't appealing.

"Thanks, Kim, but I'll pass. Sunday's a long day, plus an eight-hour drive home."

She squeezed my hand affectionately, running her thumb over my knuckles, gazing at me with lonely eyes. Disappointment raises the need for all kinds of relief. At that moment, a booth sitter popped in.

"Need any help?" she said.

"Definitely." I extracted my hand from Kim's hold. "It'll get better. You know the saying—tomorrow's the day."

When I pushed open a side door that led to the street, a cold rain smacked my face, the wind blustery. The disasters we have in life come from the choices we make. This show would not reach my minimum. I was too young for the circuit when art fairs soared in the nineties. More recently they had become financially unstable and making a viable living exclusively on the circuit was difficult. Most artists depended on a spouse to get by. I thought about Madison, pulled out my cell, and dialed her number. The phone went to her machine.

"Sorry, not in right now." Disappointing.

I marched through the rain-drenched back parking lot toward a coffee shop. The whole business of selling art was love hate. Kim said it could be the whole damn thing wasn't about money at all. That may be her survival speech to herself. The passion for art drives each of us in a peculiar way. My practical side—way too strong. There's nothing like a box full of overdue bills to temper idealism.

At the end of the block, I noticed a dirty green bill floating in a puddle on the sidewalk. As I bent over to pick it up, a foot came crashing down, almost catching my finger, splattering mud on my coat.

"It's mine!" A bristly faced man snarled, an orange scarf wound around his neck. The move stunned me. There was no question who'd been there first. Without a second thought, he bent over and grabbed the other half. Slowly, we got up, facing each other. Between us was a fifty-dollar bill. With a quick twist of his wrist, he tore it in half. His two friends wore frayed wet jackets, large black plastic bags full of aluminum cans slung over their shoulders. "Rodney, you lucky son-of-a-bitch!" one of them exclaimed.

It occurred to me there might be some danger, three of them, one of me. When a cop car drove by, I felt some relief. But the cruiser kept going and Rodney's friends stepped to each side of me.

"Looks like I have your half, mister, and you have mine." The man spoke with a thick, raspy voice, taking in short breaths, as though he couldn't get enough air to spill out one sentence.

"You see, mister, this here bill is meant for me. It's from Orlando."

"Funny, I was thinking it's from Duluth," I responded.

"Orlando's a person. Orlando Rock."

CHAPTER 4

A HOBO'S JURY

THE MENTION OF ORLANDO ROCK was astounding, but Rodney seemed clear about the name. He looked at his half of the fifty with a particular gleam in his eyes, like a child receiving a surprise birthday present. "If it weren't for Orlando, I wouldn't be standing here today."

"You've met Orlando Rock?" It was impossible they could be the same person.

"Yes, sir," Rodney replied. "A good-looking young man who was a god damn fool."

"Looks like a hobo's jury," his friend jumped into the conversation, holding a zipper-less jacket closed with one bare hand, a stubbly chin protruding just above the collar.

"Yeah, I think JC is right," the other chimed in with a woman-like voice, eyes flashing in amusement. "It's clearly a case of a hobo's jury." The two began a little chant, 'hobo jury, hobo jury,' but their friend did not join in.

"It's no joke, mister. Maybe Orlando was a fool, but he also was a king, and maybe more. I ain't one to take a name or gift in vain, especially this one, but I know that this here bill is for me. This isn't just a case of maybe or me trying to get something from you. This is an actual case of the dee-vine, of something you know is true, and when that happens, you know it, mister. You know it for sure. I mean, you can go your way and I can go mine and no one gets anything, but I think you'll find that it's not supposed to turn out that way. No sir!"

"A king?" I was astonished. It was too cold and miserable for a long, ridiculous argument. "Are you drunk?"

"Maybe," Rodney answered, obviously suffering from the weather.

"This man's tellin' the truth, mister, this here bill comes from Orlando."

I noticed the cop car parked up the street, which made me feel safer. My breath puffed out a cloud of steamed air as I paused a moment to contain myself. "Let's be reasonable," I suggested. "We can split it and be done with this."

"Listen," the one called JC talked. "It's a hobo's jury. Rodney tells why the fifty is his, then you give us your story. We all vote and whoever has all the votes gets all the money. It's got to be unanimous; no one gets a thing if we all don't agree. I think once you hear about Orlando and how we know this bill is from him, you'll see he's tellin' the truth. Everyone is the judge and jury, and we'll get this thing settled."

I was fascinated about how he knew Orlando Rock, and the proposition was the most interesting thing that happened all day. "So, we each tell our stories. Everyone agrees on which story is better and the winner gets the bill. Unanimous, right?"

"You got it, mister! No splits."

A passing city bus roared through a puddle, blasting us with freezing rain. "Okay, there's a coffee shop up the street. Let's do our story telling there. But I'm not buying for everyone." I wasn't about to pay for three coffees, listening to some diatribe.

A confident Rodney pulled a few bills out of his pocket. "It's my life savings, but I'll treat."

A city block later, we found a coffeehouse with a fireplace in the center. The smell of roasting beans filled the air and 'Make Me a Pallet,' an old John Hurt tune played in the background. A young woman with long black braided hair served us. My three acquaintances eyed her unselfconsciously. She eyed them back suspiciously. True to his word, Rodney bought two large dark roast coffees, mine with a touch of rich cream, the other shared between the three of them. Except for a window table, the place was full. Rodney faced me with his friends on each side. It was getting dark, ending the kind of cold gray day one likes to forget about.

"You see, mister, that's the whole damn thing," Rodney began, "no one knows who Orlando is or why he came around that night a little over five months ago. A damn cold night. A bunch of us had accommodations, so to speak, in the old Sandusky Warehouse a couple of blocks south of here. The night janitor would leave the back door open, and about five or six of us homeless types would scurry down in the basement during the evening hours and snooze by the boiler. It was dark but warm, with steam pipes running everywhere. We'd sleep on broken down cardboard boxes, using our coats as blankets. In the morning, we'd stash our beds in an empty storage locker and no one would be the wiser about half a dozen of us sleeping there the night before. One night, I got back too late. The night janitor finished up around midnight and had gone home. The front entrance security guard checked out early, leaving the building locked down tight. A big storm brewed, and temps went well below zero. Turned out to be a blizzard."

Rodney stuck his half of the torn fifty into his shirt pocket and picked out a half-smoked cigarette. One of his compatriots produced a light, and he took a long drag. A heavy sleety rain rapped on the window next to us, the street deserted. I stuck my half of the fifty under my coffee cup. Rodney continued.

"Anyway, this storm rolled in. It was so damn cold my face numbed. I screamed and pounded, but it did no good. No one would hear. I kept a bedroll under a nearby bridge in case of an emergency like this, so I climbed up under the steel girders, felt around for my blanket and pulled it out. My hands were numb by then. I wrapped that wool cloth around me and dozed off for a couple of hours when a coal train comes down the track across the road. Its screeching brakes woke me. Shadows from street lights outlined the heavy snow fall coming down in fierce waves. I curled up like a possum trying to keep some of my body heat under the blanket."

Rodney took another puff off his partially smoked cigarette and pulled up the collar of his old coat as if he were still in the storm and gave me a hard look. We both knew homeless people froze to death every year in the city.

"So out of nowhere, I mean out of the dead black of night, this figure comes right up to me, like the shadow of the devil himself, scarin' the livin' piss out of me. So, I asks him, 'Who the hell are you?' He shook like a newborn pup; a thin jacket and an iced cowboy hat was all he wore against bitter cold. He bent over and in a strong southern accent he says, 'The name is Orlando, Orlando Rock,' and he puts out his hand.

"Orlando had just jumped off that train. He had started from Oklahoma, traveled north to the Dakotas, then hopped a coal train coming through the top of Minnesota. His whole damn body was shivering, and he asks, 'You got advice about where a man can find a place to sleep?'

"Well, I had some advice. Get some fuckin' brains! A thin coat, no sleeping bag and wearing a cowboy hat in the middle of a goddamn snowstorm. Now that's stupid. But I wasn't in the best situation myself. He was just a young guy, maybe 25, or younger. Lodging? I held up my blanket. Hell, that's all there was on an evening like this and without hesitation, he climbed under. He looked scared, and he should've been."

Rodney lit up the tip of his short cigarette with a long drag. I thought about the Orlando I met. Certainly, different people, but odd that they would have the same name.

"You see, the thing about freezin' to death is that it sneaks up on you. Imagine a thousand needles pricking your flesh at the same time. It wears you down. My mind started playin' tricks, giving way to a drowsy feeling, same as the beginning of a cheap high. And Orlando's lips are purple and he says his eyes feel like someone has thrown sand in them, and that's a bad sign. The body sounds the alarm, but the brain's not ready to accept the facts. When freezing cold feels warm, the brain's playing tricks, and maybe it's a bit of mercy from mother nature. Who figures they're gonna freeze to death under a bridge in a Chicago suburb?"

Rodney took a long drag on the dwindling butt and let out an equally long trail of smoke. The waitress with the braided hair came over.

"Sir, there's no smoking in here." She pointed at a sign by the door. Rodney put it out with his fingers, eyeing her as she swayed back to the counter, then continued his story.

"So, the snow's blowin' something really fierce," he continued. "You can't see ten feet in front of you. The wind makes a strange howling noise and the girders creak as an occasional truck passes above. I was scared for both of us. Orlando was about to pass out on me, so I grab his hand and start rubbing it. His fingers are so cold I was glad I couldn't see them. I rubbed 'em until I felt some warmth, and then I rubbed his arms down. The poor fool just leaned against me and said nothing. For hours, I tried to keep him warm. I made him wiggle his toes and stomp his feet, but he got less and less responsive. He never complained once. I worked him until I was sweating. Well, after a while I couldn't fight my exhaustion. I felt some kind of warmth as I drifted off and wondered how in hell two men, freezing to death, could give off heat.

"Next thing I know, the 5:00 a.m. freight blows its horn, waking me. I wiped crusted ice from my eyelids and a ray of sunlight makes the new snowfall look like fresh whipped cream over everything. Orlando's head is on my shoulder. It amazed me to be alive. 'Come on, Orlando,' I gave him a poke, 'let's see if that warehouse door is open.' But Orlando isn't moving. He isn't breathing either. In fact, Orlando is dead… and I've seen dead, on the streets, and in Nam, plenty. This guy is stone cold dead! But there is something peaceful about his face that I envied. If it was a hard death, he didn't show it. Somehow, I had made it through that night and the poor bastard, he froze to death. The storm had moved on and a light breeze blew the powder off the bridge above me. It was like wakin' up from a bad dream into a glittering wonderland. I don't know how long I stared at that new fallen snow with Orlando under the blanket with me, but I heard a scraping sound from across the way. It was Ozzie, the morning janitor, shoveling off the loading dock. I attempted to dash across the large parking lot, but snow was up to my knees, lungs puffing out clouds of steam. Each step was a call back to life. Well, I made it to the door as Ozzie was closing it.

"'Hey, Rodney, you look like a dead man walking. Come on in,' he says.

I couldn't talk, just held up my arm and scurried past him, down to the boiler room like a cat that'd done something wrong. The boys put me by one of the huge steam pipes and I shook for an hour before I got my voice back. Someone gave me a cup of hot water. I was Lazarus coming out of that tomb.

"Everyone scolded me about how dumb I was spending the night out in such a storm! And they were right. As soon as words would come out, I told 'em that there was another man out there who wasn't so lucky. My voice was still quivering. Then Molly here asked what the hell I was talkin' about."

Rodney raised his cup, pointing to the person wearing the zipper-less jacket across the table. Molly raised her hand and smiled as Rodney guzzled his coffee. She had a few curly hairs sticking out of her chin and protruding brows that made her deep-set eyes hard to see. That's when I realized there was a woman among us.

"I told them the whole story about Orlando," Rodney continued. "Everyone got quiet. Finally, Molly broke the silence, suggesting I had a bad dream or maybe I should lay off the Mogen David some. So, I grabbed her arm and dragged her out of that boiler room and up the stairs to prove this wasn't just another drunk's tale of woe. We crossed the street through the deep snow to where Orlando lay. But when we got to the bridge, there was no body, and no Orlando. The blanket lay in a heap. There were no footsteps in that wintry morning snow except our own. I thought I must have been delirious, and when I looked over at Molly, I could tell she thought the same thing. But when I picked up my blanket and started folding it, something fell out onto the ground. That's when I found the fifty-dollar bill. Now I gotta tell you, mister, someone like me knows exactly how much he has and an extra fifty ain't a miscalculation. That stranger had left proof that I wasn't totally alone that night and I wasn't totally mad! A strange gift, I'll admit, but a gift nonetheless.

"That morning, we all ate well. Fresh coffee, donuts, some fancy bread and jam and I bought a jar of peanut butter from a little store on the other side of the building. We all toasted to Orlando! I divided all the leftover money with my friends. It seemed the right thing to do. I gave that fifty away and now this fifty, the one that's tore in half, it's Orlando himself saying, 'Rodney, this is a reminder.' You see, here's the point. You don't find a fifty-dollar bill but once in your life, and even then you're a damn lucky fool. But a second fifty, that's more than luck, that's something else. And this ain't nothin' to lie about, mister. Not when you've spent a night with the likes of Orlando Rock."

When Rodney finished his story, I was silent. Murmuring voices, cups clinking, the hiss of the espresso machine, the rush of warm air from a vent overhead once again filled the room. It was a story I wanted to believe, but found myself looking out the window on a cold drizzly late afternoon thinking about a life that passes by with a particular day-by-day grind that doesn't seem to afford the likes of such intervention.

Slowly Rodney put his fingers on my coffee cup, slid it back. "Your turn, mister." I shook my head and waved off his offer. He slipped my half of the fifty into his palm and folded it into his pocket.

"Thank you kindly, stranger." He pushed his chair back. "Gotta get going, there's gonna be a party down at the warehouse tonight," Rodney's voice seemed calmer.

They buttoned up coats and headed out. Molly put her arm around Rodney and as they passed the counter, he gave the waitress a couple of bucks. They disappeared around the corner and into the fold of a desperate night. A moment later, the waitress delivered a fresh cinnamon scone along with a dark roast refill, compliments of the stranger who had just left.

My pottery teacher once told me you don't see art with eyes only. "Great art penetrates," he said. "Let your whole body feel it. Letting the outer mind go becomes the key to opening your inner eye. Without that key, you remain blind." It's not a statement you get right away.

I had little faith life's disasters could be averted by some mysterious intrusion. Yet hadn't Orlando Rock saved my show from total disaster?

It occurred to me that miracles and disasters are born together. In fact, they need each other. As I looked into the tough winter months ahead, I knew this show would not give needed relief.

I finished my cinnamon scone and sweet cream coffee, then headed back to the show. A large warehouse in the distance displayed a full-sized billboard on its roof: 'SANDUSKY WAREHOUSE NOW RENTING.'

•

THE SHOW ENDED AT SIX pm on Sunday. I packed out by nine. Kim came over as I was leaving.

"You staying overnight?"

I shook my head. "Headin' home. And you?"

"I live on the other side of town. It's a long ride to Minneapolis. I've got an extra bed if you wanna stay over." Her eyes had a particular drift that said something else was in that offer.

"Thanks, but I'll make it. I always do."

"Well, see ya in Fort Worth?"

"Wasn't accepted. You doing Salina?"

"Maybe, we'll see." She gave a quick smile. "Stay safe, Willi."

"Ya, see you down the road, Kim." When we hugged, she slipped her arms all the way around me and pressed tightly against my body, then stepped back and said, "Ya, down the road."

Before I could overthink her gesture, she turned back to her booth. I headed for the van.

The drive from Chicago to Minneapolis was a lengthy one, especially when you're tired. Along the way, bitter truck-stop coffee and yesterday's donuts kept me awake. Wild-eyed truckers with big bellies ambled into the station, paying for hundred-gallon fills and a quick snack. We were all road warriors, stretching our luck, pushing back the boundary between drive time and sleep time.

While paying for gas at a truck stop, Madison left a message on my phone.

"Willi, I... I drew another picture. Totally do not understand it but I think it has something to do with you. Can't wait till your back."

Was this Madison's enigmatic voice returned? Rodney's struggle and his terrifying experience in the blizzard was a compelling story, but still, just a story. Some benevolent being saving a homeless man wasn't plausible in my world. And for that matter, Madison's voice didn't seem real either, which led me to question out loud, "Okay, Willi, what am I getting into?" I resolved to tell her we should slow down, give ourselves a break before continuing. Eight hours later I was home.

CHAPTER 5

HOMECOMING

AT FOUR AM, THE PARKING lot behind my building was deathly quiet. The single light pole threw a shadow that looked like a one-arm alien. Groggy and exhausted, I locked the van and dragged myself to the entrance leading down to my basement apartment. I inserted the key, but the door inched opened on its own—light streamed from inside. Someone banged around in the kitchen, a bacon aroma wafted in the air. Ignoring my first instinct to call out, I stealthily took a step forward. Madison entered the living room, then charged at a gallop. With open arms and a big kiss, she squeezed the breath out of me.

"Oh, Willi, I wanted to surprise you. You must be exhausted."

"How... how did you get in?"

She released her grip when my return hug was less than enthusiastic. "I... I took a key from the table last time I was here. I'm so sorry Willi... I didn't know it would upset you." Her face tensed, eyes contrite. "I grilled a tomato-bacon sandwich and bought a six of Spotted Cow."

Kicking off my shoes, I flopped on the couch. She served the sandwich and beer, which helped, but the long arduous drive had left me drained and I thought about my promise to slow this relationship down.

"How was the show?" She plopped next to me and threw her arm over my shoulder.

"Terrible. Expenses plus a little." Everything seemed awkward. "How about you?"

"I finished that painting we started in the studio last week and… I…" her eyebrows narrowed, uncertainty crossed her face, "the voice was back… and" she stopped in the middle of her sentence, eyes scanning mine. "Willi, what's wrong?"

"We should talk." My tone cold and distant. Her mention of 'the voice,' disturbing. "Maybe we should think things over."

She stood suddenly. "I should go." Delight erased from her face. "Maybe coming over was a bad idea. I was excited to see you and wanted to show you something, a picture I drew. I couldn't make sense of it. It's on the kitchen table. You can look at it some other time." Before I could say anything, she grabbed her coat, bent over and kissed my cheek.

"I guess you're right, Willi. We should talk." Then she left.

The room filled with a sudden hollow emptiness. My stomach turned to acid. How stupid could I be? Gathering my dishes, I dumped them in the sink. A bacon aroma still drifted in the kitchen, a five pack of Spotted Cow remained on the counter. Her sketch pad lay open on the table. My heart skipped a beat when I saw her drawing. There was Rodney, holding a fifty-dollar bill, staring at me. She had detailed the mole on his left cheek, the missing front tooth, sad, lonely eyes. That she could draw Rodney's face— without being there—was an impossibility, yet she'd done it.

I fell back into the chair, staring at the picture. Even after meeting Rodney and sitting with him for thirty minutes, I couldn't come close to drawing his face. Everything my logical mind had told me shattered. My gut gnarled. I'd made such a stupid mistake.

I grabbed my cell and dialed her number. No answer. Dialed again and waited. Phone machine message, "Madison, please come back. I was such a fool. It's… the picture is amazing… you're amazing, come back. I want to see you." I hung up. Called again. No answer. Left another message, then threw the phone on the counter. Rodney's eyes followed mine. I could hear his voice, 'finding a fifty only happens once, and even then you're damn lucky, but twice…' Madison was my fifty-dollar bill. The drawing was shockingly impossible. I stared at the image until exhaustion tumbled over me. In the bedroom, I dropped my clothes on the floor, drew the covers back, and collapsed. A sour feeling welled from deep within my chest. In the middle of the night, I dreamed I was under the bridge with Rodney, struggling for the blanket. Tears wet his cheek, his hand strangely familiar, soothing a troubled soul.

WHEN I WOKE THE NEXT morning, a lump was next to me. Madison had curled around my body, her arm slung over my waist, breasts pressed against my back. I could tell by her breathing she was still asleep. When I rolled over, she tucked her head on my shoulder, her face streaked with tears from the night before. Auburn hair flowed over my arm. Her eyes blinked open, and her hand slid down my chest, tickling the hairs.

"Hey. I used your key to get in."

"Hey. It's yours to keep." Her fingers moved across my cheek to my ear.

"Your ear's healed up." Tears welled at the corners of my eyes.

"Yeah… all healed. Madison, I'm so…"

"Shh," she put a finger on my lips and pushed herself up. "I know it's difficult. How about a coffee?"

"You making?"

She climbed out of bed, grabbed a shirt from my closet, half-covering her body, and disappeared out the door.

A few moments later she came back with two steaming Joes. "Where'd you get the Walmart mugs?"

I laughed. "Some potter I know made them."

She handed me a cup and sat on the edge of the bed. "Willi… It's not going to change. This thing… it's part of me and, well, it's just who I am. I've had it since I was kid. I kept it a secret for years and I thought I was crazy but believe me, Willi, I didn't choose it. It chose me. And don't ask why. I'm doing as best I can. It's… it's about marrow, it's in my bones. Holding on to this secret has been like holding my breath, and you've given me a way to breathe." She nodded her head as if saying yes to herself. "What if I had a third arm or only one leg? I can't grow another leg or cut off my arm to fit into your world. Do you understand?"

"I get it, Madison. This 'thing' you're talking about is part of the package. There's a lot of other things packed together here too. I don't want to pick you apart. I won't. Yeah, not easy to tamp down my rational mind. But... love is not rational, and not a straight line. So, I'll follow the curves. My choice... but, hmm, but a third arm? I'd have to think about it."

"Ha." She leaned over, kissed me, then rolled out of bed and walked to my dresser. Opening the top drawer, she took out a pair of my boxers and held it to her waist. "You mind?"

"Only if I can wear your pink panties," I retorted.

"No problem." She picked her panties from the floor and threw them on the covers, slipped into the boxers, then pulled on a pair of cotton meditation pants.

"You're not getting back into bed?"

"Not right now. Gotta class in twenty minutes. Drawing legs." She squeezed into low back sneakers and came over to my side. "I thought I'd show mine off."

"Can we talk about the picture?"

"Not now." Her answer was simple and definite.

"Okay. How about the arrest?"

She sat on the bed. "To keep it short, it was way over dramatized. I live ten miles from the center of a small town, just over the border, in Wisconsin. It was night, the road seldom traveled. Reid Johnson, a local cop, pulled me over. I don't know him personally except that his wife left him."

"Whoa. How do you know that?"

"Small town gossip, Willi. We all know each other, at least by sight. Local chatter says it was abuse or carousing. Anyway, he orders me to get out of my car. I politely inquired what the offense was. He said expired plates and the left blinker was out, most of which was true. He told me to put my hands on the car. I obeyed. I didn't want a ticket and asked if we could work something out. It was a stupid thing to say. He took it as a come on and spun me around, then tried to kiss me. His breath was sour garlic, his hands sandpaper rough as he slipped them under my shirt. I panicked and bit his lip. Hard enough to taste blood. He went to wallop me with a backhand, but stopped, twirled me around again and cuffed me. He stepped back and called for backup. When his buddies arrived, he accused me of resisting arrest. His lip was a bloody mess. I could still taste his blood when they brought me down to the station. The charge—assaulting an officer. I spent the night in jail. At a hearing the next day, a magistrate let me out on my own cognizance with the promise that I would check in weekly with an assigned parole officer until my court date. It was a nightmare. Her name was Judy, and she was a bitch. I wasn't supposed to leave the county without her permission, and they put a cuff on my ankle. A friend fashioned a cuff killer, one that disrupts the signal from the police tracker, making it undependable. I guess the cuff killer wasn't working when they found me at that coffee shop. My parole officer hauled me back to Wisconsin, and I spent another night in jail. Remember Jimmy the lawyer? I called him and he took my case. He did a little background checking and says they'll most likely drop all charges; it's not the first time Reid's been accused of reprehensible behavior." She let out a big breath and squeezed her lips together. "That's the reason for the arrest. I'm a felon."

"Hardly," I responded. "How do you know they won't show up here?"

"Bitch Judy granted permission to go to work."

Her hand ran down my chest and she leaned over and placed her lips on mine. My fingers ran over her arm, her skin smooth like the spinning clay on the potter's wheel, but she pushed away. "We'll make love this week, Willi. Believe me, I want to as bad as you do. But if I lose this job…" she sighed. "I can't afford any slipups, at least not now."

She rose from the bed. "How do I look?"

"Like a professor ready to teach students how a felon breaks out of jail. What are you doing tonight?"

"I model for an advanced drawing class. What are you doing tomorrow night?"

"Sleeping with you."

"You don't know my address."

"Give me a hint."

She smiled. "I'll leave it on the kitchen table. By the way, I don't cook. Bring something interesting. I'll do a salad."

CHAPTER 6

SOUP

MADISON HAD LEFT HER BUSINESS card on the table. On one half was her smiling face. The opposite side had a printed phone number and an address… in braille. A gay couple in the apartment above helped. Cupcake, who was blind, thought her idea very humorous, so did Rory, a trans African-American. They were a boisterous and friendly duo. Occasionally, I'd hear a crash on the floor above me and loud voices, but who doesn't have relationships spats? They would engage with anyone, anywhere, be it in the hallways, by the front door, or at trash collection, and on any subject. Everyone in the building knew them, whether they wanted to or not. I headed to my van in the early afternoon and found Cupcake waiting for Rory in the parking lot. His white cane leaned against the car.

"Hey, Cupcake, think you could help me out with something?"

"Hello, Willi. I'll help you if you help me." His ability to identify by voice was amazing.

"Okay, what can I do?"

"I want you to paddle Rory's ass when he comes out for making me wait so long."

I laughed. "Do I use a canoe paddle or my hand?"

"Oh deary, always with the hand! Now, what can I do for you?"

I gave him Madison's card. His fingers ran over the surface, and he smiled as he recognized the braille. "Very clever." He read the address with no problem. I scribbled it down. "She must be quite a woman."

"Maybe it's my dry cleaner."

"Not a chance, honey. Her fragrance is all over this card. Your Orbis rubbed off on her. Someone stay at your place last night?"

"What! You know I wear Orbis?"

"Willi, my nose is better than a narc canine. She used your Orbis, including a smidgen of that deodorant from Indonesia. What's the name?"

"Peking Rose."

"Oh yeah, baby. Quite the rage with the trans-folk."

"Thanks. I'll be sure to keep you updated."

When Rory came out the doorway, Cupcake shouted, "Better watch out, honey, Willi's gonna paddle your ass for being so late."

I LEFT THE COUPLE ARGUING in the parking lot and drove to a storage area where I kept inventory. After a show, the van needed repacking. I made a throwing list, completed a trip to the bank and a studio clean. There was no time for lingering disappointments, which only turned into quicksand. A couple of poor shows didn't foretell the entire summer. The Smokey Hill River Fest, in Salina, Kansas, was on the horizon.

I worked into the evening, throwing mug sets and oval forms. The following morning, mugs needed handles and oval bottoms cut out and added. Afterwards, I made Butternut squash soup and headed out. On the way, I bought sour cream and a fresh baked baguette.

Google earth showed her property bordered a wooded state park with a narrow rollicking river rolling about a hundred feet from her back porch. A large grove of pine trees lined the curvy quarter-mile gravel driveway, providing a grand entrance to her place, as well as seclusion for a small, one story, cedar sided house. A grapevine-covered arbor led to a long open front porch. A sculpture of Buddha sitting with sad, distracted eyes sat on the pedestal by the front door. Her initials were imprinted on the base. I didn't know she sculpted.

The door swung open on the first knock, and I marched in. "Madison?" I called out. A short hallway brought me to the kitchen. "Madison."

Long granite countertops bordered the ceramic sink, a pile of salad greens in a strainer. Still, no one home. The stove set separately on an island, a stainless-steel vent over gas burners had pots hanging from each side. On the other side of the island, a small kitchen table stood in front of windows stretching to the ceiling, river view, with hanging garlic braids intermingled with dried flowers on each side. Two sturdy captains' chairs tucked under. I placed my soup pot on the stovetop and walked out to a screened-in back porch. A short, curvy cement path led to a newer building, smaller than the house. The walk ended at a sliding glass door.

The studio had a high vaulted ceiling made of car siding stained natural. Eight green industrial lights hung from chains. A long workbench divided the room in two. To my surprise, she owned a potter's wheel, too clean to have been used.

"Hey."

She looked up from sorting a pile of sticks. "Can you make plaster molds?" Her eyes had that same intensity as when we met in her painting studio.

"Depends. What do you need molded?"

"Sticks." She held one up. "Maybe a half-dozen press molds of different shapes and sizes."

"Sure. Looks easy."

"Okay. Let's get to work."

I walked to the bench. "How about dinner? Remember?"

She threw her arms around my neck and kissed me. "Molds first, dinner next, desert last." She squeezed my butt. With a deep breath, I got busy.

"What's is this project?" I asked. She picked through a pile of sticks, choosing candidates for molding.

"It's a memorial for my neighbor who died suddenly."

"When did this happen?" I formed a molding box from pieces of wood Madison had cut to size.

"A week ago. I found him up on UU."

"You found your neighbor dead... what, on the street, in the woods, what happened?"

"Actually, in his car and not far from here. He stopped in the middle of an isolated country road, got into the back seat, had a heart attack or something and died."

I let out a big sigh. "That's a helluva way to go."

"He was a sweet old man, and I'll miss him." Madison oiled the chosen sticks with green soap. "I used to take him frozen dinners and we'd talk about art or listen to music."

I pinned up each stick to allow plaster to flow under it and placed molding boxes around them. "What was his name?"

"Norman. Norman Styles."

"And these sticks for his memorial?"

She smiled. "You'll see. It'll take a good week before it takes shape."

I mixed the plaster by feel, making sure I didn't stir it too much. "And how did you find Norman on that back road?"

"Early one morning I awakened to a whisper. At first, I thought someone else was in the room. Not only did she tell me to collect sticks but also where to find them."

"The voice is female?"

"Not always, but sometimes. I trekked through the woods, up the hill to county road UU, which cuts across the forest. That's where I found Norman's car."

"Did your 'voice' say you'd find a dead body?"

"No, Willi! It doesn't work like that." Her tone was sharp.

"Okay, then what?"

"I ran back to the house and called the police."

"Gruesome."

"No, heartbreaking. He was a good person."

She swept a pile of unused sticks into a box using her arm.

"Plaster is ready to pour," I said. After filling the mold boxes halfway, I explored the studio. Along a side wall, I found a potter's wheel. "You throw?"

"I never could get the hang of the centering thing. Maybe you could show me?"

"Sure. What do you want to make?"

"A couple of three-foot-wide platters, you know, like Voulkos."

"Ha! From learning how to center to three-foot platters, that's a jump."

"I like big." She ran her fingers over the plaster cast. "Plaster's set, Willi. Time for the upper half."

The plaster line came to the stick midpoints. To complete the mold, I made alignment holes, soaped the top half, then filled the casting box with freshly mixed plaster that poured like heavy cream.

"I should heat the soup while this sets up. We can crack the molds open tomorrow."

"Tomorrow?" she smiled. "You staying the night?"

"You'll need someone to crack the molds." My eyes danced across hers.

"I hope you don't wear socks to bed."

"I skinny dip."

"I like skinny dipping. You start the soup. I've got to clean up."

Peepers broadcasted their orchestral sounds from the deep woods and lightning bugs dotted raspberry bushes with their fiery glow. The sun had set, leaving a wispy stroke of gold in the sky. As I walked into the kitchen, a police car pulled up in front of the house. An officer walked under the arbor to the porch and knocked. I opened the door.

The officer was a tall man, his official blue regalia included a short-sleeved shirt showing off bulging muscles, a shiny black belt held a holstered revolver on the right side, a nightstick and a flashlight on the left. If he was surprised to see me, he didn't show it. He tipped his hat when I answered.

"Evening. I'm looking for Madison. Is she in the house?"

Stamped on his badge was Reid Johnson. My heart jumped.

"No, sir," I said. "She's out." Technically, she wasn't in the house.

"Do you know when she'll return?"

"I believe she's hiking downstream. Won't be back for a while. Is there something I can help you with…?"

"We have a few questions to ask her about Norman Styles' death. I thought it would be more comfortable to talk here than at the station." He put his boot on the threshold, but I blocked him from entering the house.

"Questions? Is there an investigation, officer?"

"There are circumstances we're hoping she can clear up?"

"What circumstances?"

"I'm not at liberty to say, but tell her to call me when she returns." His eyebrows narrowed.

"Is she in trouble, officer?"

"Just a few more questions we want answered. And your name is?"

"What circumstances would support an investigation?"

He let out a long sigh. "It's routine. No need to get upset. We believe there's a few missing pieces, that's all." He drew a card out of his pocket and handed it to me. "Tomorrow wouldn't be too soon for Madison to come to the station." I took the card as he tried looking over my shoulder.

"I'll make sure she gets it."

He sauntered back to his cruiser and, for some unknown reason, turned on his top flashers as he drove away. When he was out of sight, Madison appeared at my side.

"Thank God you were here. That's the officer I bit."

"He wants to ask you questions about Styles' death."

When she took my hand, her palms were sweaty. "Let's eat."

IN THE KITCHEN, SHE DIPPED her finger in the soup and tasted. "OMG, Willi. This is delicious! And so thick. Perfect!" She set a couple of bowls out on a small back porch table. The crickets were chatting, moon rising, the stream made a soft shushing sound. Madison had changed into a loose button-down shirt and her favorite yoga pants, no shoes. We drank wine and broke bread.

"Any idea what the police would investigate?"

"I have an idea… let's not talk about it now."

We drank wine, the soup cooled. A warm wind blew through the screens. She darted into the kitchen and brought out a two-inch brush.

"What's that for?"

That mischievous smile crossed her face. She stood behind me, dipped the brush in my bowl and slopped soup over my mouth, then licked it off with big, long lapping strokes, her tongue running around my lips. I pulled her onto my lap, grabbed the brush from her hand, and soup painted her chin, then licked it off, running my tongue all the way to her mouth. She undid the top button on her shirt and painted soup from her chest up to her neck. I lapped it up. She stood, unbuttoned her next shirt button. I threw a blanket from a nearby love seat onto the floor. We took off our shirts and painting class began.

"So, this is a technique you teach your students?" Soup dripped down my chin.

The brush, followed by her tongue, moved from my belly button to my pants' line. "It's something I learned while studying in Paris."

"Really? I don't remember this in French cooking class."

She laughed. "This class is a private lesson you'll never forget."

I lapped soup up her breast, then down her stomach. Her hips raised as I reached her bellybutton. Around her waist, the chain with the flat key fastened above her pelvis.

"You always wear this?"

"I never take it off." She pushed my head downward. "Keep going."

As the crickets and peepers sang their songs, the full moon took over the sky. We took turns painting each other with soup, dabbing and slurping, stopping along the way… to enjoy the hills and valleys of our hidden landscapes. The brush flowed over her contours, drawing her body up, the soup sweet, her body salty. She sighed and moaned, and we made slippery love. Fierce and soft, gentle and powerful, she dominated and submitted. I wanted all of her and she held nothing back.

With the bowls empty and both of us satiated, I rolled over and stared at the shadows on the ceiling. My body was still floating. She turned and put her head on my heaving chest. Her breasts were sticky. I pulled a pillow off the nearby couch and put it under our heads. She threw her leg over mine, the curve of her hips visible in a room illuminated by moonlight.

"You were delicious."

"You've done this before?" she asked.

I suppressed a smile. "Why yes. At least twice."

"Really. Is it always squash soup?"

"I thought I'd let you off easy. No jalapenos."

"Ha. Maybe next time." She bit my ear. No blood. I pulled her close.

We laid quiet, listening to forest sounds from the deep woods. Katydids and a distant screech owl joined the wind rustling through leaves in an orchestral majesty that helped float me back to earth.

"Willi, can you hear it?" she whispered.

"Hear what?"

"The geese."

"Geese?"

"They're flying south to fall in love."

"This one hasn't even made the border, and he's already in love."

"Me too," she rolled over. "I'm a sticky mess! Let's clean up."

AFTER SHOWERING, WE DECIDED AGAINST clothes and climbed into bed. I had been in love once before, but not like this. This was fire.

"It's scary, Willi." She said it as I thought it. "All I've ever wanted is to be normal, but falling in love seems far from normal."

"Normal will never fit your job description, Madison."

"Between voices and an irksome talent, I seem doomed to another path."

"Doomed? That's strong, don't you think?" She placed her head on my shoulder and pressed her body against mine.

"I want you to promise you'll always fly south to find me when I'm lost and bring me home."

"I promise." I couldn't imagine anything else.

She squeezed my fingers. "There's something really important I want to tell you."

"Now?" I wasn't sure I wanted to hear it.

"You'll know in the morning if I don't say it now."

"Okay. I'm listening." She pressed our hands into her breast.

"I have a son."

CHAPTER 7

NASH

BIRDS SQUAWKED OUTSIDE THE WINDOW as a ray of sunlight illuminated the room. We had talked into the night about her pregnancy at age fifteen, the birth of Nash, and how her hippie parents had helped raise him through tough early years. I woke with her head on my shoulder, skin touching skin, so divine. She yawned and stretched her arms out, knocking me in the head.

"Oh, sorry."

"No damage."

"You been awake long?"

"For a while. Thinking about our conversation last night. Where does Nash live?"

"He lives here, sometimes... at least his things are here. I'm not sure where he lives otherwise."

"You were pregnant at fifteen. Where did your family live?" I brushed away strands of auburn hair dangling over her eyes.

"I grew up in communes up and down the California coast. When I turned eighteen, I left commune life, found my own place and lucked into a job as a special assistant to Peter Rosenbloom, an art professor at the Art Institute in San Francisco. That's where I learned to model. I sat for his advanced drawing classes and for him personally. But our relationship went farther than modeling."

At that point, she paused her story, got out of bed and returned with a bottle and two glasses. I sat up. "A little early for the hard stuff, don't you think?"

"Life histories always require a bit of extra courage." She poured a shot for each of us. We clinked glasses, downed the first shot, then she continued.

"Stories of his wife's affairs with students on campus were rampant. She was bi, and to me it looked like an open marriage. Peter was monogamous, or so he said, which was a laugh. He meant he fucked one partner at a time, and I was his affair at the moment. To his credit, he was a genuine artist and recognized my talent went beyond my hips. With his help, I landed a scholarship."

Madison refilled our shot glasses. She slugged hers down. "Tell me when this gets boring."

"Hardly boring. Did you finish school?"

"Introductory classes were dreary, advanced courses middling. But even with the scholarship and meager wages from Peter, I couldn't support myself and Nash's daycare, among other bills. Nash was demanding, as young children are. I wanted to paint.

"The struggle to make ends meet became overwhelming. When Peter invited me to Paris for a summer internship, I jumped at the chance. Nash stayed with my parents. The professor taught a course at the Paris College of Art and knew Henri Richelet, a painter who was famous on the Paris art scene. Richelet took me on as a student. My work impressed him; he said I had 'possibility'."

Madison finished her drink and set the glass aside. "After a whirlwind summer of romantic dinners out, museums and long walks, it came to a shocking end when Peter's wife showed up."

Madison slung her leg over mine and pressed her body close.

"It was a scene out of a horror movie. I was living with Peter in his Paris apartment when Rene appeared with no warning. Rene flew into a rage and demanded Peter come back to the States or face divorce. I panicked. The night before, I had drawn Peter lying in a pool of blood. I was confused and frightened and fled to the Paris streets, walking around for hours, cold and hungry, not knowing what to do. Peter finally called, said it was safe to come home, Rene had left. He assured me they worked things out, all was well. What a liar!

"I was grateful to Peter for what he had done for me, but wanted no part of a messy, revengeful divorce. It was complicated. I flew back to LA and quit school. Three months later, Rene shot Peter dead in his studio while drawing his next pretty victim." Madison slugged her drink and poured another. I was sweating.

"My God! Rene killed him?" I puffed out a breath. "And your drawing… you predicted all this?"

"Ya, let's not get into that. Like I said, it's complicated."

"So, now you had no place to stay, no job, and a young son. How did you survive?"

"Ironically, I became a sketch artist for the LAPD. The pay was fair, and I could get by. I saw how messy investigations can get—people arrested based on poor memory and sketches I drew. What a joke.

"Eyewitness accounts are as dependable as star gazing on a cloudy night. Then one day, Nash's dad showed up. I was just a kid when I met him years before, jumping into a wild affair and knowing nothing. Screwing a fifteen-year-old? I'm pretty sure that's rape. He'd made a living supplying communes up and down the coast with harder drugs… meth, LSD, amphetamines. I'm not sure how he found us, but he was interested in Nash."

"And Nash, how did he react to his dad's reappearance?"

"Nash saw no need to begin a relationship with a man who claimed to be his father in name only. Ricardo came with apologies… and money. He said he'd changed, and he seemed less violent."

"Violent? You mean toward you?"

"The drug business was competitive and certain competitors had to be… let's say, discouraged from selling in his territory. There were plenty of beatings. He didn't hit me… much. But after moving in the second time, Ricardo was more settled and generous. Dealing drugs was lucrative. I needed the money, and I thought Nash needed a father. We lived together for two years until..." She let out a long sigh.

"Until what?"

Madison poured another shot.

"Until Nash and his dad connected over drugs."

"What the hell? Dad got Nash into drugs. Didn't you try to stop it?"

"Of course, but Nash was incorrigible for as far back as I can remember. By the time he was a teenager, interest in school vanished. But his willingness to experiment... scary. He was a natural leader, and his ability to attract friends was both magical and bothersome. Someone new was always hanging around the house. I believed the hippie philosophy—the goodness of people will win out. Turned out that wasn't true. Especially when Ricardo said he wanted another baby... with me. I told him no way."

Madison lifted the bottle, but I covered my glass. "For 8:00 a.m., I'm just right."

She splashed a round for herself, swallowed it, and placed the bottle on the bedside table. "If... if this is too much, I'll stop. I don't talk about my life usually. I mean... never. Tell me when to stop, Willi. But... I want you to know this."

"I'm in," I said. "He wants another kid—weird! What happened next?"

"Ricardo knocked up some street walker hooked on meth."

"How did you find out?"

"She appeared at my door one day with a stomach as big as a basketball and cries on my shoulder. She's the one who tells me Ricardo also employed Nash as a dealer. But it was gang stuff that terrified me. It was a shocker."

"I can't imagine you putting up with all this."

"I didn't. When a cop friend told me Nash was about to get busted, I kicked Ricardo out of the house and accepted a teaching job at the Art Institute in Minneapolis. Fleeing LA and giving Nash and myself a new start seemed the best thing to do. I was twenty-nine."

"Thus, the twenty-nine on your studio door."

"Exactly."

Madison paused. Tears dripped from the corner of her eyes. "I loved Nash so much and I didn't want to lose him. But the problem was bigger than I thought. Even after we moved, he continued his drug arrangement with his father using the biggest drug distributer in the country—the US Postal Service. Last year, he almost finished high school, barely squeaking into his senior year. Before graduating, the principal suspended Nash for selling crystal meth to classmates." Her voice drifted off as the alcohol took over.

She lay her head on my shoulder and closed her eyes. I pulled the covers up. After a soup fest and making passionate love, it was a sobering conversation. Her warm silky body twitched against mine, my heart tenderized as though sauteed with a special sauce. The warmth of our bodies twined together, lulled us back into sleep. When I woke, Madison was still in slumberland. The aroma of fresh coffee drifted in the air.

I gently pushed out of bed, put on my boxers, and headed for the kitchen. A shirtless young man poured a cup of dark roast into a mug I had given Madison. He glanced up briefly at my entrance, then puffed out a short laugh. "Who the hell are you?"

"Willi. A friend of your mother's." Nash was skinnier and taller than I imagined. His hair cut short, a serpent tattoo on his left arm, pants so baggy I wondered what kept them up. I offered my hand. He ignored my gesture as if he didn't understand what it meant. I lowered my hand to the coffeepot and poured.

He slurped his caffeine and stomped back into his bedroom. The door slammed shut. Ignored and canceled in one swing of the bat, left me stunned. With two coffees in hand, I met Madison halfway down the hallway, wearing a robe.

"You ran into Nash?" she stated.

"How'd you know?"

"Door slam and your mouth dropped open."

"Yes… we met." The two of us walked back to the kitchen.

"He's not the most talkative and can be dismissive, but don't take it personally. Nash's like that with everyone new." I set our coffees on the table.

"He's a kid."

"No, Willi, he's a man and I've been a terrible mother. Dragging him halfway across the country didn't help."

"You did what you thought right."

"Right for me, Willi. I don't even know how to talk to him. I've been under water so long I forgot what fresh air was like… till I met you." Her gaze shifted to my eyes. "Last night's soup fest was not only sexy, but fun. It's been a long time since I had plain old fun."

I smiled. "Not exactly plain… but very fun."

Her smile disappeared. "I live with this feeling of guilt about Nash. Every day I wonder, what could I have done better? So many times, I wasn't there, I had no money…"

I couldn't solve Madison's feelings of inadequacy, but I did have an idea. "Look, I have two tickets to a soccer game at Allianz Stadium. How about I ask Nash?"

"Thanks, Willi. It's a friendly gesture, but I doubt if he'll say yes." We both knew it wouldn't solve the deep-set problems that existed between them. And I agreed. Why would he go with me? But when I asked, he accepted.

•

IT TURNED OUT THE GAME between Minnesota United and Portland was three weeks out after a delay in the game schedule. I saw Madison frequently and ran into Nash several times. He always seemed in a rush to go somewhere, said little, and lived in his room when in the house. He surprised me when he called to remind me about the invite. When I picked him up, I put out my hand, and he shook it.

At half-time, I gave Nash twenty bucks for food, but he didn't return till the end of the game. While waiting for half-time to end, I heard a call over the loudspeaker system. "Orlando Rock, your party is waiting at the East Gate information booth." It was so shocking I thought I'd misunderstood the name. They repeated the announcement, which confirmed the name and place. It isn't a common name, and I jumped up from my seat, pushed my way to the main concourse and headed to the East Gate. When I arrived, the attendant said I'd just missed him. "Oh yeah," she waved an envelope. "He left this."

"For whom?"

"For WS." She put the envelope on the counter, WS printed neatly on the front.

I pulled out my license. "That's me, Will Steuben."

She didn't look at the ID and gave it to me. On my way back to my seat, my heart pounded. Impossible that this could happen. The mythical status Rodney had given Orlando was hardly believable, but it was odd that his name would be broadcast at a soccer game in St. Paul. I stood in front of a crowded food stand, opened the envelope, and unfolded the paper inside. There was only one word, 'Congratulations!' I felt like a fool. Obviously, the note wasn't for me. I slogged back to the counter and handed the envelope back to the clerk.

"Sorry, this note wasn't for me."

A confused look crossed her face. "What note?"

"You just handed me this." I showed her the envelope.

"Look, mister, I see a thousand people during a game. But I didn't give out any notes, at least not this game."

"You just gave it to me," I waved it in the air.

"If you want to leave it for someone else, put it in that wire basket over there," she tilted her head, "otherwise, put it in that square filing cabinet with the flip top over by that post." She pointed to a rubbish container, then turned to the next customer. I barged into their conversation.

"You mean you don't remember giving me this very envelope with WS printed on the front just five minutes ago? I showed you my license."

She leaned forward. "Do you know how many people I see in five minutes? Maybe you've had one-to-many beers. Got it?"

My legs wobbled as though the ground beneath me had softened. Like an astronaut floating in space, the boundary between reality and other worldliness blurred. I wondered if I'd lost it altogether. Was my mind that fragile? I crumpled the note and trashed the envelope.

When Nash returned from cavorting, he was holding hands with a young woman he met at the concession stand. Cinderella had a serpent tattoo beginning at her ankle, disappearing under her pant leg, exiting briefly on her exposed belly, before diving below her waistline. Her heavy eyeliner, tight black T-shirt with matching bandana, and a chain hanging from low hip hugger jeans indicated gang-banger all the way. She knew the team's equipment manager and had invited Nash into the team locker room with her. He got an autograph from their backup goalie on an event flyer. Nash also had an autograph of Cinderella's lips on his neck. And now she wore his belt.

WE PULLED IN AROUND MIDNIGHT. Madison met us at the door. Nash said thanks, then handed me the twenty I gave him for food, which surprised me, and hugged his mom, then trudged into his room. Madison raised her eyebrows and smiled.

"That's my first hug in a month. You made an impression."

"Yeah, maybe. I think he had a good time. What did you do?"

She led me to her drawing table in the kitchen and opened her sketchbook. She had drawn the young attendant at the information booth, with an unopened envelope on the countertop. WS printed on the front.

My head spun. "Madison, what's happening? How could you do that?"

She took both my hands and kissed me. "Something wonderful has happened."

My eyebrows furled. "What's going on?"

"I'm pregnant."

The announcement was so stunning, I couldn't talk. The pipeline between the brain and heart jammed, a thousand thoughts colliding simultaneously. I wasn't sure I was ready for fatherhood. "Yes, we've made love, but the first time was four weeks ago. How would you even know?"

"The voice told me I'd get a sign confirming my suspicions."

"What the hell. Madison, it doesn't work like that. You take the pill, right?"

"Pill shmill. Of course, I take the pill. But I've missed my period."

She flipped the page in her sketchbook. Drawn in pencil, a piece of crumpled paper with 'Congratulations' clearly written.

Madison's bright turquoise eyes stared into mine. "You've seen this?"

A small yelp escaped my throat. I was in new territory.

CHAPTER 8

SALINA

FOR THE NEXT FEW DAYS, I told myself what happened was impossible. The note, the pregnancy, the voice, all bled into every waking moment. Finally, I consciously forced it into a mental lock-box and shut the lid. I had the Smokey River Arts Festival coming on the weekend and there was a lot of preparation in front of me. I wouldn't see Madison until I returned.

The show was in Salina, Kansas, off I-70 on the way to Denver. The town lay between an occasional rolling hill and fields of wheat and corn measured by square miles. It was a twelve-hour drive from Minneapolis and I left at 5:00 a.m. for an early evening set up. Along the way, a thunderstorm rolled across the prairie with billows of heavy black cumulus swallowing up the land as it moved by. A storm like that was a show killer. I hoped the jury had put together high-quality work needed to create an atmosphere of excitement and challenge, thus bringing in money from collectors and patrons. Unfortunately, jurying procedures didn't always weed out low priced buy-sell items imitating original work. If you offered fast-food art, crowds consumed it at the expense of higher quality and more difficult ideas.

Because we couldn't drive on park grass, I would have to dolly in. I hadn't read instructions thoroughly and left my hand truck home, thinking I could unload at my booth. Packing a van with fragile artwork, along with a collapsible wind and waterproof structure, display modules, checkout, storage, lighting and sometimes a generator, proved artist ingenuity, or perhaps insanity. Forgetting my two-wheeler would make load-in a nightmare.

The clinking of metal pipes from the construction of E-Z Up and Light Dome tents across the fairgrounds mixed with blaring music, excited conversation, and sounds of laughter as on-the-road artists met once again. We stood around, catching up with tales of triumph—or tragedy—waiting for our turn to set up. Underneath all the camaraderie was an unspoken tension. For some, the show came down to rent for the next month or worse, gas money to get home. When my turn for setup came, I put on my Velcro back brace and slogged display and artwork across a hundred yards of freshly mowed lawn to my pre-assigned space. Fortunately, in one of my trips back and forth between the van and my booth, I spied a tall lanky teenager leaning against a tree with a cigarette dangling from his lips.

"Hey," I called over, "how'd you like to make a few bucks?"

"Might," he replied. "Doing what?"

"Saving an artist's life."

"Yeah? How much?"

I put a box in his hands and said, "Ten dollars, done in ten minutes," which was a lie. Without resistance, he followed me countless times, carrying boxes and display materials, telling me the story of how his father's life was spared during a tornado. I thought it was a good story, and it helped pass the time as we hauled everything to my space. Matthew Livingstone was a farmer's son, sixteen years old, strong, knew how to follow directions, and thought nothing I had was heavy. After we finished, I gave him a twenty.

He said he'd be back with friends to help at the end of the show, but I knew I'd be lucky to see him again. It's how teenage generosity works.

Two booths down from me, I saw Kim setting up her booth. She was wearing baggy jeans and a cut-off shirt, exposing a flat belly; her hair had grown out, tucked under a safari hat.

I walked over to say hello. "Hey, I didn't know you did this one. Where are you coming from?"

"Terrific show in Ft. Worth, then got called off the waitlist to this one. Just a hop from Texas."

"Lucky you." After a few seasons on the show circuit, a couple hundred miles are almost meaningless.

"Hey, Willi. Where are you staying tonight?"

"No plans. I'll find a room after setup." I figured an art fair like this in the middle of Kansas would present no problem finding a hotel.

"Bad move," she responded. "This show is a big deal here. Every farmer from a hundred miles around comes into town. I doubt if you'll find a room now." She paused for a moment, then added, "I've got an extra bed if you want to split?" It was a generous offer and a common way for artists to cut expenses.

"No, thanks, I'll find something." Even acts of generosity can get complicated.

"Don't think so," she replied. "I'm staying at the Six if you change your mind."

By dusk, the show grounds had transformed into the body of a small city. Artists put final touches on their displays. A few had just arrived, which meant a long night for them. Hammering at the music stages echoed in the twilight. Food vendors chopped chicken and vegies for the morrow's onslaught. Mother earth swallowed the sun, trees turned to silhouettes against a crimson sky. Famished and exhausted, I downed a truck stop dinner, then went hunting for a place to stay.

Kim was right. There were no available hotel rooms in town, not even cinderblock rooms at the truck stop. No-vacancy signs hung everywhere. I headed over to the Six where she was staying, found her van parked in front of her room, grabbed my bag, and knocked on her door.

The door cracked open. Two eyes peered out, then the door swung wide. "Hey, Willi, thought I'd see you. Come on in." She stood in a wrap-around towel and her hair dripping, just out of the shower. I sucked in a long breath and raised my eyebrows.

"You were right. No vacancies everywhere. Your offer still good?"

"No problem. There's still hot water if you want to shower."

"Thanks, heaven is real." I threw my small bag on a chair and headed into the bathroom. It was all steamed up, her underwear hanging from a hook on the door. I turned on the shower and climbed in, dousing myself with shampoo and fifteen minutes of glorious hot water, then it turned cold. When I walked back into the room, I noticed two things. Kim wore a silky red night shirt that barely covered her butt and there was only one bed.

For a moment, I stood bewildered. "I'll sleep on the floor."

"Willi, it's a queen. Plenty of room. If you behave, so will I. Besides, you've no one to cheat on… do you?"

I told her about meeting Madison at the Save-the-Geese rally in Minneapolis. It was a short story, but it left Kim with her mouth dropped opened.

"Madison Ayana?" She puffed out a laugh. "She's part Kiowa you know. Her parents were commune hippies."

"You know her?" It was one of those seven degrees of separation moments.

"We both studied with Peter at U Cal Santa Barbara."

She used his name so informally, it made me wonder how personally she knew him. "Peter Rosenbloom?"

Kim laughed. "Small world. Madison was his favorite." She didn't expand on the story, but there was more underneath. I wondered what else Kim knew about Madison. She pulled back the covers and climbed into bed. I got in from the other side and turned off the light. "Poke me if I snore," she said, "or if I don't."

Such a non-subtle come-on. I laid there staring into blackness. A lonely tractor trailer truck growled in the parking lot. The rosy aroma of her shampoo drifted over me. The pillow was soft, unkempt thoughts drifted by, then exhaustion overwhelmed everything. "Goodnight, Kim. Thanks for sharing the room."

"And a bed. Nite, Willi." She laughed. "Always wondered what it would be like to sleep with you."

My eyes closed like a door slamming shut. If either of us snored, I didn't hear it.

I woke early, the sun barely up. Kim's body curled around me with her arm around my waist, sound asleep. Her warmth and closeness were comforting, arousing, and my better sense told me to get up. On the road, relationships were plentiful... and complicated. I gently removed her arm, crawled out of bed, quietly collected my things, and headed over to a truck stop across the street. The faux Big Ben on the clock tower read 5:00 a.m. In the middle of scrambled eggs, bacon, and bitter coffee, my cell rang. It was Madison.

"Willi, I'm so glad you're awake."

"Barely," I said. "You're early."

"I was up talking with Nash until about an hour ago."

"Talking all night with Nash? Is that a good or a bad thing?"

"Willi, I feel like the building is crashing down around him. Something terrible has Nash cornered. His new girlfriend set up a drug deal with the equipment manager of the soccer team, but it's gone way over Nash's head."

"Let me guess, Cinderella."

"Nash said you met her at the soccer game. Why didn't you tell me?"

"Didn't think it was that important. She looked like a hooker."

Madison let out a long breath. "She's got a dragon tattoo from her ankle up her thigh to who knows where."

"That's her. What's happening, Madison?"

"The two made a deal at the soccer game. Nash promised to supply her with something called untraceable meth at cost. He heard about it from his drug dealing son-of-a-bitch father. The equipment manager bought a load of crystal worth thousands of dollars, except it *was* traceable. After a surprise drug test, the league suspended five members of the soccer team before a big game. They lost an important match."

"Can't he lie low for a while? Let it blow over?"

"It's more complicated, Willi. The team owner is a Chicago mobster, Joey Graveno. He had big money riding on the game, and he's pissed."

"What do you mean, big money?"

"Nash said a hundred, maybe two hundred grand."

I let out a long, whistling breath. "What do you want from me?"

"Graveno is a nasty piece of work. Nash thinks his life is in danger. He's asking to stay at your place for a while. He doesn't want me involved."

This was a risk. A big risk. An ambulance flew by the truck stop, siren blaring and lights flashing. The waitress came over carrying a fresh pot of Joe. "Uh oh, accident up on I-70."

"Yeah," I replied, "accidents all over the place." I held up my cup as she poured, sparking a memory of my mother serving coffee. She would invite soldiers' wives to the house during Desert Storm. My father was a medic and called into the Army reserves. I remember his whiskers against my face when he said goodbye. Four months later, he stepped on an IED loaded with nails. It was a quick war, and everyone was so proud and flag waving at how fast the US Army defeated Iraqi forces. But for thousands of soldiers, coming home wasn't easy for them or their families. The ones who didn't come home, like my father, were forgotten in the noise of victory. My mother listened to painful stories about husbands who came back changed men and memories about sons who never returned at all. She would put her arm around wives and mothers and cry with them. I was young back then, but I still recall her generosity. Nash needed help.

"Willi! Are you there?"

"Listen, Madison, give my apartment key to Nash and tell him to keep the place clean and don't touch my stuff."

"Oh, Willi. Thank you. I'm trying to absorb all this myself... It's sad and scary." Her soft breath blew into the phone. "You can stay with me... if you want to."

"I was thinking the same thing."

After a long pause, Madison continued.

"There's something else."

At that point, I couldn't imagine another complication.

"Remember, I told you I missed my period? I've been feeling ill in the mornings."

"Are you sure…" I let out a nervous puff. "Missing one period doesn't mean you're pregnant."

"I'm as regular as a Swiss watch. I know it's a lot to deal with at the moment. But… I'm sure I'm pregnant. It's our child and I want it."

My silence spoke volumes.

"Willi?" Madison's voice softened. "I know this must be shocking but… don't overthink it, just let it be for a while, Okay?"

"You're right, it's shocking, but not bad shocking. Just shocking. You're deep inside me, Madison, and I guess I'm deep inside you. There's nothing to think about and a lot to think about. The geese figure it out, don't they?"

"I miss you so much, Willi. You'll be such a brilliant father. Be careful on the road. I had a class yesterday afternoon, and I modeled in the evening. Last night, I dreamed you were sleeping with a serpent. There's so much going on and I'm so damn tired."

"You sound tired. Get some rest, okay?"

"Ya, I'll try. Good luck at the show and… yes, the geese do figure it out, and so can we."

She hung up.

I ate half my breakfast, thinking about fatherhood. A long ride into corn country and watching the sun angle over the horizon helped calm my fears. A new morning light illuminated the sky and my world.

CHAPTER 9

ANNABELLE'S STORY

"I ENJOYED SLEEPING WITH YOU last night, Willi." Kim rolled up the sides to her booth. "It was... different, very endearing. Your body runs warm. And you don't snore."

"It was sweet of you to share your bed." I pulled out sixty dollars and offered it to her. She waved the money off.

"No charge. Not that kind of girl."

"Ha!" I put the bills away.

"Where are you sleeping tonight, Willi?" Her eyes rolled upwards. There was no doubt about her offer. It was tempting....

"Look, Kim, I'm... involved. Trying to make it work with Madison. I found a truck stop room down the pike..."

"Good luck with that sparkler. Say hello for me when you get back. I'm sure she'll remember me." There was a lilt in her tone, and I wondered if the offer of a bed wasn't payback.

The show was busy on Sunday and by the time it closed, I was tired and satisfied. The People's Choice Award netted an extra three hundred dollars. I sold enough work to have a comfortable month. When Matthew and some of his friends showed up, a difficult takedown went smooth and fast. I stopped in to see Kim before heading out.

"Hey, cowgirl, how'd the show turn out?" She had barely packed anything.

Late customers had taken up her time. A red ribbon hung on the back wall. "You won a prize?"

"Yeah." She threw the ribbon in a box. "First place, painting. No big deal."

"Congratulations! That was $750 bucks, wasn't it?"

"I'm not sure. Didn't look in the envelope that came with it." She sounded somber and looked ragged. I walked over and gave her a hug.

"Thanks, Willi. That helps. I should give up the circuit. It's too damn difficult for one person."

"What else would you do?"

"I've been working with a couple of Chicago museums curating collections, especially contemporary paintings. Authentication is part of what I learned at school. Turns out I'm good at it and there's some good money to be made."

"Sounds stuffy. Will I see you at Uptown?"

"Ya, Uptown. I got invited but, ugh! It's a big show and hard for a single woman to do by herself."

"True, but the money is better than most shows. I'll look you up. Maybe you and Madison can visit."

"There's a snake pit there, Willi. I'm sure she'll be telling you about it."

When I turned to leave, she took my hand, drew close, and kissed my cheek. It wasn't a peck; it was slow, her tongue wet my cheek. I hadn't noticed her dazzling green eyes until now.

"Willi, I think you, me, and Madison are all connected, don't you think?"

"I suppose. Everyone is connected."

"No, that's not what I mean. It's a different kind of... oh, forget it. Give Madison a tongue twirling kiss for me."

•

AFTER DOWNING SOME BADLY BURNT truck stop coffee, I headed home. The plan was, drive two hundred miles, pull over, sleep in the van, drive some more. I wondered what Kim meant about being 'connected.' What was her relationship with Madison?

After an hour, I couldn't keep my eyes open and pulled into a rest area, put my seat back and didn't wake till early morning crimson spread into the deepest blue sky possible. My gas tank was on empty, caffeine level almost at zero. I pulled off at the next truck stop. The exit sign read, Minneapolis twenty miles. I thought it was a joke.

After a coffee to go and a thirty-gallon fill, I changed course, heading for the tiny town of Minneapolis… Kansas. It was a side trip I couldn't miss. I detoured north on a farm road, stopped on a small knoll, and got out. That boiling mass of burning gases, hanging somewhere in our dark universe, spread its golden arms over fields that stretched to the horizon. The scene amazed me, like opening the kiln after a firing and seeing the transformation of pieces I had spent weeks making. After glazing, they all go in chalk white, the high heat transforming them into colorful peacocks. The sunrise was assurance that somewhere all was well, and the laws of nature were working just fine, making the stupid mistakes of life seem inconsequential. Corn up to my knees had a wet, compost tang, vibrant and alive. Fluffy white cumulus floated in deep azure, one shaped like an angel lying on her side smoking a cigar. Ha! The universe had a sense of humor after all, and I wished that life could be a continuous stream of moments like this.

I thought about Nash and the troubled tide rising around him. Madison and curried squash soup made me smile. I longed to be with her. Amid these thoughts, my bladder rose in rebellion, feeling like a blowfish under attack. About a quarter-mile down the road, I pulled over, walked across a rickety wood-planked bridge and relieved myself. Under a stand of pines was a pockmarked gravestone with wilted flowers laying in front of it. The name on it clearly marked—'In Memory of Orlando Rock'. For a moment, my heart stopped. Everything stopped.

It had been months since I had heard Rodney's story about Orlando and now it all flooded back. His words reverberated—finding a fifty once was pure luck, but twice, that was something different. A tattered old mailbox with

Annabelle Livingston's name printed on the side stood by a dirt drive leading to an old farmhouse. In the distance, a dull yellow light spilled from the kitchen window. It was 5:45 a.m.; it was farm country, and someone would be up.

I'm sure she had seen the van pull into the driveway, so I climbed out slowly, giving her a good look at my face. If she trusted her instincts, she would see I was an open book. If she didn't, she'd already be calling the cops or loading a shotgun. I knocked on her door with mixed expectations.

"Yes?" an older woman greeted me, wearing bib overalls with a plaid shirt. Her eyes gave me the once over to confirm her thoughts.

"Sorry to disturb you, ma'am. Name's Willi Steuben. I saw a…" I paused, changing my story midstream— "a light on in the window and my van's overheated and I wondered if I could use your water for my radiator. I'm an artist coming from the art fair in Salina, exploring a bit, and I've run into some minor car trouble. You must be Annabelle. Your name's on the mailbox." It was a lame excuse, but I needed a reason for a visit so early in the morning. She looked out at the van.

"That's a Ford, isn't it?"

"Yes, it is," I replied.

"Why are so many of them white?"

"Not sure, ma'am. But I agree, most of them seem to be white."

"Something that size must have a 350 or better under the hood." She put on glasses strung from her neck. "Probably a one ton, and judging by the year, I'd say it was one of those new 10-cylinder jobs. You know they don't make them anymore. I'll bet it's a plugged thermostat in the radiator hose. You should let it cool down, son. I just put a pot of coffee on the stove. Want a cup?"

Her accuracy about the van was amazing, as well as her openness to my presence at such an early hour. Most city folk would already have called the police. Her crinkled face and deep spider-webbed eyes saw through the low-grade story of an overheated radiator, but she trusted her instincts and concluded I was safe enough for an invitation to coffee.

The house was tidy and full of furniture similar to my grandparents' house. There were pictures of her kids and grandkids on a buffet. I stopped for a moment in surprise. There was Matthew Livingston, the sixteen-year-old who helped me at the show. I told her I met Matthew, and he had hauled things to my booth. Matthew was the genuine break. We both relaxed. I had come for a reason, and she would wait for that reason to come out. Annabelle went for the Corning Ware pot on the stove. "If you want a little cream, help yourself. It's in the fridge."

Annabelle poured strong black coffee in two wheel-thrown mugs, then sat down at the table. "What are you doing on the back roads so early, young man?"

The feeling of stranger fell away. She held her mug with crooked arthritic fingers, her skin worn and leathery from years in the fields. She had already been up for a while. A couple of mixing bowls in the sink and a heavenly aroma signaled something was baking. There was nothing fancy about Annabelle, just a straightforward what-you-see-is-what-you-get kind of person.

"I live in that other Minneapolis, the one up in Minnesota. So, I got curious. Thought I'd catch the sunrise and a country breakfast."

"Well, this ain't no restaurant, but I do have a few biscuits in the oven." Annabelle pushed up from the table and checked the oven. "Be a few minutes though." She saw there would be no arm twisting here. "By the way, welcome to Minneapolis," she chuckled. "It's not fancy, but it has perks."

"I can't imagine living alone out here?"

"Alone? You're never alone in nature, son. There's more life out here than all the people in that city you come from," she answered in a friendly manner.

"My husband died years ago. I grew up on a farm nearby, raised crops, cows, rode horses. This is my life. How could I leave it? Now, most my kids live nearby."

"Whose marker is that at the beginning of the drive? 'In memory of Orlando Rock' written on the face."

Annabelle's eyes changed. She got up from the table, walked to the window, and looked out. Her stare seemed to go beyond the fields and far beyond Kansas. I had touched a sensitive memory.

"I had a friend named Orlando Rock," I said. "Is it possible there could be two people like him?"

Annabelle turned. Not only did she see right through that fabrication, but her gaze continued down to my fibbing soul.

"The world would be a different place if Orlando had lived," and without prodding, in an easy even tone, she began.

"It had been a bumper year for the crops. The hardest part was bringing in the harvest. We needed help, and that included whoever was coming down the road. That's how we met him. He was walking into town from who knows where, with a small rucksack thrown over his shoulder. He was young, single, handsome, and smart. As he passed the upper 40, he spotted our son, Thomas, having a tractor problem. As it turned out, Orlando was handy with tools as well as figuring out mechanical-type problems. He fixed a plugged fuel line, and we hired him on the spot.

"He grew up on a ranch somewhere in Oklahoma, or so he said. I never saw our boy take to anyone like he did Orlando. He became part of the harvesting crew like he'd lived here his whole life. When the weather changed, everyone was nervous about getting the harvest in. Back in those days, farm families worked together. That meant a lot of mouths to feed, and the womenfolk would keep the home fires burning while the men worked from dawn to past dusk. It wasn't community you learned about from a book or from some classroom discussion; it was community because we all needed each other to survive. The weather was hot one day, freezing the next, but the men didn't care. Bringing the crops in was all that mattered. Orlando worked as hard as the next man.

"Toward the end of harvest, daylight was short. One late afternoon, when the sun was almost down, the boys came in early on Ollie's flatbed. We could hear that old rattletrap a mile away and the call went out—the men were back! There would be hustle about the kitchen the likes of which you'd think the king's army was coming to dinner. I met the boys and told them food was on the table. A storm had come in and pea-size hail made a ruckus bouncing off the shed's metal roof. The ice stung when it hit 'cause the wind was so strong. Dark clouds were hanging low.

"We all sat down to dinner and I asked where Thomas was. 'Still on the middle 40, tractor problem,' one of the farmhands said. Orlando excused himself and I followed him out to the porch.

"I remember him saying, 'This ain't no regular storm, Annabelle.' A greenish tint covered the sky. He walked off the porch and headed down the road. He was worried about Thomas, and so was I.

"Not fifteen minutes after he left, our phone rang. It was the Halvorsons on the other side of town giving us the warning—funnel cloud coming. There was a flurry of activity. Everyone knew what to do. Tornadoes are common in this part of the country. The shutters slammed closed, machinery moved into the barn with the horses, doors secured. No one panicked, but there was plenty of fear. I grabbed our lock box with all our papers it in and we all headed out to the shelter. Orlando and Thomas were nowhere to be seen. In the distance, I could see the funnel dancing across the field heading our way. I stood by the hatch that opened into the shelter until someone finally yelled, 'Close the door, Annabelle, they'll be alright.' But I knew all was not well, and I was right.

"Thomas was under the tractor when the funnel cloud suddenly appeared about 40 acres away. He told me later that the sky was so black it looked like night, the air thick with debris. Orlando ran down the road shouting to get out of there. Thomas said the last thing he remembered was the tractor leaving the ground. Instead of everything speeding up like you'd expect, he said everything slowed down as the funnel swallowed everything in its path."

Annabelle walked over to the stove and brought the pot of coffee to the table. "Want some more?" I held up my mug. Tears welled in her eyes.

"What happened to Thomas and Orlando?" I asked.

She looked out into the barnyard as though yesterday was today.

"I stood by the shelter door for what seemed like a lifetime, waiting for those boys. Thomas was only eighteen. Dirt, hay, anything not nailed down began to move. The sky blacker than any soul that ever lived on this earth. Out of the dust and rain comes Orlando. They're both drenched, and he's carrying Thomas. I ran out to meet them and he laid my son right in my arms. 'He'll be okay,' he says in the softest, calm voice you could imagine. And Thomas feels so light you'd think he had given me a baby. Thomas was my baby.

"'Gotta let the horses loose,' says Orlando. 'It's gonna take the whole damn barn. Your house will be okay.'

"The wind was howling like a pack of wolves and the dust stung my eyes. What's burned into my memory is that as he's walking to the barn, the air filled with debris swirling about, but nothing touches him. Nothing! A wind strong enough to take down buildings and he walks with ease. And it's all in slow motion. Time itself had slowed down in some miraculous way. I yelled at him to get into the shelter, forget the damn horses, but by that time the noise was so great I could barely hear myself screaming. The funnel was fully visible, coming over the front forty. A minute before it hits, all the horses come running out. And then hands were around Thomas and me, pulling us down into the shelter. The doors slammed shut, and I was shaking all over, like a truck had run me over. I broke down sobbing. Thomas lay on one of the bunks. His face was all bruised and his arm twisted around backward. He just lay there hanging onto life itself.

"It's true what they say about a tornado. It sounds like a freight train passing right over you. And when the noise died down, there was just silence in that shelter. Seemed like hours before someone moved. The men finally opened the hatch and the smell of manure smacked us in the face. Everyone came up out of the shelter and just stood with their mouths dropped open. It was really something. The storm was already a mile to the east. I could even see some blue sky out in the western sky. The barn was just plain gone. The silos were still standing, so the harvest was safe. Debris was everywhere and the house… untouched, just like Orlando said."

Tears streamed down Annabelle's face. I took her hand, choked up myself. She put her other hand over mine and squeezed, then pushed away from the table.

"Those biscuits are done by now." She pulled a cookie sheet full of newly baked biscuits from the oven. She placed a bowl of fresh butter and a jar of home-made strawberry jam on the table. "After the storm, we searched for Orlando. We never found his body. Swept away, I imagine. His small bag of belongings gave no hint of relatives or where he lived. The only thing I kept of his is this coin." She pulled out a necklace that hung from a chain around her neck. It was hexagonal with a bird imprinted on one side. "If it hadn't been for Orlando that day, you would've had no help yesterday at the fair. Thomas is Matthew Livingston's father."

I sat there in some kind of suspended animation for a moment. I couldn't even talk. Finally, I picked up my cup and took a sip of coffee.

"Matt mentioned that his dad's life was saved, according to some family story. He didn't know how true it was."

"Mostly, my family thinks it's a crazy story carried on by an old, slightly confused grandma. Thomas seemed to think the whole incident was just a dream. He remembered little. But it's not something that comes and goes on a memory or a belief. If I hadn't felt Thomas in my own arms and seen the bright eyes of Orlando next to me, I might have forgotten the whole incident. But for me, it's more than just a memory. It lives right here," she put her hand over her heart, "right where it's supposed to."

There was no doubt something had touched her. Sitting together in that kitchen, a field of wonderment surrounded us. Whoever or whatever Orlando was, he became the common denominator between our two different lives.

For the next hour, I ate some of the best flour biscuits I've ever had. Annabelle talked about the farm and her family. It was like we had known each other forever. It was like two humans who never met ought to be. That was breakfast in Minneapolis, Kansas.

ON MY TRIP BACK TO Minneapolis, I couldn't get Orlando out of my mind.

"This here fifty is for me," Rodney had said just months ago. "It's from Orlando." I didn't know what to think. To each of us, our experience is real. But do our hopes and dreams, fears and beliefs shape what we want to believe, make them more than real than they should be? Somehow, all my complicated problems seemed quite small. The sky was deep blue from horizon to horizon, my window was down, and cool morning air washed over me as I sped back into the maze of events I call my life.

CHAPTER 10

TROUBLE

LATE MONDAY AFTERNOON, I PULLED into the parking lot behind my apartment building. Living with Madison while Nash used my place was a big change, but I'd take it slow. Packing up fresh clothes along with a few other belongings would be a start. Friends and my mother needed updating about the address change, but posting on social media didn't seem appropriate, at least not yet. Most of all, after the long drive, I needed a shower. Rory was standing outside the entrance, smoking an unfiltered Camel. His dark skin contrasted against the white pants, white shirt, and white Nike Airs. A perfectly smooth face with high cheekbones, a high voice, and purple hair belied the fact he was a successful trader at a brokerage firm.

"You look beat, Willi. And this is probably bad timing, but we need to talk."

"Now?" I set my rolling suitcase aside. "What's the problem?"

He blew a plume of smoke into the air. "It's your new roomies, Nash and Cinderella."

This was news. I didn't know Cinderella was also living at my place. "They're not my roomies."

"Whatever. The young guy, Nash, seems okay, even headed, smokes too much pot but I like him. Cinderella is a wild card, Willi. How do you know her?"

"What do you mean, wild card?" I sat on a nearby bench.

"One, I've seen her standing here by the door, blouse wide open with nothing on but a bra and panties underneath, which I don't really care, but the underwear should at least match. There are plenty of others in the building grumbling, and it's not about her underwear. She solicited Cupcake, trying to sell him 'untraceable meth,' whatever the hell that is. Who knows what else she's selling? She's trouble."

I let out a deep breath. After living in my place for only four days, Nash had already screwed things up. "Christ! I'll talk to Nash."

"That's not all, Willi. A black SUV has been hanging in the parking lot since you left. Someone is surveilling them. I've been watching out our window. They're gang-bangers. The driver gets out occasionally, leans against the vehicle and smokes a reefer. His black leather jacket has a lightning bolt on the backside. We took a photo, just in case."

"In case of what?"

"Look it, Willi. We're no spring chickens. Something is coming down. And it's coming down soon. Last time there were four of them in the van and I thought this is it, but something spooked them, and they drove away fast… like wheel-squealing fast."

My mind was spinning. "Thanks for the heads up, Rory. I'll speak to Nash."

"You've got yourself a real problem." He took a last puff on his cigarette and we both went inside.

The heavy odor of marihuana hung in my apartment, clothes strewn all over, my desk turned into a weighing station for pot. Ash trays overflowed with cigarette butts and reefer leftovers filled one of my green glazed salad bowls. Dirty dishes, trash cans overflowing with order-in food containers and empty beer bottles piled high in the kitchen. The couch had a big stain on the center cushion, with Cinderella's pink panties thrown on the back. Only one normal bulb lit the place. Everything else was blue light. It would take a professional cleaning service to make the place livable again. No sign of Nash or Cinderella.

I opened a window, skipped the shower, threw a few things in a larger suitcase, and headed out. Rory was right—I had a problem.

•

MADISON WAS IN THE STUDIO when I pulled in front of the house. The early evening sun set behind uncertain clouds, threatening rain. The sound of crashing from inside the studio made me hurry in. Glass shards were all over Madison's workbench, a hammer in her hand.

"Hey." I stood in the doorway.

"Willi!" The hammer stopped mid-air. Madison came around the workbench, and gave me a bear hug, then returned to her project. "I need some help."

"Who doesn't these days?" I set my suitcase on the unused potter's wheel. She continued cracking a six-foot mirror into jagged fragments.

"Madison, we need to talk."

"For sure, lots to talk about, Willi, but I can't get distracted right now. This… thing, this project is like fire in my brain. I've got to follow it through. I promise there'll be plenty of time to talk, okay?"

I nodded. There was no stopping her.

"I want you to sort out the odd-shaped pieces of broken mirror at least six inches long."

I laughed. "They're all odd-shaped." I put my arm around her waist and pulled her against me. She returned my squeeze with a quick hug, then drew away.

"I know, breaking up a mirror is a cold welcome home, but if I get started with you, hugging will lead to kissing, which will lead to…" she took a deep breath. "Self-control, right? Later, we'll let loose."

"Okay, what are we doing?"

"Finishing my sculpture. I need about seventy-five irregular shaped pieces."

"Glass shards and ceramic sticks. I don't get it."

"Perfect." She handed me a pair of gloves. "I'd be disappointed if it was obvious."

She scored the mirror and tapped the mirror. I picked through the shards, taking off sharp edges with a whining Dremel. She inspected every fragment before setting it aside for further use. Whatever she was making clearly existed in her imagination, with each element having a specific place. After an hour of Madison imposed no-talking, she announced, "Finished." I powered down the Dremel, leaving my ears ringing. We closed up the studio. I grabbed my bag and headed for the kitchen.

"Coffee or wine?" she asked.

"Got anything stronger?"

She laughed. "Sounds like it's going to be an evening. You hungry?"

"Starved." I set my luggage on a chair.

"Put your things in my bedroom." She pointed down the hallway, then said, "Our bedroom."

I tromped down to a small, cozy room. A large cactus almost touched the ceiling in one corner. The low dresser had a carved front with a wood-framed mirror over it. Lip balm, deodorant, and jewelry scattered about the top. A pair of curtained windows looked out over the pine studded drive. Her flowered fragrance filled the air. A nightgown hung from a hook in a small closet. On the unmade bed were four pillows. Balancing my suitcase on a stool, I laid out fresh clothes, then stood under a delicious hot shower for half an hour. When I returned, a bottle of Jim Beam and a turkey avocado sandwich awaited my arrival. I raised my eyebrows.

"You said strong." She had changed into shorts displaying the curve of her long legs, a loose studio shirt with tails tied around her mid-section. A bottle of Beaujolais sat on the counter, a goblet in front of her. "The show went well?"

"Yeah. Enough to make bills for the month, so I'm happy… kind of. When I went back to my apartment, I found it trashed. Did you know Cinderella was part of the living arrangement?" I picked up the oversized sandwich and took a bite.

Her eyes narrowed. "Cinderella is living with Nash?"

The whiskey went down in one slug. I poured another shot.

"That explains something. Nash stopped out here today." Madison sipped her Beaujolais. "I'm so sorry about the mess. His life seems so… mixed up."

"It's not your apology to make. He's an adult… I think."

"He was vague about what he was doing but told me he's never made so much money. I couldn't tell whether he was really happy or just stoned."

"Happy… I doubt it. Money… I'm sure it's coming in bundles. Cinderella is a dealer selling some kind of 'untraceable meth' at my apartment door." Madison bowed her head, listening silently as I retold Rory's story.

"Here's a twist, Willi. Nash told me he's never loved anyone as much as Cinderella."

"Drugs, sex, and money. What kind of love triangle is that?"

"Half the world." She finished her wine, but she didn't refill it. "Speaking of love triangles, I've got some good news."

"I could use some good news."

"According to the doctor, my pregnancy is normal."

"Boy or girl?"

"How about human being? Half you, half me."

Her face glowed. Our fingers laced together, and I leaned across the table, our lips met, wine mixed with whiskey, making the kiss sweet and slippery. Her hand reached behind my head and pressed our mouths together, tongues playing tag, bodies drawn upward from our chairs. We fell into a full embrace, the kiss continuing through my body, to the ends of my extremities. In that one moment, I never loved or wanted a woman more. I swept her into my arms and carried her into the bedroom, her arms slung around my neck.

"What, no soup?" her eyes excited and playful.

I unbuttoned her shirt. "Should we take a break while I make some?"

"Don't you dare leave." She unbuckled my belt. A moment later we snuggled under the handmade quilt, our bodies bound like a leaf pressed between the pages of a book.

•

WHEN I OPENED MY EYES, the sun beamed through the open window. The covers drawn back, the space next to me empty. I never heard her get up. My jeans hung over a chair, shirt folded. Her fragrance remained under the covers. I dressed and walked out to the kitchen. The coffee pot was already half-empty with a note, 'we didn't need soup.'

I laughed, poured a cup, and headed out to the studio. Where else would she be? I met her coming in the back porch door.

"Hey, Willi. You found the coffee."

I raised my cup. "And the note."

She smiled, and we walked back into the kitchen. She sat at the table, cupping her morning coffee.

"You been up long?" I asked.

"Four a.m.," she responded. "There's a lot going on, Willi. Things we didn't get to last night." She lowered her head onto her palms, squeezing her cheeks together. Strands of hair fell over her shoulders. "I wanted to tell you, but we were... busy. And you were exhausted."

"So, what's up? I'm listening." I nursed my coffee.

"The good part is... the police dropped all the charges against me. You know, the ones about assaulting an officer. Jimmy, my lawyer, did a great job snooping around. Reid had lots of complaints against him, and the cops didn't want to stir up a bees' nest. But..." She let out a breath, tears welled.

"But what?"

"Jimmy said some kind of investigation into Styles' death includes me."

An antique Arts and Crafts fixture hung on a low chain over the table, projecting a squared beam of light. Madison sat back. A shadowy figure lodged between a dark kitchen and the bright surface.

"Should you be worried?"

"Willi..." she started, "what if you know something... but that something might be taken as something else?" She rested her head in her hands, long frizzy auburn hair falling everywhere, individual strands silhouetted like snow crystals on a windowpane, her face subdued by shadows. I ran my hand over my eyes. Our fingers connected across the table.

"That's a little vague. Does that something connect you to Styles' death?"

"I wasn't going to show you this, but now is as good a time as any."

She went to her drawing table, opened the top drawer, and pulled out a large manila envelope. With a sigh, she spread photos and drawings on the table. There was Norman Styles laid out in the back seat of his car, staring lifelessly at the ceiling with sticks surrounding his head. There were a dozen of these pictures in different configurations.

"Christ, Madison! You put sticks around Norman after you found him dead?" I was horrified. "Isn't there some law that prohibits fiddling with a dead body? Who the hell knows how he died!"

"Believe me, Willi, it was upsetting to find him all stiff. I even tried to drag him out, but he was too heavy. A dead body isn't just a dead body and life isn't what a mirror reflects back at us." She shuffled through the pictures. "There was something very jagged and unpredictable in the way he lay. Besides, I didn't disturb him, and it gave me some insight into death."

"Insight into death?"

"Forget that I said that."

"Do you know how incriminating this is?"

"Don't you get it? It's all a damn experiment. Life is the laboratory. What we do in it is all experimental. Even Norman told me that art is nothing more than test runs and trials, overturned convictions, and jailbreak ideas, things that don't work, and then, that one thing that sparks the soul."

"The law will not see this as some art experiment!" When she looked into my eyes, I saw someone as fragile as the mirrors she had broken in the studio. "Oh God, never show this to the police, and for your own sake, burn these images."

"Never. They're part of the piece I'm building."

I rested my chin on folded fingers, head shaking involuntarily. "Then hide them. This is damning evidence."

"According to Jimmy, they're going to charge me with accessory to murder or worse. They found stick pieces in his hair, similar to pieces in a bag I carried. They say most victims know their murderer. I was the closest one to Styles and the last to see him alive."

"Pieces of sticks? Pretty flimsy evidence."

"There's more. And it has to do with Reid."

"Reid, the cop?"

My eye caught movement out the hallway window. When I stood, a police cruiser had just parked in front of the house. Madison saw it too. She panicked.

"I can't do this right now." She grabbed her coat, flew out of the kitchen. The back porch door slammed, and I could see her disappear down a path into the woods. A moment later, there was a knock. It was Reid Johnson.

I opened the door. "Hello, officer," my smile was as phony as the law he pretended to represent, "come on in." Reid tipped his hat.

"You're Willi, the new boyfriend. We met before, didn't we?"

I didn't go for the new boyfriend bait. "Yes, we have. Can I help you?"

"Is Maddy here?" he used her name as if she was a friend or casual acquaintance. She hated to be called Maddy. Well over six feet, he wore the full regalia of an armed officer, including nightstick and a buttoned-down holstered gun attached to a shiny black leather belt. It looked like official business to me.

"She's somewhere out in the woods, probably be gone a couple of hours. What do you want from Madison?" I kept the tone light, but I could feel a nervous knot in my stomach.

"I've got a few questions about the death of old-man Styles." There was something incriminating in the way he looked around, his eyes darting down the hallway toward the kitchen, then across the open living room.

"Can I help with anything?"

"Only if you know something about how Styles died."

"I never met the man, but I understand Madison knew him."

Reid gave me a hard look. "Oh? How did she know him?"

His question had turned into probing. I would do my own probing.

"How about a coffee, officer?"

"Sure," Reid answered.

As we walked into the kitchen, I remembered Madison's pictures still spread out on the table.

"Hey, Reid, there's the coffee pot." I pointed to the other side of the kitchen. "Pour a cup, I'll clean up this mess." I quickly shoved the images back into the envelope and casually threw them on the drawing table. Reid brought his cup and sat. His weight made the captain's chair creak and his nightstick poked through the spindles. It didn't look comfortable, which was fine. Staying long wasn't part of my plan.

"So why all the interest in questioning Madison?" I began.

"Nothing serious," he sipped from the steaming cup. "She was the last person to see him alive, as far as we know. That makes her an important witness."

"Witness to what?" I asked.

"Well… medical examiner's not sure how Styles died. They're saying it wasn't a heart attack."

"What do you think?"

"I can't really say, Willi. That's why there's an investigation. If there was foul play, we have to investigate."

"The police suspect foul play?" I was sounding like an interrogator.

"I really can't talk about it."

"And you believe Madison had something to do with Styles' death?"

He slugged down his coffee like he was drinking a cold beer. "We're just looking at evidence."

"What kind of evidence? Are you saying Styles was… murdered?"

Reid's eyes scanned the room, as if some clue lay on the counter. "It's just an investigation, Willi, nothing more… at this point."

"And Madison's connected with this investigation?"

He pushed himself out of the chair. "She's not telling us everything she knows, and I'd suggest you help her fill in the blanks."

"That's crazy to think Madison had anything to do with this."

"Calm down, Willi. It's only a few questions." He took a card out of his shirt pocket. "Have her call me when she returns."

I followed him to the front door.

"Thanks for the coffee." He tipped his hat and clomped out to his cruiser. The entire visit was shocking. I needed to calm down.

I walked out to the studio with murder indictment rumbling in my brain. It was a puzzle with many pieces missing. I wiped off the potter's wheel in the corner. It was a Brent CXC, a lot of power, impressive. There was plenty of space to build shelving and the shed behind the studio would be adequate for a kiln.

"Hey." Madison appeared in the doorway, looking pale. "Reid's gone?"

"He's gone." I gave her his card. "The cops want to ask you a few more questions about Styles."

"That's the second time he's hassled me. I'll call Jimmy and let him handle this."

"Lawyers are expensive. Why not talk to the police?"

She walked across the studio and sat on a low stool, ignoring the question. "You cleaned up the old Brent?"

"You made a good choice. Brent is a top line potter's wheel."

Her eyes flicked upward. "Maybe you could do some of your work here? There's space, and a shed out back for a kiln." She'd been thinking about this too.

I nodded. "You and I never finished our talk. How about a cup of tea for a change?"

"It's not going to be an easy talk, Willi."

"Let me guess. You killed Styles." It was a joke, but her gaze dropped to the floor. She turned away without answering the question.

My heart dropped into my stomach.

CHAPTER 11

MADISON'S CONFESSION

WITH STEAMING MUGS OF GREEN tea and a few homemade cookies, we sat across from each other. On the other side of the river, eight thousand acres of deep woods stretched into a state park. During the night, the view was abject darkness, a bit terrifying for a city boy. Madison nibbled a cookie, her fingers around the mug.

"How well do you know me?" she started.

"Sometimes I think I know you pretty well. At other times, I wonder if I know you at all."

"Okay, that's fair. But what I'm about to say will take you into new territory. My life will literally be in your hands. Should I continue?"

"Absolutely. You're the mother of my child, and I love you."

"Love can be a relative term, Willi." She took a deep breath. "There was more going on with Norman than anyone around here really knew. He was an incredible human being… his end-of-life situation was sad, you know what I mean?"

She was trying to find words for something that she hadn't yet been able to verbalize.

"I don't know what you mean. You're being vague. What was Norman's end-of-life situation?"

"Well, that's it exactly. He wanted to shorten his life. It was dragging out."

"What are you talking about?"

"Norman had Parkinson's. It was advancing quickly. His hands shook, he had trouble walking."

"You never mentioned that to me. I mean, that's bad, but was it an end-of-life situation? He could still drive, cook food, couldn't he?"

"In those last few weeks, I fed him and drove him to the neurologist. He was in a lot of pain, physically and emotionally. He knew he was deteriorating.

"His mother had died of Parkinson's—the disease was in his family history—and even advanced treatments weren't slowing the tremors.

"Norman loved life and wanted to die with some dignity, not rot like a vegetable." She put her head down on her arms. The chair creaked as I leaned back into the shadows. Storm clouds had darkened the sky, turning the bank of windows by the table into mirrors. Our ghosts seemed to have their own conversation within the panes.

"Are you saying Norman wanted to kill himself?"

Madison pulled herself straight in the chair. "Well, not exactly by himself. He had put a shotgun to his mouth but couldn't pull the trigger."

"That's a relief."

"Because of tremors, hand movements were becoming uncontrollable. Norman asked me to help him commit suicide." Madison went to the stove, poured more hot water into her mug. The overhead light swung when she nudged it, making our shadows jump to the floor.

"He what?" I steadied the light. "Madds, you didn't… did you?"

"Willi, say you'll still love me if I tell you this." Her eyes narrowed.

"Madison! For God's sake!"

"Promise!"

"OK, OK, I promise." My hands nervously tapped the tabletop.

"I was part of it. Norman showed me a book he bought on how to kill yourself. There were many choices with precise details and even ratings about how fast and painful each method was. We went over it together and he finally decided on asphyxiation. After many long conversations, he resorted to begging for help and, after thinking about it, I agreed. We planned the whole thing out, including what to do with his body. I thought it would be so simple, even beautiful. We both cried on his final day, just before he backed that green Ford of his into the shed and started it up. It belched so much exhaust I thought it'd be quick. He wanted me to lock the shed doors. If he knew there was no escape, he could go through with it. I couldn't believe our goodbye. It was like... see you later. With the vehicle running and Norman in the driver's seat, I locked the door and stood outside. The engine raced... maybe ten minutes, probably more, and then nothing, not one sound. I felt like a lonely atom lost in an enormous universe surrounded by all of creation. Something inside of me could feel him crying out until I couldn't stand it. I tore off the lock and threw the doors open. He was standing right there facing me, tears pouring down his cheeks. He collapsed in my arms, gasping for air, and I cursed myself for agreeing to go through with it. I dragged him into the house and laid him on the couch. Hours later, he began breathing normally, but he still looked sick, really sick. I wanted to call the doctor, but he wouldn't let me. Willi, I couldn't go through with it. The man was too precious. That seventy-two-year-old bastard was too precious. That night the voice came, soothed me and told me I would have a vision."

Madison sat there in a heap, staring out the window. Tears streaked her face.

I couldn't move. My mouth went dry, hands and legs frozen in place as our ghosts watched us from the window reflection. My fingers inched to the mug of hot tea.

"When did this happen?" I whispered.

"The day before Norman died out on TT," she answered quietly.

"And you think this relates to Norman's death?"

"At first, I was sure of it. He was in terrible shape, but he was conscious and talking. I told him I'd see him through to the end. He wouldn't have to die alone. Suicide wasn't going to work. He nodded in agreement. After feeding him soup, he seemed better. I took the path from his property back to the studio, feeling relieved. That's the last time I saw him alive.

"He didn't want anyone to know he tried to commit suicide, especially his daughter." Madison sat back into the shadows, leaving only one ghost in the window staring back at me.

"Norman had a daughter? Where was she through all this?"

"She lives in New York City, teaches at NYU. I've talked to her a few times. She hardly knew her father."

"How did Styles get out to TT, find his way into the backseat, and wind-up dead? Did you drive him out there?"

"No! When I left him, he was alive! Something happened after I left."

"And what about the vision?"

"The vision was about missing pieces—I wasn't seeing the complete story. That's when I started thinking Norman was murdered. It's also when I started building 'Fractured'."

I leaned forward, clasping my hands together. My shadow in the window looked like someone saying prayers. And maybe I was. Praying that all this was a dream, and I'd wake up to find it all washed away. But that wasn't the case.

CHAPTER 12

FRICTION

IN THE MORNING, WE ATE fresh bread from a local bakery, drank ground Nigerian, which made a rich dark coffee, and finished breakfast avoiding last night's conversation. Madison's plan: finish her sculpture. She refused to chase Nash around trying to fix his life. She would have a 'talk' with her ex. She'd also talk to her lawyer, Jimmy, about the investigation.

I had to get back to my studio and return to work. The next show was in Des Moines. If successful, I could pay back loans that fueled the first six months of the year. I had walked on the financial edge of disaster for so long, it seemed miraculous I'd made it this far. It was mid-morning when I pulled into the parking lot. Rory was waiting by a new Tesla.

"Where did that come from? The car is amazing."

"What? Gay people don't have money?"

"Ha! So exposed," I retorted. I ran my hand over its smooth contours. "She's a beauty."

"Be careful, honey. She's a he."

"Nice butt." I ran my hand over the rear quarter panel. Cupcake came out, waving his white stick back and forth.

"Hey, Willi."

"Admiring your new wheels. Spectacular car."

"Isn't it wonderful?" Cupcake said. "I love that new car aroma and the warmed leather seats. The downtown brokerage firm hit pay dirt when they hired Rory. He's sooo good at the markets and his gay customers love him. We've waited two years for delivery."

I laughed. "Some things are worth waiting for."

"Listen, Willi," Rory opened the door for Cupcake, "I've got news about that van hanging around the lot. They weren't spying on your roomies."

"They're not my roomies. What were they doing?"

"I think those gang bangers were there for protection. After you left yesterday, Nash and what's her name, Cinderella, showed up with a U-Haul and moved out."

"Moved out?"

"Two Asian men got out of the van wearing black leather jackets with a lightning bolt embroidered on the backs. They helped your friends load out."

I puffed out a breath and shook my head. "Why would Nash and Cinderella need protection?"

"Oh baby, it gets complicated from there. Another car pulls up front next to the U-Haul. Some guy with two young girls with him, both blossomed out, you know, the pushed-up boobs, lots of cleavage, and spiked high heels. They all get out and the girls hug Cinderella. I doubt if they're much older than fifteen. But it's obvious Cinderella is their go-to girl pimp. They all pile into the car and drive off. Good riddance to all of them."

"Thanks for the heads up, Rory." I headed to the door.

As I passed by, Cupcake grabbed my arm and whispered, "I think the Supe wants to talk to you."

"I bet he does."

Rory slid behind the wheel of the Tesla, rolled down his window and waved with both hands as the vehicle drove itself out of the lot. I headed to my apartment.

THE PLACE WAS A SHOCKING mess, even with all their belongings gone. But on my desk was a plastic bag with a note: 'Willi - Sorry, the place is such a pit. This should cover any clean up expenses. Nash.'

In the bag was at least a pound of dope. I had stoned my way through college, but had given the habit up. This amount would last a lifetime and I didn't want it. Caught with a reefer is a misdemeanor, but a whole pound of grass, that's a felony—in this state. I called an old potter friend of mine.

"Bear," I said, "I've got a little problem you'll love. Too much dope."

There was a moment of silence on the phone. "You're joking, right?"

"Free," I retorted. "A pound, maybe a little more."

Bear had saved me one time when I blew my transmission on I-90 crossing the bottom of Minnesota. We were both heading to the same show in Sioux City. When he saw me pulled over on the side of the road, he stopped and drove me to U-Haul. Instead of dropping me off, he followed me back to my fully packed van, helped load up the rental, and waited with me for the tow truck. It was an act of generosity common between artists.

Twenty minutes later, he showed up at my door and almost squeezed my guts out with his hug. We talked about old times and upcoming shows. I gave him the bag of dope.

"This has to be worth over a thousand bucks, Willi. You sure about this?"

"Ya," I replied, "treat me to coffee next time we meet on the road."

"Hopefully it won't be over a broke down trani. Thanks, Willi." He rolled a joint, lit up, and offered me a drag. I declined. He left, swinging the bag all the way to his van in the parking lot.

I packed essentials out of my apartment, thinking about the extraordinary change I was stepping into. Madison's house was now my home, and I was about to be a father. I wasn't sure who I'd be to Nash, but there was no doubt he was a big part of Madison's life.

That afternoon in my small garage pottery, I threw large bowls with a heavily grogged clay, hoping they'd dry by Wednesday, in the kiln, glazed and fired on Thursday, cooled and packed out for Des Moines on Friday morning. It was a tight schedule. I didn't get back to Madison's place until after midnight. The lights were on in the studio and once again, the sound of crashing echoed in the night. But this time, Madison was furious.

CHAPTER 13

A DANGEROUS CONNECTION

"I JUST HUNG UP ON Ricardo, my ex-husband, child rapist, father of Nash." Madison held up a hammer.

"Husband? Child rapist?"

"What should I call him—the man who fathered my son? Nash's non-parent interventionist? The man who got me stoned and drunk one night, then knocked me up, a fifteen-year-old who knew almost nothing, then left to continue his drug-run down the California coast. He's got no idea!" She hit a piece of mirror, sending splinters all over. I gently took the tool from her hand and laid it on the workbench.

"You're making a mess. What did he say?"

"Nash called him a few days ago and explained the 'situation'. Ricardo said he knew of Joey Graveno, a small actor on a big stage. Sells meth in Chicago. Ricardo then connected Nash with some… 'friends'," she air-quoted friends.

I nodded my head. What Rory and Cupcake described fit. "I assume his idea of help was connecting Nash with the Lightnings or whatever they call themselves."

"The Asian Bolts. They're an offshoot of a larger gang based in Chicago." Madison leaned against the workbench, lips curled in a snarl. "How could that son-of-a-bitch do that to his own son?"

"Do what?"

"Tell him he's got untraceable meth when there's no such thing, then connect him with a gang that will only draw him into a more dangerous situation. My God, Willi! The man's insane."

"How much trouble is Nash in?"

"Every time Ricardo says small, I'm thinking big. I have a feeling Graveno is no small-time actor, and he's going to exact pain for such a loss. And protection via an Asian gang? What's that mean—Nash in the middle of a gang war? Good God!" She picked up the hammer and smashed more glass.

I walked to the other side of the workbench, swept glass pieces into a pile with a hand brush. "Nash is a smart kid. He'll work this out. I'm not sure how either of us can help. What else did Ricardo say?"

"He's got some Chicago connections. He'll see what he can do."

"Okay, so at least Ricardo is on Nash's side. Maybe that will help."

"Ricardo is the small-time actor. And he's self-serving. I'm not even sure why Nash called him." Her head hung low. There was no simple resolution here.

"Furthermore, Nash warned me to stay out of his business. Says he doesn't want me to get hurt. I'm scared, Willi. Really scared for him."

"Let's sleep on this. There's nothing we can do tonight."

With a last swing of the hammer, glass shards scatter across the workbench. "You're right. But I'll be damned before some thug hurts Nash!"

CHAPTER 14

FRACTURED

OVER THE NEXT FEW DAYS, her anger mellowed. When I woke Friday morning, as usual, Madison had been up for hours. The van was packed, ready to head out to the Des Moines Art Fair. Rumor was it could be a great show, but a crowd's taste is difficult to predict. I had decided on artsy, and loaded up with bigger pieces. Madison was at the kitchen table, drinking Kona out of a mug I made, and sketching. I poured a cup, gave her a hug, and sat across from her.

"I enjoy sleeping with you, Willi. It's your rhythmic breathing and soft shoulder. I'm a boat snuggled next to its mooring. Everything seems calm and Okay."

"It is calm and Okay, Madds. I love how your contours fit mine. You're like cuddling a soft pillow."

She sipped her coffee, closed up her sketch pad. "I finished the sculpture."

I had seen it from across the studio as she worked on it over the past few weeks, but she wouldn't let me view it front side or close up. It was seven feet tall, three feet wide, a piece that would hang on the wall.

"Finally! Let's go see it." I pushed back from the table.

"You go. I'll make pancakes. I found a blueberry patch in a field close by."

A WOODEN FRAMEWORK SUPPORTED THE piece vertically. Cast ceramic sticks lay like you'd see them on a forest floor, framing mirrored fragments cleverly grouted together. She had set each jagged piece precisely, some raised and angled, reflecting different planes. When I stood before the sculpture, my reflected image fractured, parts of my body missing. I looked like an incomplete puzzle. It was a metaphor, but its power was unnerving. I'm not sure how long I stared at myself—stunned.

When I walked back into the kitchen, Madison met me at the door. The aroma of bacon grease, pancakes, and fresh coffee filled the air. She put her finger to my lips. "Shh. Don't say a word. I want you to absorb it. We'll talk after pancakes."

By the time we finished breakfast, I was bubbling over. "I've got to say it."

"Okay, Willi, belt it out."

"The whole thing is not about the piece itself."

"So far, so good. Continue."

"It's the reflection that completes its purpose."

"And what about the reflection?"

"Fractured. Perhaps we're all fractured."

"Bingo! Let's make love."

"Ha! Don't you want to hear more?"

"I want to feel more." She grabbed my belt and tugged me down the hallway but stopped halfway. "Maybe we should make love in front of my new piece?" She changed direction, still pulling me by the pants. "Come on, Willi."

In the studio, we shed our clothes and angled the piece to give a side view. Throwing her arms around my neck, she jumped up, scissoring her legs around my waist. She was lighter than expected and we made wonderful love, laughing at our reflections as we bounced in front of the mirror. No matter which way we turned, there were missing pieces. She pressed into me, kissed my face and lips. We finished with her leaning over the workbench, both of us howling like wolves. I collapsed, my throbbing heart beating against her smooth, sweaty back. We stood in that position for some time, feeling each other's rapid breathing, enjoying the marvelous energy surging between us.

"You smell divine. Hey, did you use my Orbis?"

"I love its gentle aroma, doesn't attack the nose, and it reminds me of you." She turned, putting her arms around me. "I wish you didn't have go."

"It's not for long, I'll be back Monday."

With pounding hearts, we stood naked in front of 'Fractured'. Naked and fractured were part of our relationship. "That was quite the initiation ceremony," I said.

Her face turned serious. "There's another part of this sculpture you're not seeing."

"Okay, what's that?"

"We're all trying to fit the pieces together, and mostly they don't fit as we want them to."

"That's only natural," I said. "Everyone's trying to shape their future."

"The future is like ten thousand rain drops collected in a cloud. What I see the is storm that's coming."

"What does that mean?"

"Forget that I said that. I don't want to charge up your over-thinking brain." She laughed, slipped into my boxers, and threw her panties at me. "See you in the kitchen." She grabbed her clothes and walked out.

I dressed in front of the piece, watching my missing pieces change in the reflection. When I moved, the voids changed size and position, never the same. Could I ever fully know myself or another person or a future that had so many changeable parts? Madison's missing pieces were an unsolvable mystery. Yet somehow, she could see the storm those pieces produce. It left me with unanswerable questions, which I'm sure was part of her intention.

MADISON POURED COFFEE WHEN I came in. "I read the list of artists at the show. I know one."

"Really, who's that?" I sat at the table.

"Kimberly West. A painter."

"Kim? We meet all the time on the road. She's a good friend. Where do you know her from?" I hadn't told Madison about the shared hotel room in Salina.

"Kim and I met at the Art Institute in San Francisco. She was Peter's 'darling' until I came along. I had no idea about the bees' nest I was getting into. Kim and Peter were having casual sex. I don't think it was anything really deep. But Kim was attractive and used it to get her way with Peter. And when I arrived, she helped me learn the dos and don'ts around him. As a painter, she was far beyond other students; an enormous talent, and I could see why Peter took her on. I fell under her spell. She was... alluring, understanding, easy to talk to, and always touching me. Then one night, after sharing a bottle of wine, she asked if she could kiss me. I said yes. It only took one. We made love."

"Wait. You had sex with Kim?"

"More than once, Willi. She was a marvelous lover and experienced, and she opened a whole new world for me. I think she fell in love and was jealous that Peter turned his attention to me. As my 'study' with Peter matured, Kim moved on. She went after Rita, his wife. Peter and I became lovers, while Kim and Rita had their own affair. It all fit together... at least for a while. Kim gets off on doing both the husband and the wife."

I thought about how close I came to falling into Kim's obsession.

"So... you're Bi?"

She laughed at my seriousness. "So... I'm one at a time, Willi, and I hope you are too."

"Well, let's get married."

"We're living and sleeping together, just had sex in the studio, we're about to have a baby, and devoted to each other. If you want to have a ceremony, sure, let's do it. But I don't need government papers to prove our partnership."

"I don't need to prove anything either," I replied. "I've seen one of the most magnificent sculptures of the late twentieth century. My partner is a genius, and I couldn't love her more."

"Okay, then. Your partner/lover has a request." She set a steaming mug in front of me and put her arms around my neck.

"Anything."

"I want you to take the sculpture to the show in Des Moines."

I lost my breath. "Take that huge mirror piece to Des Moines? I don't think I can do that. Outside of the logistics, the booth is only for work made by the exhibiting artist."

"Make yourself a collaborator."

My mind spun, heart skipping beats like a jazz pianist. "Why so important to exhibit at this show?"

"The awards jurors, Willi. Two are from the Smithsonian."

CHAPTER 15

DES MOINES

BY LATE AFTERNOON, WE HAD built the sculpture's wooden crate and packed it in the trailer. I made it to Des Moines after set-up hours, which was fine with me. Navigating the narrow path between rows of booths with a trailer is easier if no one is there. By midnight I finished set up, with Fractured boxed but in place. I sacrificed half of my display space to fit it in. I also risked being ejected from the show for bringing another artist's work.

My reservation at the Hilton was a splurge. I was exhausted and grateful it was only a couple of blocks from my booth. Even at such a late hour, the hotel tavern overflowed with artists and travelers. I found a seat at the bar and ordered a beer. As I sipped a local IPA, a hand ran over my shoulder and down my back. When I turned, Kim kissed me on the cheek.

"You're salty. Late set up?" She wore jeans with leg pockets and a button-down shirt, her hair cut short.

"As ready as I'll ever be," I answered. Knowing a piece of Kim's history made for an awkward meeting.

"Where you located?"

"On the bridge."

She winced. "Ouch. That can be a windy spot. Be sure to weigh down your tent." She slid onto the stool next to me.

"How about you, ready to kill it?" I asked.

"All new work. It's a gamble. Have you seen who the awards jurors are?"

"Yeah, some mucky-mucks from out east."

She ran her hand up my back, which gave me shivers. She was a temptress.

"Not just any jurors, Willi. They're scouting. The Smithsonian show is a crack at big time collectors."

I finished my brew. "Well, I'm going to take a crack at a soft pillow and a few hours of shuteye. Good luck tomorrow."

"Hey… did you say hello to Madison for me?"

I slugged my beer. "She remembered you from college. Didn't say much, but she says hi." Kim's eyes turned down, then she smiled.

"Madison lived on the wild side. We should talk, if you wanna hear a few good stories."

Before I could respond, a woman carrying two mixed drinks slithered up to Kim. "There's a free table," she gently bumped Kim's hip. "Let's grab it."

"See you later, Willi." She kissed me on the cheek again, leaving her lips pressed against my skin for an uncomfortable second too long, then disappeared with her friend into the crowd. I headed to bed.

EARLY THE NEXT MORNING, I rolled up my tent sides and unscrewed the box holding Fractured. With the sides removed, I pushed the piece vertically, using the back of the box as its holder. The weather couldn't have been better, sun and no wind. My booth neighbor was a leather worker, Sein McGovern, a six foot four two hundred seventy-five pounder from Dublin. He had moved to the States when he was a kid but still had that Irish twang. I knew him from the circuit, but we had never been neighbors. He self-tanned and dyed the hides, made backpacks, computer bags, and tight leather pants for women who want to show off their legs. His beautifully crafted boots came in various colors with custom embossed designs, including a pair with diamonds embedded around the top edge.

Over the course of the show, we became friends, sharing road stories and tidbits of personal history during slack moments. Divorced and obviously not over it, his ex-wife, Josie Wallflower, had worked with him for years. Their yelling matches during set up were legendary. He needed money for alimony and a little spending cash. I didn't think artists made enough to pay alimony, but I was wrong. He was busy both days.

"Willi," he said, "I've seen you on the circuit many times, been meaning to say hello. I love your stuff. Josie bought something from you in Springfield last year."

"I remember Josie. We traded for a leather cowboy hat." Trading goods was common between artists.

"Well, my trading days are over for a while." He wiped sweat from his brow. "I need cash."

I nodded. "Don't we all."

"That colossal piece in your booth, the one with the broken mirror pieces, it's unworldly."

"Unworldly. What an excellent description."

"It's so out of place, different. If that's a new direction, you should definitely follow it." He stood for a minute in front of the piece, stepping to the right, and to the left. "It's a showstopper."

Well, it was a new direction. Not exactly what he was thinking, but it made me worry that Madison's piece didn't fit my work or the display.

"Hey, Willi." I heard a familiar voice. Kim entered. "Hello, Irish."

"Hello, Kim." For a moment an acrid energy filled the space between them.

"I gotta finish setup," he said and left the booth. I turned to Kim.

"Hey, Kim. You ready to go?"

"A bit under the weather," she replied. "One of those nights."

I could only imagine.

She walked directly to the mirror and stared. "That's the problem, Madison was always so damn good." Kim stood mesmerized by her reflection, then turned to me. "You're taking a risk, Willi. It's pretty obvious the piece is her work."

My heart leaped to my throat. There was no wiggle room. Kim could see through any explanation I could muster. "It means a lot to her to be here."

"It's a magnificent piece. I'm sure it'll be a prize winner. She always was the best… and she knew it. Good luck." She ran her hand over the ceramic stick framework. I walked her out of the booth. There was more than a drop of bitterness in her tone that made me worry. With such high-powered award judges, even a hint of impropriety would be trouble—big trouble.

Irish watched her walk away. She wore a loose blouse and tight jeans that left little to the imagination. I heard him sigh.

"You know Kim?" I asked.

"Yeah, you might say we've had our ins and outs."

Before I could get an explanation, my cell phone rang.

"Willi," it was Madison, "I've been worried. Did the piece make it okay? Are you set up?"

"It looks great, Madds. Even Kim thought it looked great."

A sudden silence fell between us. Then a long sigh. "Be careful around her, Willi. She's well aware of the stakes. Maybe you should board it up."

"No way! It's here, I'm here. All engines engaged; this show is a go. I'll call you later." My voice was far more confident than I was. When I looked up the street, the jurors were just starting their first round. The art fair was open, and I was sweating.

Awards jurors start with a quick glimpse of the show. After a walk-through, they'd settle into the business of judging each booth individually. On the first round, a long look was not more than a studied stare. With over two hundred booths to ferret through, there wasn't much time to get awards out by the artist dinner that night. They made a slight pause at a glassblower's booth up the way, and a brief stop at Irish's. As they passed my booth, they not only stalled, they entered. As if my work didn't exist, they stood in front of Madison's piece, mesmerized. One juror approached me.

"Does this have a name?"

Serious work had titles. "Yes," I responded. "Fractured."

"Indeed," she said in an icy voice. "You should make sure the title is in view."

"Yes, ma'am. I will."

Her gaze briefly fell on my larger pieces and without another word, they left the booth, continuing to walk the long row in front of them. Irish came over.

"That's a good sign."

"You never know with judges," I retorted. "What catches their fancy one moment disappears in the next."

"Good strategy," he replied, "keep expectations low. But jurors rarely stop on the first round."

"Keep expectations low," I repeated. "There's a ton of great work here."

LATER IN THE AFTERNOON, THE same jurors made their second round. Sometimes they introduced themselves, sometimes they walked by. When they arrived, the first juror introduced herself. Evelyn was the granddaughter of Joseph Hirshhorn, who founded the Hirshhorn Museum in Washington, D.C. My armpits turned to waterfalls.

"Interesting piece," she began. "What inspired this creation?"

My mouth opened, but no words came out. Conversations with Madison bubbled up. "What we see here is our fractured image, thus the name. The piece suggests who we are is more than the sum of our parts. Parts of our reflection are missing, leaving mysterious voids." I could hear Madison laughing at my answer.

Evelyn's partner, the second juror, came over. "And how does it relate to your other work on display?"

"Only that clay is the contributing media," I explained. "It's a one hundred-eighty degree turn from functionalism. Totally different direction."

"It certainly is," Evelyn proclaimed. "I'd almost think someone else made it." Her comment made me shudder. They stood in front of the mirror, whispering to each other, then walked out of the booth, pausing, looking back in and writing copious notes. When they left, I let out a long breath. Irish came over and shook my hand.

"Congratulations, Willi. Did you see them scribbling on their clipboards?"

"Don't be so sure."

About six o'clock that evening, just before the fair closed, a messenger from the show office delivered a note requesting my presence at the artists' awards dinner. They would announce three best of show winners and merit award finalists in seven different media. First place would receive three thousand dollars and an invitation to the Smithsonian show. Second place was two thousand, and third place, one thousand dollars. All winners would receive re-invites to next year's festival. As I closed up, Kim popped in.

"Hey, Willi, are you going to the artists' dinner?"

"Ya, I'm going."

"You got invited, didn't you?"

I took a deep breath. She already knew.

"Ya. How about you?"

"They asked me too, you know, to make sure I was there. They announce runners up and place winners, so who knows if we won anything? Wanna go together? Disappointment loves company."

I said sure before I could think through all the ramifications.

KIM MET ME AT THE happy hour for free wine and beer. Pay for your own mixed drinks at the bar. The crowded room was noisy and stuffy. I hated these affairs. Kim was good at schmoozing, which relieved some of my uneasiness. After a few drinks and a lot of small talk with artists we knew, bells rang. Doors to the banquet swung open. Sculptural centerpieces made by various show artists adorned cloth covered round tables. Servers wore white gloves, circling with wine bottles keeping our goblets full, and chefs cut slices of prime rib to order. Salads and side dishes, sauces and fresh breads filled the buffets. Kim sat next to me. Neither of us ate much. After dinner, servers cleared dishes and brought dessert. While we ate, the show coordinator began the awards ceremony with endless thank yous and acknowledgements, especially to the jurors. Finally, he announced seven merit award winners. Kim took my hand. Even if you weren't a place winner, a merit award was good for the resume and an invitation to next year's show. Seven runners up later, we clapped for all of them. There was a mixture of excitement and disappointment in the eyes of these award winners. Kim's palms were sweating. My heart was in my throat.

"And now the finalists for the three top prizes." The announcer was spotlighted and spoke into a microphone. "Third place finalist—Philip Johns, glass." The crowd went wild. Phillip was well known and liked on the circuit. The tall lanky glassblower strode to the front of the room, a big smile on his face, while a picture of his work appeared on a large screen behind the podium.

After applause subsided, the speaker paused and looked down at the list on the podium. "Second place finalist…" he looked up at the crowd, then back to the sheet of paper in front of him, "Kim West, painting. Come up here, Kim." Again, applause and whistling. Kim squeezed my hand and whispered, "You're next." She walked to the front and stood by Phillip's side. An amazing painting appeared on the screen. After the clapping subsided, the Master of Ceremony paused, looked down at the podium, purposefully delaying the big announcement. A cloud of silence covered the room. My heart was in my throat.

"And our winner… William Steuben… ceramics!" Again, applause, but as I walked to the podium, Irish stood and shouted, "Go Willi!" which brought the crowd to their feet. When the image of Madison's mirror appeared, I blushed with guilt. The crowd roared. I wanted to run out of there.

Kim whispered in my ear, "Steady, Willi, steady."

The gush of praise was overwhelming. My face was beet red. Kim held my held as my knees wobbled. When the ceremony ended, Kim gave me a nudge. "Let's get a drink." I couldn't agree more. We pushed our way out of the crowded banquet room as artists heaped congratulations on us. I couldn't get out fast enough.

I headed for the hotel tavern, but Kim tugged me toward the front entrance. "Let's go somewhere quieter. There's a place a couple blocks from here." I agreed. One more congrats and I'd explode.

WE SAT IN A DIMLY lit corner, and I paid for the first round. "How does it feel?" Kim asked.

"Shitty." I let out a breath that almost blew out the candle on the table.

"She's such an enormous talent, Willi. I've seen no one like her. Neither did Peter."

"That's right, Madison mentioned you both studied under Peter Rosenbloom. Was he in love with her?"

"Peter? I don't think he was capable of loving anyone. Her talent captivated him. They were like Mozart and Salieri, one a genius, the other struggling with his limited abilities. The thing he could do was seduce her."

I said nothing about Kim seducing Madison.

"What kept her in the relationship?"

"She got what she wanted, a trip to Paris, study under a famous master, all expenses paid for. What she didn't expect was to get pregnant."

"Pregnant? Are you saying Nash isn't...?"

"No. Nash was about three years old. I admired Madison for being a single mom and a student. But screwing Peter turned sour. After Peter's wife discovered Madison was pregnant, she exploded and flew to Paris. I begged her not to go." Kim's stare fell to the tabletop. "I had my own attachments."

The waitress interrupted, asking if we wanted another round. I ordered doubles for both of us. We sloshed them down and Kim ordered more of the same.

She pursed her lips. "Madison had an abortion in France, then flew home and quit school. I looked for her, but she didn't want to be found. Later, I learned she worked for the LAPD as a sketch artist. I made my own sketch of her, which I keep as a remembrance."

She pulled a small pad from her purse and flipped through pages of visual thoughts and doodles, pulling out one loose page slightly yellowed with age. The image, so detailed you'd think it a photograph, left no doubt about Kim's talents. It was a drawing of Madison's face, but it was the depth of her eyes that got my attention. Kim was still in love.

"I'd love to sketch you, Willi. You're such a perfect model."

She scooted next to me with her pencil in hand. And as the waitress delivered another round of doubles, she leaned over and brushed her lips over mine, putting her hand seductively on my thigh. Her whiskey breath was a hundred proof, and when I didn't move back, she pressed her lips into mine. My alcohol brain lit up, breathing turned heavy, heartbeat fluttered.

"Maybe we should do this drawing in my hotel room?" Kim suggested.

I was about to answer when Irish ran up to our table. "Jesus, Willi, I've been looking all over for you. Didn't you get the text messages? A storm with strong winds is moving toward the show. Artists on the bridge are already taking their work down."

He nodded at Kim. "Hello, Kim."

"Hi, Irish." She turned to me. "You'd better go. I'll text you my room number. Let me know when you're done. I'll be up." Our eyes touched like branding irons.

I shook my fuzzy head back to semi-reality.

"What do you mean strong?"

"I mean booth-shattering strong. Let's go!"

I ran out with Irish. A ferocious wind smacked us as we ran toward the bridge. Tents shuddered in gale-force winds. Artists ran to protect their work. Some had already driven in their cars. I retrieved the wooden sides of Madison's sculpture from behind my booth and began screwing them together. Despite weights on each corner, the tent jumped. The wind roared over and under the bridge. Nerve-racking gusts hurried my fumbling fingers. A stranger appeared out of nowhere and asked if I needed help. "Grab a pole and hold the tent down," I yelled. I laid the sculpture horizontally and screwed on the sides. When the rain came, I had just finished fastening the top to the coffin-like box. Icy droplets beat down in the rhythm of a hundred drums. The stranger didn't budge. He held the forward post like a cement block, standing in the wind-whipped rain as I placed my pots down on the bottom shelf. I grabbed the tent pole across from him and both of us stood in the screaming squall, our bodies punished by a horizontal downpour. The tent held firm. I yelled out thank you, but the noise drowned out my voice. Sounds of crashing up the street made my heart skip a beat. For thirty minutes, we held down a tent that should have blown away. The wind died as quickly as it came, but the deluge continued. I promised myself to give him a pot for his help. But when the storm lifted, he disappeared. I never saw him leave, and he never said a word. Without him, I would have lost everything.

My drenched clothing felt like a wet sponge. I was stone cold sober by then. On my way back to the hotel, I passed booths crushed by the wind, tent frames bent, canvases tossed into the street and torn. As I headed for my room, Kim texted. I never returned the message.

THE NEXT MORNING, THE DAMAGE was shocking. The storm had blown ten booths off the bridge, twisted aluminum tent frames testified to the power of the wind, work scattered on the pavement. One tent dangled above the river, held in suspension by its anchor ropes. Displays laid shattered, countless hours of struggle and determination ruined, artists in tears. We helped each other, the first responders in a disaster zone. The fever of disappointment and pain were palpable. Artists held each other in their arms. It looked like a bomb had gone off. Miraculously, my booth and Irish's were untouched. Outside of a slightly bent frame post and one broken pot, I had escaped catastrophe. Fractured laid untouched, horizontal where I left it the night before. Irish put his hand on my shoulder.

"We were lucky." Irish stared at the mess. "Do you think the show will open today?"

"Absolutely," I replied. "The show must go on. The bridge took the worse hit. Everyone else was fairly unscathed."

"Remember that guy who held down our tents?"

I looked at Irish with a confused look. "I saw him hold *my* tent."

"He had one hand on your corner post, one hand on mine. That stranger must've been a muscle man, because those posts didn't move. He saved our asses."

Holding down Irish's tent? That was new. "I wanted to thank him," I said, "but when the gale blew through, he… disappeared."

"After the winds died, I gave him a pair of maroon boots. He said I didn't have to give him anything, but I threw them in a plastic bag and tucked it under his arm."

"What the hell," I replied. "We both were lucky."

"Well, because of him, we still have work to sell. A lot of folks here weren't so fortunate."

Irish disappeared back into his tent, and I unpacked Fractured. My front flap was down, and someone called my name. Two officials from the committee were standing outside my booth. One was the show director, Carl Walters.

"Mr. Steuben, can we talk a minute?"

"Sure," I had no choice. They both entered. Fractured laid horizontal in the box.

He looked around. "You were one of the fortunate ones."

"Ya, lucky, I guess. Can I help you with anything?"

"The jurors awarded you first place." My heart jumped to my throat.

"Yes, thank you so much."

"Normally we'd be giving you a ribbon. But we have information about the piece that won you this award." He nodded at the partially unpacked sculpture. "We believe someone with the initials MA created the piece." He crouched by the boxed sculpture and pointed at the tiny initials on one of the ceramic branches. "The piece is amazing, but with a little help from an observant artist, we traced those initials to your partner, Madison Ayana. Did you make that piece, Mr. Steuben?"

I was shocked into silence.

The world crashed down around me. Only one person could have made that connection for them—Kim. I shook my head, totally humiliated. "No," I confessed. "I helped Madison make it."

"I hoped that wouldn't be true, but you have violated an important rule. The committee talked it over and concluded you may remain in the show on the condition you remove the sculpture. You will forfeit the award and receive no award money. You will have to jury for next year's show, like everyone else. I suggest that next time you bring only your work and no one else's." His final words were biting. "I'm sure you would've won at least a merit award on your own work, Mr. Steuben." They walked out.

My body shook, teeth clenched. Displaying Madison's sculpture was a foolish thing to do. I wanted to break every pot in the booth. I had been Kim's chump.

Irish stuck his head between the tent flaps.

"Hey, Willi, how's it going?"

"A kick in the ass is in order." I knew he heard the whole conversation. It's not like Light Dome tents are sound proof. "You probably heard."

Irish made a weird face and nodded. "Not good," he said. "How'd they find out?"

"You know Kim? She's the only one here who knew Madison's work."

Irish's face paled. "Yeah, she's a piece herself."

"Sounds like you know her."

"The word 'know' has many meanings."

"Hey—would you give me a hand carrying this thing?" We moved the sculpture behind the booth. I spread out my display unit and filled it with my work. Irish looked on, drinking a Pepsi.

"Your partner is an amazing artist," he said.

I nodded. "Ya, she is. Seems like the distance from stardom to the bottom of the mud pit isn't that far."

Irish puffed out a laugh. "Listen, Willi, if it makes you feel any better, my ex-wife designed all those leather pants and a lot more. When we split, she quit the circuit and our partnership too. She said I could use her designs, but it'd cost me a yearly new pair of boots."

"So, the boots are yours, everything else essentially her designs?"

Irish looked down and nodded. "I may have talent, but she's the genius."

"Hey, Irish, watch my booth for a minute. I've got something to do."

He agreed. I walked swiftly up the block, passing artists opening up. I knew a lot of them; each living out their own soap opera lives. Making money from what your heart tells you is like plucking wild honey from a bees' nest. I stopped in front of Kim's booth, put my hands on my hips. I faced the first prize ribbon that flew from her tent. Inside, she was leading a customer through the sale of her largest piece. She glanced up, saw me standing out front, then looked away. Nothing more needed to be said. The show wasn't even open yet and people gathered, waiting to enter her booth. She had used me. Her betrayal not only hurt but was degrading.

When I got back to my booth, Irish was setting out leather bags. "Any action?" I asked.

"A juror stopped by asking for you, Willi." She left something on your checkout counter.

I found Evelyn Hirshhorn's business card with a note. 'I'll be back in Washington in a few days. Tell your amazing partner, Madison, to call me.' I almost fell over.

CHAPTER 16

THE RETURN

SWADDLED IN MIDNIGHT MOONLIGHT, I turned into the long, winding drive leading to the house. Des Moines to River Falls had taken five hours. My headlights cut into the darkness like a flamethrower. For a change, studio lights were off. A dim glow from the kitchen threw shadows down the front hallway. I had called Madison about the humiliating outcome. She met me at the doorway, wrapped her arms around my neck. It was a full body hug and hard pressed her lips to mine, flattening my mouth.

"Hey, I need those lips."

"So do I," she retorted. "Oh Willi, I'm so sorry."

"I'll admit, it was... different." We walked to the kitchen, a steaming teapot on the table. "How are you feeling?" I asked.

"Besides throwing up occasionally in the mornings, I'm fine."

She pulled a mug from the sink and set it next to hers. "You did well...? I mean, outside of my foolishness."

"I made the decision to display Fractured. And it wasn't a total disaster. I sold four thousand bucks." She knew nothing about Evelyn's note or Kim's betrayal.

We settled at the table. She poured tea, lopped honey into my mug.

"What's new?" I started.

The arts and crafts light hanging over us once again invited our window ghosts into the conversation, each of our movements copied in the reflection. She sipped Earl Grey, eyes flitted upwards into my gaze. "The night you left... I didn't sleep. The voice came back, and I went to the drawing table." Her smile disappeared.

"And this is like someone whispering in your ear?" I still couldn't wrap my head around 'the voice.'

"It sounds real, Willi... maybe it's an urge or a vibration or implanted thoughts. It's so hard to describe and yes, I've wondered if something is really wrong with me." She drew a deep breath. "I followed instructions." Madison opened her large sketch pad to a twelve by sixteen-inch pencil drawing. Kim's face stared at me, her wet whiskey lips beckoning. "As soon as I drew this, I knew she'd try to seduce you."

The picture was so perfect I could almost smell Kim's alcoholic breath. My cheeks flushed. Feelings of guilt and anger raged at myself and at Kim. With a brief glance, Madison saw it all, but said nothing. She flipped to the next page.

"I don't know what this means." A man pelted by driving rain, water dripping down his face, gripped a tent pole. In the background, other tents flew in the air. My mouth dropped, chisels ran up and down my body.

"Oh my god. That's the person who helped save the booth."

Madison looked confused. "What are you talking about, Willi?"

"During the storm, a man appeared out of nowhere. Holding one booth down in fierce wind takes both hands, but this guy anchored my tent with one hand and my neighbor's tent with his other. He saved both of us. Extraordinary!"

Madison walked to the cupboard and pulled down a bottle of Jack, poured a shot for me and a sip for her. "That deserves a toast."

"To what?"

"That was no normal human being. His name is Orlando Rock. You're being followed."

"Followed?" I almost laughed, yet the suggestion struck me in the gut.

"By the inexplicable." We clinked glasses.

"What the hell does that mean?"

Our reflections stared at each other in the window. Like an Edward Hopper painting, they lived in their own solitary world.

"Things like this happen for a reason," she said. "Another realm, an alternate reality touches us. The reason hasn't unfolded yet... but it will."

"Ya, well..." I didn't really believe in fantasy land, but my experiences were mounting a solid case that something extraordinary was occurring.

"It's not about what you believe or don't believe."

I downed the liquor. She poured me another, and I changed the subject to Evelyn's note. When I showed it to her, Madison shrugged it off.

"What... you're not going to call her?" It was incredulous.

"I'll think about it," was all she said.

After a few more drinks, my head fogged over. I needed a hot shower and a pillow.

We climbed into bed. Her presence and her warmth felt like home. Her body exuded a divine aroma.

"You're lavender."

"New soap." She pressed herself against my body and kissed me. Taking my face in her hands, her bright turquoise eyes suddenly flared. "Did she fuck you, Willi?"

My heart skipped a beat. "No!" I thought of Kim's lips brushing mine and how close we came. "I was drunk, she was drunk, I said too much, and so did she. She's a siren, but I didn't screw her. She still loves you, Madds. But it's turned into revenge."

Madison rolled over, head on her pillow. "Love leaves its scars." Lying side by side, she laced her fingers into mine. "There's so much more to talk about, Willi."

I closed my eyes, stomach churning. She was right, but exhaustion won me over. Madison laid wide awake. I could feel it.

NEXT MORNING, I WOKE WITH a surge of energy and a head full of new ideas. I wanted to throw large platters, two feet to three feet in diameter, wall pieces with handprints, but I wasn't sure what handprints or where I'd get them from. Madison was up and working in the studio, coffee pot half empty. I walked out to the studio, leaned against the sliding door jamb, holding a cup of Joe. She was deep into her next piece.

"Mornin'." I sipped my coffee. She looked up briefly.

"I need some help."

"We should talk," I reminded her.

"We will, but right now, this comes first. I want your molding skills to make tiles, thirteen-inch square, which should shrink down to twelve-inch when finished."

"A tile sculpture? What's it about?"

"I'm building a wall."

"What kind of wall?"

"Do you want to help or not?"

"Of course, I'll help."

"Okay, get to work."

She had already made the clay prototypes. A tile is easy to cast, no edges to catch, everything rounded, flat surface. Within an hour, I had made and poured six plaster molds. They all needed to dry, so we took a break and walked into the kitchen. Somewhere in those twenty feet between studio and house, she relaxed.

"Sorry, Willi, I know I can be such a taskmaster. I'm building a commemorative wall."

"For whom?"

"For every woman murdered using her vagina to make ends meet. And this would include wives, girlfriends, flings, prostitutes, and more."

We entered the kitchen, I poured two cups of Nigerian and set the mugs on the table. "And this includes... you?"

"For the two years I was with Peter... I was his whore."

"But you weren't murdered."

"There're many ways to murder a person without killing them and even more ways to seduce a young woman."

"What about Kim?" I asked.

"She used Peter's wife the same way Peter used me. Kim would withhold affection to get things. Rita bought her what she wanted. Kim was easy to love. Believe me, Willi, I know. Peter's wife got caught in Kim's softness and availability. Rita fell in love. But when Kim found out I was pregnant, she was furious, and told Rita she still loved me."

"Kim told me about it. You had an abortion."

"I had no choice. I couldn't afford another kid that would only pull me more deeply into Peter's fucked up life. A child with him would turn into a nightmare."

"So, Peter's wife flies to Paris to reclaim her husband and blasts you."

"Exactly. Set up by Kim. I was glad it happened. Peter would eventually move on to the next young thing with talent, and I wasn't willing to be in the middle of his messy his marriage. So, what happened in Des Moines wasn't the first time Kim's exacted revenge."

Madison pulled a container of fresh fruit from the fridge and popped English muffins into the toaster. As she filled two bowls with mangoes, grapes, and persimmons, I opened her sketch pad to the picture of Kim. Strands of hair fell perfectly on one side of her round face, eyes searching, but wet, seductive lips were the dominant feature.

"There's something else, Willi." She delivered fruit and English muffins to the table. My rising appetite suddenly squashed.

"You mean Nash?"

"No. Reid, the cop. He stopped me a couple of nights ago on the back road to our street. It's like he knew I was avoiding town. He claimed I was speeding, which was most likely true. I mean, who goes the speed limit on UU?"

I popped a grape into my mouth. It was cold and round and smooth. I just let it sit there.

"I rolled down the window with my license ready," Madison continued, "but he made me get out of the car and put my hands on the hood. He checked the inside of the vehicle with his flashlight but found nothing. It was all a ruse.

"'You're in trouble, Maddy,' Reid said, releasing the safety strap off his holster.

"'The name is Madison,' I retorted.

"'I've got evidence you were involved in Styles' murder. Enough for an indictment.'

"I turned around, seething and almost spit in his face. 'You've got nothing,' I shouted. 'Stop harassing me!' I wanted to smack that sick smile off his face.

"Then he said, 'We both know why you went up to Styles house after you killed him, don't we?'

"It shocked me he knew I'd been to Styles' place after he died. I'm not sure how the cops knew. He could see my reaction. 'What do you want, Reid?'

"He reached down and unzipped his pants. 'One blow job and it all goes away.'

"I was livid. 'If you touch me, Reid, I'll scream till every animal in this forest wakes up. You have read me so wrong. I will fight you to the end.' My fists clenched, ready to swing.

"'Have it your way.' Reid zipped up. 'But you know exactly what I'm talking about. So, think about the consequences of abetting a murder. You might change your mind.'

"He acted so fucking confident, but he backed off, got into his cruiser, and drove away. I stood by the side of the road, shaking."

The story was so shocking I swallowed the grape whole. An electric wave passed through every nerve in my body, hands and feet tightened. I wanted to smash something. Madison sat frozen like a statue in a graveyard. When I touched her hand, she jumped.

"What did you do after that?"

She got up from the table and opened a kitchen drawer. "I bought this. It's a Glock, 9 mm and two magazines." She brought the gun to the table. "If Reid comes to my door, I want protection."

"Do you even know how to shoot that thing?"

She slammed the magazine into the stock and released the safety. "There," she said, "loaded." With two hands, she pointed the weapon out the kitchen door and squeezed the trigger.

The gun went off like an M-80 firecracker. My eardrum shattered by the sound. A metal casing flew out of the firing chamber, bouncing onto the floor. The bullet made a clean hole in the back porch screen and who knows how far into the woods it went? With her thumb, she ejected the magazine and set the gun on the table.

"I know enough to protect myself."

"For God's sake, Madison, you can't shoot a person for just any reason. It's complicated. Why don't you call Jimmy and tell him what happened?"

She picked up the weapon and the magazine, put it back in the drawer. "I did. He wants a meeting with you there, too."

"Why me? I'm peripheral."

"I don't know, Willi. Jimmy has connections. He said he knows things about Reid, things that may concern you."

A moment later, Nash ran into the kitchen. "What the F was that noise?"

I didn't know he was home. Nash stood in the doorway, his shirtless body revealed a mahjong symbol tattooed on his chest, a serpent curled over his shoulder. He was tall, thin, wiry, his hair slopped back. "Was that a gunshot?"

Madison rose from her chair and gave him a bear hug and kissed him on the cheek. "Hey, when did you get home?" Nash pulled away.

"Did you buy a gun?" His eyes narrowed.

Madison walked to the drawer and casually took out the Glock. "Home protection."

"Whoa!" He took the weapon from her hand and pulled back the carriage. A cartridge ejected. "You know, taking the magazine out doesn't mean there's no live ammunition in the chamber." He glanced in the drawer and grabbed the magazine. "You should load this with 20 caliber bullets. They go farther and do more damage." He looked over at me.

"Hey, Willi. Good to see you."

"Ya, good to see you, too. What brings you home?"

"Picking up a few things, you know, personals." He threw the magazine back in the drawer and turned back to his mother. "This isn't home protection. It's Reid protection, isn't it?"

Madison looked surprised. "What do you know about Reid?"

"I saw him pull up the drive the other day. He didn't stop, just swung around the circle and left. He was snooping."

"I can take care of myself. Reid's just a jerk."

Nash shrugged. "If he ever touches you..." He pointed the unloaded gun at the window and pulled the trigger.

CHAPTER 17

AN ARGUMENT

A COUPLE OF DAYS LATER, Madison and I were in the kitchen having an argument.

"What the hell made you think you could touch my work?" I yelled. I had thrown six large platters that were drying under plastic. Madison had tampered with two of them. "And who gave permission to do what you wanted without asking?" I was livid. "Not only my work but my idea!"

She stood her ground. "What idea?"

"I don't know, maybe handprints?"

"Handprints?" She let out a long breath. "Those platters spoke to me. The form is gorgeous. They drew me in. I know it's your work and I apologize, but I'd do it again. It was spontaneous combustion."

"What the hell, does that give you a free pass to alter what I make? What if I drew all over your tiles?"

"Depends what you drew."

"Damn it, Madison!" I slammed the back door and stomped out to the studio. The invitation to work together seemed idyllic to begin with. This was a bump, perhaps a wake-up call.

Uncovering my platters revealed she had not only tampered with them but ruined them. On the bottom shelf, the largest piece was a complete mess, destroyed, obviously an experiment gone bad. The next one, also an experiment, she had quickly changed her approach, learning how to control the flow of colored slip. When I pulled down a third platter, I was aghast. She had meddled with that one too... but she had altered the symmetrical character of the piece, and mastered dipping her hand in slip, pressing it onto the surface without blurring the image or overly crossing colors. Repeated handprints in different colored slips covered the surface. It was— breathtaking. Better than I imagined possible with such a sloppy substance, and most likely better than I could've done myself. I hated and loved it simultaneously, which made me more furious.

The platter next to it was still fresh and untampered with. I dipped my hand in black slip. Fingers shiny and dripping in the creamy slurry, I pressed my hand on the leather hard clay, imprinting the surface. With my other hand, covered in grey slip, I did the same. Alternating hands, I repeated the process, covering the platter. Each imprint left a deliberate mark, each angrier than the one before it. My nails dug into the flesh of the surface. By the time I finished, my teeth clenched, muscles taut, fingertips leaving deep gouges and scratches. My body tingled. Bolts of electricity racing over my skin. The last handprint included rugged marks that looked like an animal had clawed the surface. I could certainly destroy my work if I wanted. It was far from a masterpiece, but raw emotion had emerged. I wanted to destroy the piece. Instead, its tattered ruins remained on the workbench. This wasn't the way I usually worked, but I felt better.

While I washed the gooey slip off my hands, I could see Madison doing a yoga exercise in the front yard. In the distance, a car came barreling down the road, leaving a dust trail behind. A moment later, Jimmy, in a baggy suit got out. He was paunchy, but the black-rimmed glasses were new. He was wearing the same ragged overcoat and I wondered if he really was a lawyer. At the car door, she gave him a bear hug.

When I walked through the back porch, Madison and the lawyer were coming into the kitchen. She walked across the room and kissed me on the lips. When she went to pull away, I pressed in and kissed her back.

"Thank you, Willi. I need you on my side."

She pulled down a couple of mugs and headed to the coffee pot. "Jimmy, this is Willi."

"Sure, I remember you from the coffee shop."

"Willi's my partner and father of my child."

"You picked a hell of a time to get pregnant." Jimmy's surprised expression quickly turned deadpan. "Do you have any idea what's going on?"

CHAPTER 18

JIMMY

IN A QUICK CHANGE OF mood, he shook my hand. "Congratulations, Willi." He said it un-wholeheartedly, then sat at the table and put his briefcase by the chair.

"Would you like a coffee?" Madison was at the pot.

"I think I'm going to need something stronger." His gaze shifted to the tall windows and beyond. "How far do those woods go back?" he asked.

"I'm not sure, a couple of miles at least." She carried steaming pot of Joe and a bottle of Woodford Reserve to the table. It was tempting, but I waved off the whiskey—too early. She poured Nigerian for herself and me. Jimmy got the Woodford.

"Well, at least the rear flank is protected."

"Are you saying Madison needs protection?"

Jimmy leaned into the curved back of the captain's chair. "She's about to be indicted on abetting a murder, or possibly more—that's one situation. The other is Nash and Cinderella selling 'untraceable meth,' a fictional drug, to Joey Graveno's soccer team. He's a Chicago mobster. I'd say yes, some kind of protection is in order."

"What makes you think I'm in danger?" Madison said as she poured cream into my coffee.

"Word from the street." Jimmy's mouth set in a straight line. "And I can tell by your reaction you know some of this. But it's more complicated than you think."

"Reid's involved, isn't he?" Madison refilled Jimmy's empty glass.

"There're all kinds of connections," Jimmy said, "which I don't understand, so I thought you could help."

"What don't you understand?"

"Joey Graveno has a side business selling stolen art."

An abysmal silence fell between us. My mind spun like a jet turbine. Madison tensed. Jimmy's eyes shifted between us.

With a stabbing sigh, Madison spoke. "What the hell is going on, Jimmy? What's my indictment got to do with Graveno and stolen art?"

"Reid's a wildcard, Madison. A rent-a-thug kind of cop. I'm not sure about his connections to Joey Graveno. But you're an artist and Reid knows enough not to approach Joey unless he's got something valuable. Maybe he found a rare painting in Styles' house." Jimmy slugged down the Woodford. "You have any ideas about this?"

Madison shifted uncomfortably in her seat and shook her head. "No idea."

"Whatever it is, Reid's in over his head and Graveno will exact pain to get what he wants. There're lots of possibilities to this game."

"Does Graveno want Madison's artwork?" I asked.

Jimmy looked over at Madison. "What do you think?"

"I'm not famous or expensive enough."

"Well, someone is." Jimmy raised his glass and downed his drink. "There's a missing piece here and if you know anything," he eyed Madison, "I suggest you tell me now. Graveno's not stupid. It gets complicated because Cinderella and Nash burned Graveno with their drug deal. As far as the kids go, Graveno will wrap both of them around his little finger. Maybe he wants to own Nash as one of his dealers, and who knows what he wants Cinderella for. Maybe she's got a nice body."

Madison stared with a pallid face. A ton of granite dropped into my stomach. "How do you know all this?"

"Before I came to this hole-in-the-wall town, I represented plenty of

Graveno type mobsters in Chicago. I saw prosecution witnesses disappear and politicians cave. To them, it's business, serious business. And gangsters play for keeps."

"Can Nash and Cinderella buy their way out of this?" Madison was thinking way in front of me. "Pay Graveno for his losses?"

"I heard his losses were upwards of two hundred grand. Depends how he's feeling at the moment."

"What connections do you have?" I asked.

"I have associations with a couple of Graveno's henchmen who owe me… so I could approach them with an offer."

Madison stared at the table. "Two hundred grand is out of my league, Jimmy."

"Listen, I've talked to dozens of thugs like Graveno. He might think this is too small to make a big deal out of, or he might be angry as hell at losing money. Can't say, but I have contacts who can feel out the situation. Graveno fences stolen artwork, so there might be a possibility there. My hunch is that Reid's got something pretty valuable."

"I assume you're not doing this pro bono?" I asked.

"For this kind of work, I usually charge a thousand a day, but I'm not busy right now and I like you both. A couple of G's as a retainer should get me started."

Madison looked at Jimmy with gloomy eyes. "A couple of thousand?"

"I'd prefer Venmo, but I'd give you a discount for cash."

I got up from the table and walked into the bedroom. In the bottom of my suitcase was an envelope with art fair cash. I brought it back. "How much of a discount?"

"Nineteen hundred. How's that?"

"Seventeen fifty," I retorted.

"Okay, that's fair. But it's only a retainer. This could cost a lot more."

I counted out the money. Madison watched as Jimmy scooped up bills and pushed away from the table. "Gotta get going. I'll be in touch. You might have a talk with Nash. He could make things a lot worse. Cinderella too."

"How about Reid?" Madison asked.

"Two things—one, if you have a gun, don't shoot him." Jimmy threw back his drink. "And two… don't fuck him."

"You mean, don't fuck with him." I said.

"No. I mean, don't fuck him."

CHAPTER 19

HELP ARRIVES

A DAY LATER, I PICKED up the rest of my personal stuff from my apartment. I couldn't believe two people could destroy a place in such a short time. Rory from upstairs stuck his head in the partly open door.

"I thought it was bad, but this is worse than bad. What's that sour odor?" He invited himself in. "Anything we can do to help, Willi?"

"Ya, two hundred bucks, you guys clean the place up, keep or throw out anything I leave."

Rory looked down at a puddle on the floor. Soda or something sticky spilled, imbedded with ashes. "Ewe." He wrinkled up his nose. "Two fifty and it's a..."

"How about free?" A voice came from the doorway. We both turned toward a tall, lean figure.

"Hey, Nash. Come on in." Sometimes the distance between surprise shock and rational thinking is shorter than one would think. "Free sounds good." Nash entered and threw a cloth shoulder bag on the couch.

"Two hundred would be fine, Willi." Rory finished his sentence. "We'll make sure it's done right." He edged carefully past Nash and clomped up the stairway.

"Cinderella and I were in such a rush to get out... I didn't realize how much of a mess we left. It'll go faster if I help."

He looked ragged, tired. His shoulders slumped and the fierceness in his eyes gone. "How 'bout a beer?" I asked.

Nash followed me into the kitchen. When I opened the fridge, I found a couple cans of Coors, a squeeze bottle of ketchup, an old hotdog still wrapped in foil and something in a plastic bowl covered with green mold. Nash leaned against the counter and popped open his drink. I sat at the table. His skinhead hair had grown out a bit, lips were plump, like Madison's.

"So, how's the new place?" I asked.

"You living with Mom?" He avoided the question.

I nodded. "We're giving it a go."

"She's crazy. You must have noticed?"

"Then it's a perfect fit." I picked up a sponge and began wiping out the refrigerator. "How is Cinderella faring?"

He guzzled about half his beer. "She's pregnant…"

I sipped my beer, a way to hide my un-surprise. "Congratulations. Have you told your mother?"

"Not yet."

"You know, Madison's pregnant too."

"I know. I'm going to have a baby sister."

That was a revelation. Why hadn't Madison said anything? I squeezed my lips into a sour line. "You can start with the dishes in the sink."

"You didn't know, did you?" His sharp eyes had caught my expression.

"Let's say she omitted that piece from the conversation. I'm sure there's a reason."

"No reason, Willi. She just… does stuff."

It was an accurate observation, but I decided not to respond. Nash set his beer down and began piling dirty plates on the counter in an orderly manner. "We're trying to clean up. Go straight, get rid of the drugs."

He didn't see my raised eyebrows and doubting expression. "Cinderella feeling okay?"

"It's her first trimester, so… she needs help. Getting off meth isn't easy. She's going to a methadone clinic."

I opened the fridge and dumped the bowl of its rancid contents. "That's a healthy start. Especially for the baby." It seemed he had dropped his 'I'm a punk' attitude.

"Ya, we both want this kid, even if…" he let out a long sigh.

"Even if what?"

"Even if it isn't mine."

"What do you mean, not yours?"

Steam rose from the hot water as Nash washed dishes in the same meticulous way Madison made her ceramic sticks. "It's most likely mine and…" There was a long pause. "I love her, Willi. I really love her. She sold more than meth, so she was always at some risk. Now all that's changed."

For a moment, I had to think what else she would sell. Then it struck. "Oh my…" I stopped there.

The hard shell around Nash had cracked. We were both in love and expectant fathers. But our situations couldn't be more different. I had to respect him for accepting Cinderella for who she was. I'd done the same for Madison. In some ways the two women were alike—spontaneous, head strong, and irreverent.

As we cleaned, Nash talked about his hopeful future without drugs. I said nothing about the abyss he and Cinderella faced. He brought it up.

"We were in trouble when a couple of Graveno's lackies made contact. They could've just killed us, but they said 'the boss' was in a generous mood. He'd settle for a hundred fifty G's."

Nash's tone was so straightforward it sounded like pocket money he owed the local bank, except it wasn't. My mouth dropped open.

"Shit, Nash, that's a pile of money. What are you going to do?"

"We have friends. An Asian gang on the north side. We made a deal. I supply them with cheap drugs. They give us protection."

I wondered if that was a deal brokered by Ricardo, his dad. There were so many downsides to that solution I couldn't count them.

"Why not negotiate with Graveno? He can't get what's not there."

"These guys can exact a lot of pain, Willi." Nash picked up the mop and started on the floor. "We made an offer, but his counter was unacceptable."

"What was that?" I set the washrag on the table and faced him.

"Graveno would lower the debt, maybe even forget it, if Cinderella came to work for him. Of course, we both knew what that meant."

"She's pregnant, Nash. What the hell."

"Some Johns pay double if the prostitute's pregnant."

At that point, I lost my breath.

After a couple of hours of hard work, we finished basic cleaning. I offered to buy dinner, but he declined. 'Rella' wanted him back before dark. He slung the cloth bag over his shoulder, similar to what Madison hauled around.

"You don't draw, do you?" I asked.

He smiled and extracted a sketch pad. "Wanna see?"

I sat next to him in a somewhat functional kitchen. He flipped it open. The drawing was breathtaking. Cinderella laid naked on my couch. He downplayed her abundant breasts by keeping them in shadow, emphasized the curvature of her hips. But he also caught her innocent, sad eyes and part of the threatening snake tattooed on her thigh. There was no doubt Cinderella was a beauty or where his talent came from.

"Have to go, Willi." He closed up the pad and stuck it into his sack. "Let's do another soccer match."

"Sounds good." I walked over and put out my hand. "Thanks again for the help." We shook. So different from how we first met.

"See ya around, Willi."

Hopefulness had returned to eyes so like his mother's. When I thought of the events swirling about him, it made me shudder.

The place was orderly, but nowhere clean enough to pass inspection. I walked upstairs and knocked. Rory answered the door.

"Hey, Rory, the apartment needs a deep clean so I can get my deposit back." I took out my wallet.

Cupcake came up from behind. "Are you and what's his name... Nash, all buddy-buddy now?" Rory poked him in the ribs.

"Put your wallet away, Willi. We'll make sure it's super clean."

I put out my arms and we all hugged. "I'll miss you guys."

"And gals," Cupcake added.

I gave notice to the Supe, and with that, a chapter of my life ended.

•

A FULL MOON PERCHED OVER treetops, a fully lit sphere spreading dream-like figures throughout the woods, shadowed arms clutching each other. The long gravel drive to the house crunched under the tires, crickets wailed in their monotone song. Only one lonely light from the pole barn pierced the night. I pulled up in front and got out. The house was dark, but I could make out a figure sitting on the front porch next to the sad Buddha statue. With halting steps, I called out. "Madison?"

"It's me." Her voice pierced the night choruses from the woods. She met me on the front walk and threw her arms around me. "Willi, I was so afraid."

We walked up the stairs to the front porch. In the moonlight, on the table, was a loaded Glock. I let out a long sigh.

"I thought Jimmy said don't shoot anyone."

"It… I felt safer in the dark with a wall to my back."

"Let's put the gun away and talk."

She ejected the weapon's magazine, and we walked to the kitchen. I pulled a bottle of chilled burgundy from the fridge and poured two goblets.

"I don't know if I can do this, Willi," she started.

"What's got you so upset?"

She brought over her sketch pad and opened it under the antique light that hung over the table. Images of flames filled one page, and on the next page a vague face stared out from an inferno.

"I don't know what it means but whatever's coming looks frightening. The voice insisted that the flames be larger." She put her head on the table. "I can't make out the face, but I think it's Nash's."

I turned the pad toward me. "Nash? I don't think so. I saw him today. He's growing his hair back."

She lifted her head. "Nash came to your apartment?"

"Not only did he help clean, but apologized for the mess. Said he was going straight."

"He told you something else, didn't he?"

Rummaging in the fridge, I found Brie. It paired well with the Burgundy. We sat at the kitchen table, lights low. Madison opened her sketchbook to a drawing of Cinderella, very pregnant. "Nash said he didn't tell you."

"He didn't. I drew this about two hours ago."

"Well, she's not that pregnant, still in the first tri. But they're happy and they both want the baby."

Madison grinned. "We'll have two girls in the family."

"Thank you for telling me."

"Sorry, Willi… it's just that…"

"Wait! How do you know Cinderella's having a girl?"

With eyes turned down, her cheeks flushed. "The voice."

She came over and sat on my lap. "It's all so mixed up. Maybe you should keep the Glock."

"Ya,' I said it in a low voice. "Stick 'em up."

"Maybe I should stick you up."

"Indeed, you should!" I picked her up and carried her into the bedroom.

We made love to erase the anxiety, the worry, to forget the world and remember each other. We gave into desperate embraces, and our sweaty bodies fell into rhythmic delight. It was love-making to reunite with our life together and be overcome by raw pleasure. It was beautiful and satisfying. I tickled and teased with an eagle feather she kept on the dresser, which made the moment feel like kids playing. We ended with her body stretched over mine. Like a blanket, she relaxed into my contours, our hearts pressed together, and we fell asleep.

In the middle of the night, she rolled over and slipped out of the bed. Her naked body silhouetted in the moonlight, eyes glowing. Without a word, she left the room. She was in the grip of the voice.

CHAPTER 20

JOSIE WALLFLOWER

WHEN I ROSE THE NEXT morning, more pages of flames filled her notebook, but she was nowhere to be seen. By the coffee pot, she'd left a note—'don't you dare throw out that bear-clawed platter you made. It's gorgeous.'

While waiting for a fresh pot to percolate, I unloaded the van, putting most of my belongings in the small pole barn. Stuffed under the back seat were the pair of pink boots from Irish to his ex-wife, Josie Wallflower. She lived on the Iowa border, two hours down state, which was a short hop for most art fair artists. Madison came into the kitchen through the back porch door, the eagle feather tucked behind her ear.

"Hey… mornin'." I poured a fresh coffee. "Tough night?"

"You saw the pictures." She sat at the table, robe sliced open, exposing her naked body. "I wish I knew what they meant, Willi. It's a future place, but I don't know whose future or when that future may arrive."

I brought two mugs and sat next to her. "I can't imagine how confusing that must be."

"That's why last night was just what I needed." She plucked the eagle feather from behind her ear and ran it between her breasts. "Sometimes sex can be… such a right remedy." She leaned over and gave me a wet kiss.

"You, Madison Ayana, are a lovely siren!"

My fingers wrapped around the steaming cup. "Yesterday, Jimmy talked about something missing from the equation, something you might know. Are you holding back important information?"

"Not now, Willi. There are missing pieces…" She shook her head. "But not now."

"Okay, you're not ready. I get it. It's gotta come out, eventually."

She sipped her coffee. "I know, I know, but… it's complicated, and I'm not ready."

"It's all complicated. Irish's divorce is a good example. He's still giving presents to his ex, Josie Wallflower. I'll drop them off today. Her place isn't far… Iowa border."

"To a normal person, Willi, that's far."

"Speaking of normal, should I take the gun?"

"I've put it away. If I get rattled again… we know the remedy, don't we?" She stuck the feather in her cleavage.

I raised my eyebrows. "Yes, we do."

•

JOSIE WALLFLOWER LIVED ON THE end of a two-mile-long dirt road. Her house was the size of a triple car garage, with a porch extending along the entire front, a stone chimney protruded from the side. The only thing that brought it into modern times was a satellite dish on the roof. Green pasture gently sloped to a corral next to the cabin where two horses stood grazing.

There was the unmistakable crack of gunfire from behind the homestead. When no one answered my knock, I walked around the house where the sounds came from. A woman in jeans and a tucked-in loose shirt fluidly drew her six-shooter from its holster, firing at cans sitting on a fence about thirty feet distant. She spun the weapon back into place, then drew again and fired. I leaned against the house, watching the string of targets blown away. The bend of her knee, the motion of her arms, the spin of the six-shooter, had the syncopation of a modern dancer. With that same deftness of motion, she turned suddenly, drew her pistol and pointed it at me. I dropped Irish's gift and put my hands up in the air like a bank robber caught in the act.

"Christ," she said, looking at the package on the ground, "another emissary from Irish." A ponytail stuck out the back of her wide rim hat, adorned with a beaded band. She walked with a slight limp, legs bowed. Her low-cut red sneakers fit her free-wheeling style.

"You're right, it's from Irish. Mind if I lower my hands, or if you're gonna shoot me, get it over with." I picked up the package as she spun her six-shooter back into her holster. "I'm Willi, a friend of Irish's."

"Josie Wallflower." She gave a firm handshake. "My apology for being so short-tempered. I've come across some weird ranch hands out here lately, not excluding emissaries sent by Irish. Come on in, let's get out of this wind." At the back steps she turned, spontaneously drew her gun, and blew away the one can that remained on the fence, then spun and holstered the revolver in one unbroken motion. When I jumped at the unexpected explosion, she laughed.

"Not a gunslinger, are you?"

"Turned in my gun for a potter's wheel." I climbed the stairs behind her.

"You're a potter. I like that. Earthy kind of guy."

"I'll take that as a compliment."

The kitchen was simple, a four-burner gas stove, an oven underneath, a small table with two chairs by the window overlooking the corral where a couple of horses ran loose. She took off her Stetson, unbuckled the holster belt, and hung it on an antler hook.

"So, Willi, coffee or something stronger?" She had one hand on her hip and the other on the fridge door.

"Coffee," I replied. "Still have to drive home."

"And where is home?"

"A little town outside the Twin Cities. Riverfalls." While she made coffee, I wandered into the living room. An antelope's head hung above a stone fireplace. A Karl Bodmer print of a Dakota woman was on an adjacent wall. Upon closer inspection, it wasn't a print, it was a painting. The artist's signature shocked me—Kim West.

"Wow! Small world. Kim painted that?" I asked.

"You know her?" Josie pulled two mugs from her cupboard.

"I do, from the art fair circuit. She's a fabulous painter."

"I told her I liked paintings of Native American women. She liked a leather purse in my booth and wanted to trade. Next show we met at, she brought me that painting. After a visit to the Joslyn Art Museum, she said she painted it from memory."

"From memory?" I stepped back. Kim had caught all the nuances of Bodmer's genius. "It's extraordinary."

"She's extraordinary."

"Seems Kim has fans all over the place."

Josie gave a wry smile as she set a couple of mugs on a side table and lit logs in the fireplace.

"Where'd you hook up with Irish?" she asked.

"At the Des Moines show. Our booths were next to each other. He said you two were once a team."

"Ya, way back when." She blew over the steaming mug, then sipped. "He was a warm, cuddly teddy bear with a devilish penis."

I wasn't sure what that meant, but the wind caught the back screen door, slamming it hard making an exclamation point to her sentence. She talked about growing beans, keeping cows and running a small ranch, a hard life she enjoyed. When asked about her limp, she got up and brought out a bottle of Jack.

"A few days ago, I met my neighbor's new hire. We had a brief run in, and I probably should leave the whole incident at that—but it's the reason I'm limping, and the memory keeps twisting my brain into a knot."

She threw a few more logs on the fire, added a shot of whiskey into her coffee. She held up the bottle. "Want some?"

I raised my mug, she poured, and we settled in front of the fire's cozy warmth. "So, what happened?"

"I say new hire because this guy had spent most of the morning fixing my fence posts. He spoke with a southern drawl, wore chaps and a wide rim hat; a

Colt hung in a holster on his belt. I've seen a million just like him, except he wore maroon-colored boots, which I'm sure got him more whistles than he wanted.

"I told him to follow me to the fence line his boss wanted fixed. He was sunbaked, mid-thirties, thick callused hands and gorgeous deep blue eyes.

"He'd found a human skeleton a mile or so to the west of where we were standing. There were rumors that bank robbers found safe haven out here during the days of Jesse James. The prairie isn't as harmless as most folk may think. I wanted to see the remains, so I followed him. He was a smooth rider, easy in the saddle. I could tell the horse was enjoying him as well, which impressed me."

Josie poured another round. Her horses snorted in the corral and one, named Ranger, stuck his head through an open window, but Josie paid no attention.

"After a short ride, a parched skeleton appeared between two small boulders. I dismounted, walked around searching for the skull. Fifty feet from the ribs, I picked up a white rock protruding through the dirt and yelled that I'd found it. But when I turned, he'd drawn his gun and pointed it directly at me.

"Well, I was livid about my miscalculation. I was stupid to trust a stranger, but I wasn't going to be taken advantage of, not without a fight. I flipped the skull toward the cowboy and leaped to one side, reaching for my weapon. Both our guns went off simultaneously. My horse reared and ran down the hill. I swear I saw my bullet float through the air, heading directly at this stranger. Now that's never happened before. I mean, a bullet travels some six hundred miles an hour, yet I saw that bullet go through him. By the time I fired, two rounds were coming at me. He wasn't like lightning—he was lightning. I felt a warm rush. The impact dropped me to the ground. I remember a red-tail hawk flying above, diving in slow motion toward an unseen prey. For a moment, the world appeared in dimensions I have never seen before, a veil had lifted. My gun lay several feet away in the dust by the skeleton. The cowboy stood over me with a copperhead hanging from his gun barrel. Apparently, when I picked up the skull, the serpent had been hiding inside. He put his hand out and helped me up. I faced him in stunned silence. My foot hurt, but damn! — I shot him."

Josie got out of her chair, stirred the fire, then poured more Jack. She casually shoved Ranger's head back out the window, closed it, and settled in again.

"Willi, he was one lucky son-of-a-bitch. I swear that bullet passed directly through his shoulder. But he stood in front of me, untouched. And ya, I cussed and let him know how pissed I was. Not only did he ruin my boot, but my sock, too. It was a bloody mess.

"The cowboy apologized, then fetched a first aid kit from his saddlebag and tended to my wound. Killin' a snake in midair is an Annie Oakley type shot... I'd say miraculous. He asked if I could get home on one boot. I limped over and gave that snake a solid kick. The cowboy dusted himself off with his hat, picked the snake up and placed its limp body on a boulder.

"I apologized for my foul mouth. I'll admit I was feeling confused. He sat next to me chewing a piece of prairie grass and said I'll be getting a new pair of boots soon. And his maroon boots? Made by Irish. I recognized the eagle embossed on the top half. What the hell... I could hardly believe it.

"Without another word, he mounted his horse, tipped his hat and said, 'You be careful.' I stood there watching his dust trail as he rode the distant fence line. I hobbled over to where the cowboy had placed the dead snake... but there was no snake... anywhere! And it wasn't any dream 'cause my foot throbbed like hell. I mounted up and headed home with this weird feeling that the world around me wasn't real. The whole incident was... well, it just was. But it's been bothering me ever since."

Josie stared into the fire. The incredulity of her story sent shivers up my spine. I thought about the maroon boots Irish gave the stranger who saved our booths in Des Moines. It was too damn impossible to believe.

"By the way, this is for you," I said, and pushed Irish's gift over next to her chair. When she opened the box, tears welled. I hadn't noticed the boots had a snake imprinted around the top and down the side. It was astounding.

She invited me for dinner, and we talked about the art fair circuit and Madison and the Des Moines debacle. Josie's life with Irish was difficult. At home, he was a hard drinker and a ladies' man when on the road. Tired of his affairs, Josie divorced Irish. But when Kim's name came up, lines formed on her forehead, her eyes dodged mine. After a half bottle of Jack, another story emerged, related to the Bodmer painting. Kim and Josie became art fair friends after the trade. Josie, now on the circuit by herself, would go out drinking with Kim after the show.

"She was soft and seductive, Willi. I fell for her. She was smart, talented, and lovely. Irish had wounded me. Kim soothed and… encouraged me. She filled a hole."

"That's Kim in a nutshell."

"You've slept with her?" she asked.

"We've had our run-ins."

Josie laughed. "I didn't know that question could be so elusive. Kim told me she only slept with exceptionally talented artists."

"There's something about Kim that is… experimental," I said. "She attracted creative types." Secretly, I doubted she limited her field of lovers to the exceptionally talented.

"And experienced," Josie added. "Her touch comforted. I admit to sleeping with her. No regrets. I'd do it again."

It didn't surprise me. Irish had slept with Kim too, but I said nothing. It fit her lecherous pattern. The array of relationships on the circuit is like a loosely woven fabric with lots of connections.

After dinner, Josie showed me her work. Her jaw-dropping piece was a pair of leather chairs made from hides of different animals—cow, buffalo, and zebra. No doubt she fit Kim's pool of exceptionally talented. We had a last cup of her special blend coffee before I hit the road. At the door, we gave each other an affectionate hug. Josie said if I ever needed anything, to call her. In a short time, we had become good friends.

CHAPTER 21

INDICTED

THE CRUNCH OF GRAVEL UNDER van tires announced my return along the long, dark drive. It was around midnight; the studio lights were blazing. Hooting owls and crickets chirping filled the nocturnal forest. Moon shadows cast their dark pallet across the front lawn. Light flooded the kitchen, but the house was silent. Madison's sketch pad lay open on the drawing table. The picture, done in pencil and watercolor, was of maroon boots with a snake embossed on top. It took my breath away. Her clairvoyance astonishing. I sat on the stool and stared until the distant sound of music drifted in from the studio. Through the sliding glass door, I could see Madison working. She looked up and waved me in.

"Hey, Willi, how'd it go?"

"It went well... Josie's an interesting woman." I walked over to my workspace. Only one large platter remained.

"What the hell...? You used another platter? I thought we made an agreement."

"Look, Willi, I'll put your name on this sculpture as a collaborator."

"Sculpture?" I walked to her workbench.

She had disemboweled the mid-section out of my three-foot platter and squeezed the edges together, making it a large oval shape. Taking the leftover clay from the middle, she made an inner lip rolled against the larger thick lip of the rim. It was a five-foot vagina, mounted on a tiled background, one side cut into the curvy shape of a woman. Handprints on the outer lips applied in colored slips, wavy concentric ovals within the opening led to a suggestion of infinite space. The piece laid flat on her workbench, easily seven feet when turned vertical.

"It's taking shape, but far from done."

"A vagina?" I was speechless. An eight-foot ladder stood next to the workbench with her camera clipped to pipes extending over the piece.

"Go ahead." She pointed up. "Take a look."

The view from above was... extraordinary. Graphic. "So, what's the point?"

"You don't get it, do you?" She ran her hands over the soft, pliable clay, pinching out a clitoris. "The form is smooth elastic lines. I wanted the in-your-face size to make the object itself commanding, the subject unavoidable, exposure to it indelible and its presence undeniable, and that's just starters. It's the most powerful opening in the universe. Nothing comes close to what arrives from it or the miracle machinery behind it. And no part of the female body has been more abused."

"And the title?"

"Haven't decided. Maybe 'Yoni'."

"Why not call it what it is?"

"Giant Vagina? Is that what you're saying? Or should I use some other description men have for a woman's genitals?"

"Okay, I get it." The ladder shook as I climbed down.

"Maybe, Willi... maybe if you had one, you would get it. It's a Yoni, a divine opening."

"But who wants that hanging on their wall?"

"I don't work for the consumer, Willi. I work for what's inside me. And what's inside me is growing... every day."

"So, all is well?"

"As far as our baby goes, all is good. But this piece is far from finished. Listen, would you take the camera down?"

"Why the camera?"

She stood with her hands to her side, staring at the floor, then let out a sigh. "There's been some developments. Let's go in and talk."

My stomach scrunched. Developments sounded ominous. I fetched the camera, and we covered the piece with a thin plastic sheet.

I RETRIEVED A COUPLE OF glass goblets from the kitchen cupboard and grabbed a chilled bottle of wine from the fridge. We sat at the small table in front of the tall kitchen windows and once again our shadow reflections had a drink with us. "So, I'm listening."

"That's one thing I like about you. When you say you'll listen, you listen." She sipped her wine. "I got a call from Evelyn today."

I squinched up my face. "Evelyn who?"

"Hirshhorn, the juror from the Des Moines show whom you met."

"She called you?"

"She wanted to see more work, recent work. I sent her a few images, including pictures of my new piece."

My back stiffened. "The Vagina? It's not even finished."

"I sent pictures of the unfinished piece and drew a sketch on paper with other details. She liked it… a lot." Madison turned the goblet in her fingers, Burgundy sloshed up the sides. "She wants to see more and asked if I had enough work for an exhibition."

"In Washington?"

"No. At her New York City gallery."

"Evelyn Hirshhorn called you and asked if you want a show in NYC?"

"She said I came highly recommended."

The whole thing seemed too bizarre. "An international gallery owner wants you to show in NYC. Wow! Unbelievable. Who did the recommending?"

"Norman Styles."

I looked at my reflection in the window. A blank ghost stared back. "You mean dead Norman Styles?"

"The same one."

I shook my head and puffed out a long breath. There were so many crossed connections my brain could hardly function.

"Why did Evelyn Hirshhorn, a famous gallery owner, value a recommendation from your hermit-living neighbor, Norman Styles?"

"Because his name is Norman Edgar Styles."

"What! Edgar Styles, the painter?"

"Exactly. The painter who won the Grand Prize at the Paris Painting Exhibition two years ago. The Styles who's represented in multiple museums around the world, and the same Styles who sold one painting at Sotheby's for half a million dollars."

"You brought frozen dinners to the famous Edgar Styles and sat around talking about art?"

"I told you, I don't cook."

"But he's dead. How did he know Evelyn?"

"She handled a few of his paintings internationally. He said she should take me on as a client."

"Oh my God, Madison, that's… a breakthrough. No wonder Evelyn called." I raised my goblet in a toast. But Madison neither picked up her goblet nor responded to my enthusiasm. Instead, she gazed into the forest, then shifted her stare to the table.

Resting her forehead on her hand, she mumbled, "I… I turned down her offer."

My heart sank. "Madison! Any artist would jump at an offer like this. It goes into international recognition, your work shown worldwide. And you turned it down? I don't get it."

"I had to tell her the truth."

"What truth?" I was beside myself.

"I've been indicted for aiding and abetting a murder. It would stain the show, the gallery, and her reputation. I couldn't keep that a secret."

"Indicted? When did this happen?" My head spun with thoughts and questions.

"After you left, Jimmy called. He said the DA just issued the indictment. We go to court next week to enter a plea."

"And what was Evelyn's reaction?"

"Evelyn said indictment wasn't conviction and believed in my innocence. We'd go slow, follow events, maybe push the exhibition back into next year."

I released a deep breath. I noticed my shadow figure had disconnected from me. His head on the table—I stared at Madison. "What is the indictment based on?"

"Evidence, Willi. Strong evidence."

"What kind of evidence?" I sounded like a police interrogator.

Madison's long auburn hair draped over her shoulders, individual strands framing her face and bathed in light from the antique fixture above. She stared at me through tear-blurred eyes. "Evidence, Willi... that could easily put me in jail, maybe for murder."

CHAPTER 22

EVIDENCE

A LONG SILENCE FOLLOWED. BEYOND the window panes dark mysterious forces lurked in the forest, primal forces in the fight for survival, and its presence infiltrated the room. I pulled my chair closer and entered the beam of light flooding the table.

"Willi... I'm not sure where to start. Norman was a dear friend, you know that, and he shared a lot of personal things with me."

"You're being vague... what kind of personal things?" She turned her head so that the overhead light cast a deep shadow covering half her face. A black line separated pale red lips.

"In the end, I couldn't do it. I couldn't help him commit suicide. You've got to believe that."

Teardrops fell to the table, her head down and shoulders shaking. She sobbed until the trembling stopped and she raised her head, looking for my eyes.

"I believe you, Madds. You would never hurt Styles. But who drove him out to UU where they found him?"

"That's the problem. The indictment claims he was murdered in his house and moved."

"And there's evidence that you... killed Styles in his house? Why would you kill Styles?"

"There's another part of the story I haven't gotten to yet," Madison replied.

"For God's sake, Madison!"

"Please, Willi…" her tear-stained eyes were red. "You can't imagine the horror story I'm living."

"Okay. It's shocking. You've done nothing wrong. What came next?"

"After I found Norman that morning, I didn't come straight home. I went to Norman's house."

"Whoa, you went to Norman's house before calling the police?"

"He had told me that when he died, he wanted me to take the four drawings he made of me. He showed me a metal box and said it was important that I take that too, before the cops started going through things."

"You took a metal box from his house?"

"Yes."

"And that key around your waist. It's to the metal box?"

"Yes."

"Did you open it?"

"No. He said I'd know when to open it and should wait."

I raised my eyebrows. It made no sense. "Okay. You're in the house. What else did you see?"

"Things weren't right in the house. Someone had been there before me. There was evidence of a struggle. Two of the four drawings were missing."

"Edgar Styles made four drawing of you posing for him?"

"Yes. Detailed drawings and typically in his realistic style. The four were a series that got more bizarre as they progressed. I searched all over but only found two."

"What do you mean, bizarre?"

"He wanted to draw the stages of lost innocence. He did this by posing me in… unique positions. One pose was like a Vargas style pinup, but the others were… revealing in different ways. The pinup drawing and one other are missing. All were nudes."

"He posed you like a Vargas pinup?"

"Only one Vargas pose. I suggested other poses using shadows…

withholding exposition, letting the viewer finish the reveal within the mind's eye, which he liked."

Vargas was a master at posing women, and Madison had the kind of body Vargas would paint. But she also had a mind full of creative ideas. "Did Styles plan to sell them?"

"Norman said he wasn't interested in the money. After he was dead, I could do whatever I wanted with them. We had a... a deep relationship. I'm sure the set was worth in the upper six figures."

I furled my eyebrows. "Did you sleep with Norman?"

"I would have... but he never approached me that way. Instead, he drew what was still within me. Something I thought I'd lost."

"What was that?"

"My body, Willi. My beautiful, deep body." Her turquoise eyes peered into mine. Hands ran through her hair; tear stains ran like watercolor down her cheeks. "Peter took something from me I thought I could never recover. Norman helped me find it again... and so have you."

I drew in a deep breath and paused. Her revelations were stunning and damning.

"Do the police know about these drawings?"

"No... or I don't think so. Someone stole two of them, and I have the other two."

"Who would that someone be?"

"You're going to think I'm crazy when I say this, Willi, but... I'm pretty sure it was Reid Johnson. When I went back to Norman's house, I found a Rothman cigarette butt on the floor. Reid smokes Rothmans. Norman gave up smoking years ago and one other thing."

"What's that?"

She rose from the table and brought her sketchbook over. Flipping through the pages, she came to a drawing of Reid's face, blood dripping from his eyes like teardrops. My mouth dropped.

"The voice made me draw this. Reid killed Styles and stole the missing drawings. It wouldn't take rocket science to find out their value."

"Beyond the missing pictures that no one seems to know about—yet, what evidence do they have against you?"

"When I found him dead in that back seat, I…" she took a deep breath. "I kissed him. I could have left lipstick on his lips."

"You kissed dead Norman Edgar Styles?"

"That's right. I kissed him goodbye. I suppose I left everything from my cinnamon lip balm to my DNA on his lips. Together with the missing drawings, there's plenty of evidence against me."

I put my elbows on the table and hung my head between my hands. Thoughts cascaded. The first time I looked through the spyhole of a wood-fire kiln, I witnessed the hellish world of an inferno. The long flame from dried red pine licked pots glowing bright yellow, flames dancing like ballerinas in a tornado, an ethereal river of fire rushing over vases and jars, whirling within bowls, searching for oxygen, transforming the chemical structure of the glaze and the clay. But firing by wood is often unpredictable, leaving scars and ash, both surprise and disappointment. And this was Madison, an unpredictable fire that transformed everything that came close to her. Mesmerized by her energy, by her devilish heat, I had thrown caution to the wind. A skilled kiln master controls the fire, but Madison had blown beyond every boundary. Would there be anything left of me when the fire cooled?

As if reading my mind, she took my hand. "If you want to leave me, Willi, I understand. It's… complicated and… I don't want you to get hurt in this mess." She let out a mewling breath.

"You are the mother of my child and love of my life." I took her hand. "You come as a package, Madison. I'm all the way in."

"Then let's make love. Hot flaming love. Burn me up and we'll become embers floating in the night sky, forgetting the troubles of life." In one motion, she threw off her shirt. We tossed a blanket on the back porch floor, and minutes later we were flames dancing in the kiln, whirling like raptured dervishes.

CHAPTER 23

STORKS

THE NEXT MORNING I ROSE early, ground fresh Kona and made poached eggs on English muffins. Madison's sketchbook was still open when she came in. I pointed to a drawing I hadn't seen before.

"The maroon boots… how did you come to draw them?"

She closed her eyes and shook her head. "The voice, Willi. Then the images. They took hold of me. I drew what I saw in my head."

My eyes glazed. It was outside my limited understanding of the unnatural.

"I'm sorry, Willi. It's… something I can't figure out about myself. I don't know why I drew boots or what they mean, but I know they're connected to you. Something big is coming toward us…" she paused, "toward you, Willi."

My heart leapt into my throat. "What thing is that?"

"Can we not talk about this? I don't even know why I said that. Let's drop the whole thing, okay?"

"You draw pictures of people and things you've never seen, then say something is going to happen to me and you want to stop the conversation?"

"I hate this… this thing! Don't you understand? I don't want it, but it keeps coming back, okay? I don't know what's coming exactly, but I can feel it coming. That's all. Can we be done with this?" She was annoyed, as was I. But she made clear the conversation was over. It's not like we hadn't been through this before.

As if on cue, my phone rang. It was Nash. He wanted me to come over. I was about to tell him I was busy preparing for my next show when Madison mouthed, 'go see him.' An hour later, I headed west on 94 toward Minneapolis.

·

HIS PLACE WAS AN OLD Victorian house converted to a duplex. The stairs to the front door needed fixing, and the building overdue for a painting. Each unit had its own entrance and buzzer. One read 'Olsen', the other had no name, just a tag that read, 'upstairs'. I pressed the button, and the door clacked open. A long stairway with a single bulb barely illuminated the way. I knocked on the door at the top. When the door opened, I gasped.

"You must be Willi." Cinderella opened the door, wearing a bra that barely contained bulging breasts and bikini panties. There was no doubt she was pregnant. "Nash will be out in a moment. Can I offer you something? A beer or a snort?"

"Do you always answer the door half-naked?"

"You're offended?" Her mouth twisted into a half-smile. "If I answer naked, you're a paying customer. Half-naked is for friends… or perhaps a stranger. It depends."

I grabbed a robe off the back of a chair and threw it at her. "Well, I'm paying a visit, not a paying customer. Distractions aren't helpful. I'll have a beer."

"I'm used to distracting. It's my business." She slipped into the robe, which only came to her hips. "Spotted Cow or Crazy Lady?"

"Crazy Lady. Thanks." As she marched to the kitchen, Nash came in.

"You remember Cinderella?"

I raised my eyebrows.

"She can be shocking, but she's a good person, Willi. We want to have this baby and make a life together."

The room was orderly. A simple wool rug lay by a coal fireplace and a rocker in front of it. Furniture was new, no piles of dope or overflowing ashtrays. A vase with flowers sat on the dining room table. Except for Cinderella's panties on a line by the window, it looked almost normal. I took a deep breath. "I'm happy for you, Nash. Glad you called... why did you call?"

He sat in an oversized leather chair across from the couch. "I would've talked to Mom, but she gets emotional too quickly. I'm hoping you'll see what Cinderella and I are trying to build and give her the message."

"What message?"

"It's all under control."

"What's under control?"

"You know, the drug thing. We've worked out a deal with Joey Graveno, the owner of the soccer club who got upset over losing a bet."

Cinderella came out wearing a loose pair of cotton pants, her robe open. She set a bottle of beer on the coffee table in front of me, lit a joint, and snuggled next to Nash.

"What do you mean, working it out?"

"We've agreed to pay him a hundred grand. Cinderella averages four grand a week. I won't sell meth in his territory, but I still make money selling grass to students, which covers our expenses. One of his lackey's stops by once a month to collect."

Nash said this so matter of fact, it almost sounded normal.

"Graveno is dangerous, Nash. It sounds like he owns Cinderella and has side-lined you."

"Occasionally an associate of Graveno comes to town and Cinderella has to service him for a reduced price. But mostly, Graveno keeps his distance. Besides, we've got insurance. Connections with an old friend are keeping us safe."

"You mean the Asian gang?"

"How'd you know?"

"Ricardo talked to your mom."

"Yeah, he helped with the protection. I already knew Seng, the leader."

"And what's their price?"

"I supply them meth at cost."

"Thought you didn't sell meth anymore?"

"I don't. I just supply them. They do the street selling and give me a small kickback."

His thinking was so incongruent, it took my breath away. I slugged my beer, Cinderella held the joint to Nash's lips, then took a drag herself.

"And why did you call me here?"

"I want you to tell Madison I'm okay. That it's all under control. She's gonna be a grandmother, you know. Cinderella and I are trying to build a new life and we're doing well. When we've paid off Graveno, we'll save a little, have our kid, and leave this life behind." Cinderella bent over and kissed Nash on the lips, practically sucking the breath out of him. "I want to show you something."

He pushed up out of the chair and led me to a small room down the hallway. They had painted it blue, with storks flying on the wall and a fat pink dinosaur smoking a reefer—Nash's work, Cinderella's idea. The crib was baby ready with a mobile hanging overhead and a changing table with shelves filled with diapers and wipes. A small pink dresser sat in the corner, a penguin stuffy on top, and a Mickey Mouse lamp. It was darling… and heartbreaking at the same time. They were doing the right things and wrong things simultaneously.

When I left, Nash gave me a warm handshake. "Tell Mom it's all going fine. We'll have a family, she'll have a granddaughter."

"A girl? Congratulations."

Cinderella had tied her robe closed and kissed me on the cheek. "I know you have your doubts, Willi, but we love each other. We're just different."

I couldn't agree more. Outside of selling her body, I wasn't sure what Cinderella's talents were, but Nash's artistic ability abounded. As I trudged down the dimly lit stairs, I thought about their hopes and dreams of a normal, happy life, a life in love. It's an illusion everyone carries, but in reality, such happiness comes in glimpses and at unexpected moments. It's not permanent, and I trembled for their future.

When I returned to the house late in the afternoon, Madison was at her drawing table. The feeling of home had seeped in, and I gave her a big hug from behind. She turned and threw her arms around me, tears in her eyes. Over her shoulder, I could see her latest drawing—a burning baby crib carried by storks.

It was shocking. I closed the sketchpad and held her tight. I couldn't believe she'd draw such a tragedy.

The next day, I was on the road heading toward my next show in Ann Arbor, Michigan.

CHAPTER 24

MURDER ON THE ROAD

INCLUDING SETUP, THE SIX BROILING days in Ann Arbor, Michigan left me exhausted. Five simultaneous art shows take over the city. A thousand artists alongside blocks of non-profit booths and stores with sidewalk sales pushing everything from import clothing to cheap perfume made it the largest fair in the United States. It's always part circus, part art event, and you'd think making money there impossible. But enormous crowds come with lots of money. Collectors from all over the country descend on the town to add to their corpora. The show was insanely difficult to do, staggeringly hot in mid-July, and expensive—at least two grand if you slept the first and last night in your van. I made eighteen large, most of it cash, which would ease a lot of financial pain.

The road home was a drive through torrential rain as I headed west toward Chicago. Thoughts about Nash and Cinderella haunted me. It pleased me they wanted to change their life, but their plans to pay back Graveno were a nightmare. They underestimated how non-discriminate the forces of brutality can be. With the torrent continuing non-stop, I needed dinner and a cup of three-B Joe—bottom of the pot coffee, black and bitter.

As I peered into the murky distance, I passed a stalled motorist. The hood was up, and a man waved for help next to his pickup. With no raincoat and water cascading from all edges of his wide-rim hat, he looked desperate. I slammed on the brakes and the van skidded to a stop a hundred yards beyond his vehicle. Shoving my things from the front seat to the van floor, I unlocked the door.

"Thanks, mister." He got in, dripping like a water-logged sponge, and threw his wet backpack between the seats. "I've been standing out there for twenty minutes. No one seemed to notice I needed help. I owe you a big one!"

"It's quite the storm," I said, already regretting I'd stopped. The seat and my papers on the floor were now soaked. "There's a truck stop up the road where you can get service for your pickup."

"Name's Rolland, Rolland Cole." He spoke in a southern accent and extended his hand, giving me a firm grip.

"Hello, Rolland. I'm Willi." I turned on the heat.

"Oh, you don't have to do that. I'm used to the rain. But my vehicle isn't. The weather got to the gas line. It's an old Ford, simple straight six, too old for computerized fuel injection. She sputtered and then died on that hill where you picked me up. Got all my stuff in her, too."

"You must come from Oklahoma." I grabbed a loose towel and tossed it to him. The first thing he did was wipe his boots.

"Exactly right, mister, and moving to Kalamazoo." His chin had the sharp angles of an anvil, nose a pointed triangle.

"Kalamazoo! Why would a Southern boy head to an inhospitable place like Michigan?"

"I'm getting divorced," he stated. "Decided not to prolong kicking a dead horse. I packed my things, left a note, and started life anew." He let out a short, nervous laugh, took off his hat, and ran the towel over his face.

"I wish it were that easy!" I said. He seemed a likeable fellow, early twenties and starting over. It made me think of Nash and Cinderella.

I turned the heater to low, and we traveled on, the wind and rain blowing hard. A billboard along the way pointed to Lloyd's, a truck stop, fifteen miles away. Talking is one relief valve for the pressure cooker of human emotion, and as he talked, I realized his valve was dangerously plugged.

Rolland bluntly began with the demise of his marriage. "I caught her in bed with another man."

"Whoa, that's tough." The downpour became fierce, shortening the reach of my headlights. Taillights in front of me were my guides. The downpour sounded like drums against the van, a background beat to his story.

"I usually went to the bar after work," he continued. "But on this one evening, I had an early out. When I arrived home, the lights were off, so I tiptoed up to the bedroom. At the door, I heard all these groans and thumping. It was obvious what was happening. I stood there for the longest time, wondering if this was real or too much alcohol. The worst part was Tamara's cries of pleasure. It was a shock that spun my mind like a roulette wheel that wouldn't stop. I went back out to my truck and took the shotgun off the rack, loaded it, and walked back in. Somethin' snapped inside me. At the bedroom door, I crouched down, hand on the long barrel, and waited. Not sure what I waited for. I just waited."

I looked over at Rolland and wondered what kind of nut I had picked up. Beads of sweat rolled down his shadowed face and he stared blankly into the night, as if he were watching a movie of the whole thing outside the windshield.

"My thoughts were jumbled like a tangled-up fishing line," he continued. "I wasn't sure if I should smash the door, shoot both of them, or set the gun to my head and pull the trigger. And in the middle of my confusion, there's a tug on my arm. It's my little girl saying, 'Daddy what are you doing with your gun?' Her eyes were as big as the moon. After tucking her back into bed and kissing her goodnight, I went out to the truck, placed the rifle back in the rack and sat thinking about my next move."

Rolland squeezed the wet towel, causing droplets of water to fall onto his lap.

"You must think I'm crazy." He looked over at me.

"No, no," I lied. "Just a fellow in a bad situation. What happened?"

"After a long think, I went back into the house and kicked in the bedroom door. My wife screamed. The man jumped out the window, no clothes on, and ran away. When I asked Tamara what the hell was going on, she ignored me, put her robe on and marched out the front door for a smoke. Our six-year-old woke again, adding to the commotion. I followed Tamara out the door, screaming at her. She threw something at me, calling me a worthless, lazy, mostly out of work, drunk son-of-a-bitch and if I really cared for my family, I'd find a job that made real money. I slept in the pickup that night. I could hear our little girl and my wife crying for hours afterwards. Tamara left at six the next morning to drop our daughter off at her mother's. She had to make the seven o'clock shift at the meat packing plant.

"After she was gone, I went into the house and just stood, frozen like ice on a river, but underneath, things were raging. She was right. I was worthless. I knew I had to leave, and in that one moment my whole life changed." He put his wet cowboy hat back on his head. Swishing wipers cleared the windshield, filling the silence between us with rhythmic consistency.

"So…" I glanced at Rolland, "didn't you think about going back home to your folks or talking the situation out with a friend… you know, cool down a bit, think things over?"

He shrugged. "My sister lives in Kalamazoo. That's what made most sense to me." He reached into his shirt pocket, pulled out a folded piece of paper and put it back in again, as though to prove he had an address to go to.

"How about some dinner?" I suggested. "My treat."

"I'd be grateful, mister." Rolland looked like he was going to cry.

At Lloyd's, we parked in front of the restaurant. A young waitress seated us at a booth. Travelers packed the place, waiting out the storm.

"You believe in God?" Rolland asked.

"Can't say that I do, or I don't," I answered. "What's your point?"

"I want to," said Rolland, "but it's a difficult belief to trust when your life falls apart and there's no one but yourself to figure it out."

Rolland's deep loneliness seeped into my gut. Life can be mean. Being flush with cash, I decided to give him a hundred dollars to help. I told him I had to make a call and drifted out the door to retrieve money from my van. Being on the road is not glamorous, and I missed Madison. When I called, there was no answer. She was most likely in the studio.

The rain had slowed to a drizzle, with fog drifting in, softening the glare of outside lights. It was a night to be inside, at home, next to a fire, snuggled up with your lover and sipping a glass of wine. Under the glow of phosphorescent lighting, I watched two pickups pull up behind each other at the gas pumps. Two men got out of the forward pickup, one wore a backward baseball cap, an enormous belly spilt over his belt. He had a stubbly beard, his eyes sunken into a fat fleshy face that made them look like he was continuously in a squint. He spat on the ground as soon as his feet touched the ground, a blue work shirt half untucked. A brief glance sent shivers down my spine. The driver, a man about the same size, stepped out and zipped up his pants.

"I'm going to look around, Sly," the driver called out. "Why don't you fill it up."

"Okay, Rivera," the man answered.

Sly yanked the gas nozzle out of its holder like he was pulling a six-inch nail out of a wooden beam. His thick fingers held the nozzle at full throttle while he guzzled a beer. His hands, permanently stained with grease, had rings adorning every finger. The spiked middle ring could have been a weapon from the medieval ages. He leaned against the truck with a boot up on the curb, waiting for the click of the pump, studying details of the station—the layout of cars parked in front, the dead-end driveway to the back, the two aprons giving approach to the station. His gaze fell upon the cowboy, who was gassing up behind him. The cowboy stared back. Their glances collided, as if the boundary between night and day met in some unfashionable way. Sly spat again.

"Hey, ain't them maroon boots of yours somethin' special," he snarled. "You get them from your sister?" He put his hand on his big belly and laughed. The cowboy tipped his hat and turned his back, finishing at the pump.

"Bro, get your fat ass over here," Rivera shouted from the doorway next to me. "Let's get this over with."

Rivera was bigger than his brother, less fat, more muscle. His scraggy beard hid a pockmarked face and his head and neck seemed as one unit attached to giant shoulders. He wore a black leather jacket that would never make the zip around his stomach. They looked like the type that fix motorcycles for the Hell's Angels.

"Fuckin' Christ," I heard Rivera swear under his breath, "don't blow this thing." Anger and intimidation radiated from them like heat-soaked bricks after a kiln firing. The cowboy backed his truck into a parking spot, turned his lights off, but left the engine running. I grabbed a hundred from my stash and went back into the building. The two big men sat in a booth across from Rolland and me.

Our server was just pouring coffee, so I ordered. "Selma," I read her nametag, "I'll have the special and some of that famous pie of yours." Her eyes turned to Rolland, and he followed suit.

"You gotta trust it'll all work out," I said, but Rolland watched Rivera and Sly in the booth across from us. There was an undeniable evil exuded by their presence. It's often the wounded who sense danger first. Their bruises lay close to the surface, and, like an antenna, it allows them to see beyond a horizon others can't see. Rivera left, heading toward the john. Sly looked over at Rolland and then caught sight of his boots.

"Hey man, nice boots. Give ya a hundred bucks." His face bore a natural snarl and his tone intimidating.

Rolland looked up. "Not for sale!"

The big man slid out from his table and stood in front of us. I could smell his beer breath and body odor. The hair on my arms rose. Sly stepped on Rolland's boot as he swung into the seat next to me. I barely got out of the way as 350-plus pounds of flesh came crashing down, shaking the whole booth. Years of abuse and violence, jails and whorehouses, an absent father, an alcoholic mother, radiated from this man. There were forces so deep and twisted you could almost reach out and touch them. He spilled Rolland's coffee as he settled. The act was so outrageous that for a moment both Rolland and I sat in shock. Selma, our waitress, came back carrying our specials. For an instant I felt relief, as though reinforcements had arrived, as though she had the power to change the course of events unfolding. Encouraged, I looked Sly in the eye and mustered up the courage to speak.

"What the hell are you doing?" Sly slid closer to me, effectively pinning me against the wall, his way of saying, 'shut up.'

Selma had no clue what was going on. Efficiently, she delivered the hot plate specials and wiped up the spilt coffee. "Should I set another plate?" she asked.

"Yeah baby, me and the boys are having a little powwow. Get me one of those specials." As Selma wiped the table, Sly grabbed her arm, "Whatcha doing later, baby?" his beer breath all over her.

In a cool and restrained voice Selma answered, "Listen, honey, after work I'm goin' home to three kids, a husband, and a pile of laundry. Now take your filthy hand off me or I'll have you thrown out real fast. You boys better look after your friend, or you'll be following him out!" Now she was looking to us for help.

The cowboy in the maroon boots stepped inside the front door, not twenty feet from our table. He leaned against the wall, calmly surveying the scene. His boots looked so familiar, I wanted to shout out.

"Get your God damn hands off her!" Rolland screamed. He put his hand over a steak knife lying next to his plate. I remained pinned by a wall of flesh. At the register, I could see Rivera scooping piles of bills into a paper bag. Panic seeped through my body. His brother was robbing the place. The whole scene was like an elevator cut loose from its cables careening down the shaft to certain destruction.

"Hey, little man, what you gonna do?" Sly taunted Rolland. He twisted Selma's arm so her elbow slammed on the table.

"You're hurting me!" Selma cried out.

Rolland jumped to his feet, the steak knife loosely held in the palm of his hand. The big man laughed. I was completely vulnerable to every move he made. But Selma was no rookie. With her free hand, she swung around and smacked Sly across the face. Her diamond ring left a bloody mark on his cheek, but he hardly flinched. He just tightened his grip on her arm. You could hear the wrist bone snap. Selma screamed. The restaurant went stone cold silent. When I looked back at the register, Rivera swung around facing the commotion, a gun in his hand. Rolland slashed at Sly with the knife. Sly batted his arm away. Rivera raised his pistol and squeezed the trigger. The sound was deafening. The bullet swept across the room in slow motion, ripping the air apart as it sailed above a candy display and over the booth next to us. If the bullet was meant for Rolland, it was off course. It came straight at me.

All sounds disappeared. Small droplets of moisture appeared in the air, reflecting light like polished diamonds. Within this phantasmic dimension of time, the cowboy raised his arm, spreading his fingers apart. His eyes were pure white, no irises. When he closed his fist, the bullet's trajectory curved. Constraints on time and space made the room rubbery, no longer solid. The projectile struck Rolland in the head, knocking him clear off his feet.

Rivera's angry voice reverberated across the room, shouting at his brother. People all over the restaurant were screaming, looking for cover. Dishes crashed to the floor and tables tipped over as people tried to save their lives. Selma, on her knees, held her wrist and whimpered. I froze with my mouth open.

Sly grabbed my coffee cup, took a slurp and said, "Pick up the bill for me, would ya ace?" Selma slumped to the floor next to Rolland's shaking body.

He walked to the register. His brother rapped him on the head with the palm of his hand and, as they headed for the door, Rivera grabbed the cowboy by the shirt and sent him crashing into a stack of newspapers.

A moment later, their truck roared off into the fog. I remember helping Selma up, then stooping over poor Rolland. The side of his head was blown away. I stared at the bloody mess, my heart drowning in adrenaline. The whole side of his skull was missing and everything inside was spilling out. I thought I was going to pass out. His body twitched a few more times, and then it was over. He lay still, one eye staring up at the ceiling fan overhead.

A few minutes later, four truckers charged in with their rifles and posted themselves around the restaurant, just in case the brothers returned. It was more a gesture of helplessness. It was unlikely that Sly or Rivera forgot anything. I remember the police arriving, a full squad of them, and then three ambulances and the fire department. The damage was more than just poor Rolland. An old man had a heart attack and flying dishes cut several people. Lloyd, the owner of the place, brought out blankets and gave them to those in shock. He also served free coffee and pie. We huddled in groups, repeating the story over and over. It was curious how one story could have so many versions. Many people thought Sly had been firing directly at them. No one mentioned the cowboy. In fact, when I asked, I was the only one to have seen him. The spilled newspapers he crashed against were neatly restacked by the doorway.

I told the police about Rolland's pickup stalled on the side of the road, and his sister's address was in his pocket. By the time they got through with questions, it was 4:00 a.m. Adrenaline had worn off and complete exhaustion set in. My body, my heart, my soul ached. I was drained to the core. Even with a blanket around me, I shook, and a medic gave me some pills. The pink ones were Ativan for anxiety, the others, Trazodone for sleeping. He said don't take them all at once, but I popped them all. As I left the restaurant, the cashier called me over.

"Did you see that cowboy by the door?" he said.

I puffed. "Yes, yes. You saw him? Maroon boots, right?"

"I didn't want to say anything because no one even mentioned him, but…" he took a deep breath, "he changed the trajectory of that bullet. I saw it. Don't know how he did it, but I think you saw it too—he saved your life."

At that point, every logical structure with me crashed. Tears fell in droplets as big as the world. He touched what I couldn't admit to myself. An overwhelming urge to escape came over me. I put out my hand.

"Willi."

"Bid Ed." He reached under the counter and pulled out a plastic bottle. "You look pretty shaken. If you can't sleep, take one of these. The pills the medics give are child's play compared to this."

"Yeah, thanks." I stepped back… then ran out into a rain-soaked night.

THE GYROSCOPE FOR THIS TRIP had spun out of control. A tow truck pulled in with Rolland's pickup angled up on the carrier. I quickly crossed the lot, got in my van, and popped one of Big Ed's red pills. Rolland had left his cowboy hat on the floor between the seats. I couldn't touch it. Across the highway was a motel. I wasn't going any further.

This tragic event had turned success upside down. Questions rose about purposeless death—babies dying in their sleep, soldiers killed by friendly fire, or drunk drivers who run over innocent people. Was Rolland's death just a matter of bad timing—a poor fool in the wrong place at the wrong time, another victim of random chaos? Or was his murder the result of some deep karma, a retribution that had to be lived out on this night in this truck stop? Could it have been a preordained script that Rolland played to perfection? Was I appointed to be the Judas to deliver Rolland to his murderer? But the big question—was the cowboy the Orlando Rock of countless stories, who holds down tents in straight line winds and kills snakes and saves the homeless? And if so, why did he save me and kill Rolland? Is that mercy or twisted justice?

There was an inner bruise I reeled from thinking about Rolland's flesh and blood life extinguished in one senseless act of murder. I felt as though someone had slapped my heart. Something inside was vibrating, something I was unfamiliar with.

I was about to enter the motel office when the manager turned over a sign in the window, 'No Vacancy'. He saw me peering in and shrugged out a sorry. As I turned back to the van, a voice rang out, "Willi?"

A familiar face came out the door. "Kim? I can't believe it. What are you doing here?"

"Same as you, heading home from Ann Arbor. All the rooms were taken going west, so I came back this way. Got the last room here."

The rain started again, and a lightning flash burst across the sky, deep rolling thunder rumbled in the distance. The light under the portico dimmed, then brightened again. I could feel the pills taking hold.

Kim stepped close. "Willi… you look dreadful. Did you have a bad show? What's wrong?"

"I feel terrible. I just saw a guy murdered." When she took my hand, it was shaking. She put her arms around me.

"Oh my god, Willi. I've never seen you like this. Come on, you can stay with me."

I pulled the van in front of her room. When she unlocked the door, a musty odor from a worn rug greeted us. The queen-size bed had a drab painting screwed to the wall above it, two nightstands on each side with push-button lights above them. A flatscreen TV set on the dresser. With thoughts spinning and eyes barely open, I sat on a spongy mattress and put my face in my hands.

"We've shared a bed before, Willi. You're welcome to share it again." She threw her suitcase on a stand, then sat next to me. "What happened?"

My insides were vibrating. Maybe it was the pills or emotional upheaval, but tears welled, and the story of Rolland's murder poured out. Kim listened quietly, stroking my back as the events of that night spilled out. I never mentioned the cowboy or seeing the bullet strike Rolland.

At the end of my tale, I fell over into the pillow. She took off my shoes, propped me up and unbuttoned my shirt. As I took off my pants, she pulled back the covers. I got in. She undressed, slid into bed, and put her arms around me. I remember her comforting warmth and soothing touch. She kissed my face, running her hands down my chest. She whispered, "Shh, it's going to be alright." Her breath was minty, lips velvety like downy feathers against my neck. She stretched herself up and buried my face in her soft breasts. Lightning illuminated the room, and the lights dimmed. My body trembled. The pills transported me into a different realm. The last thing I remembered was kissing her breasts before the world disappeared.

WHEN I WOKE THE NEXT morning, sunshine burst through the curtained windows. The only trace of Kim was her minty aroma on the pillowcase. The events of the night before were dreamlike, and I staggered out of bed.

On top of my neatly folded clothes was a pair of her pink panties with a note. 'You're still a virgin—so no worries. Your member refused to standup and join the membership. You're amazingly difficult. Still, I enjoyed being next to you. Look me up next time in Chicago. Hope you're feeling better. Love, Kim.'—her phone number scribbled on the bottom. I crumbled the paper and threw it on the floor—Kim's version of twisted love.

In the shower, I scrubbed to get her fragrance off my body, but the groggy feeling of a pill hangover remained. I should have been outraged, but I had made choices no matter how impaired. Kim's ability to take advantage of a wounded soul was deviant. When I opened my suitcase, she'd left a drawing on top of fresh clothes. The image, a curving bullet sketched in pencil, almost jumped off the page. The picture slammed me in the chest. It came with a note: 'I couldn't sleep, Willi. In the middle of the night, I kept seeing your image, not Rolland's, in front of that bullet. I don't know why I drew this. So happy you weren't hurt. I think we're connected. Love, Kim.'

That bullet floating through space, a piece of deadly metal meant to strike me, then inexplicably curving away hitting Rolland, became vivid. The note and the image were startling. I sat on the edge of the bed, hyperventilating. Bending forward, elbows on my knees, I stared at the floor. Did Kim hear voices too? I never told her about the cowboy or the curving bullet. Madison's words reverberated — 'Let it be, Willi. You can't think this one through.' I snapped back into reality and forced myself to head out.

In the motel lobby, bottom-of-the-pot coffee looked like sludge from a sewer. Lloyd's would have something better than mud. I walked out to the van, greeted by my cell flashing on the center console. Messages showed Madison had attempted three calls. I called back, but no answer. If working in the studio, she wouldn't pick up, or her prescient voice had already told her about Kim, and she was angry.

I drove across the bridge and pulled up to a pump at Lloyd's. The world churned on as before. People gassed up, a couple by the front door smoked cigarettes, a family with two kids headed inside. The sky was powder blue, not a cloud in view. Only a few puddles hinted that a major storm had passed through, and nothing showed the mayhem of the night before. The gas nozzle clicked, and I headed inside for a takeout coffee. Big Ed was back at the register.

"Hey, Ed."

He glanced up, a bit confused, then said, "Oh yeah, Willi, right? You're the guy who was here last night."

"Thanks for that pill you gave me. It was a lifesaver."

He wrinkled his forehead. "What're you talking about?"

"After the shooting, you said you saw the cowboy with the maroon boots... you gave me a pill to help me sleep. Remember?"

"Cowboy in maroon boots? I don't remember any cowboy and I don't dispense pills—period! I mean, you looked rough... we were all in shock."

His denial took my breath away. Not only did he talk to me about the cowboy, but he gave me that red pill, and it knocked me out. When I set my takeout coffee on the counter, he waved off payment. "Stay safe, Willi." — and moved on to the next customer.

I slid into the front seat, took a deep breath, and started the van. My phone buzzed, showing a voicemail. I could hear Madison's heavy breath, her voice breaking into sobs, the message short.

'Willi... Cinderella is missing.'

CHAPTER 25

A Sobering Talk

FIFTEEN MILES LATER, I CALLED Madison again—no answer—then called Nash. No answer either. I wasn't sure Jimmy would remember me, but I phoned him anyway. Madison said he didn't have a secretary or an office, only an answering service. He worked out of his car. Knowing too many secrets kept him mobile.

"Who is this?" he answered after two rings.

"Jimmy, this is Willi Steuben, Madison's partner." There was a brief silence as Jimmy connected to who I was.

"Oh yeah, Willi, the boyfriend."

At least I was in the loop, which saved a lot of explaining. "Listen, I'm on the road and got a disturbing call from Madison last night about Cinderella."

Another pause. "What did you hear?"

"Cinderella's missing."

"And why does that concern you?"

I could feel Jimmy's cautiousness. "I... I'm afraid of Madison doing something dumb, like going directly to Joey Graveno to get her back."

"Well, it's not Madison I'm afraid for. It's Nash who would do something stupid. I'm not sure what your girlfriend is up to."

"Do you think Graveno has Cinderella?"

"My Chicago source says she's been trunked."

My heart raced. "Trunked? What's that mean?"

"They took Cinderella to Chicago in a trunk… to soften her up. After a couple of days of bread and water and pissing in her pants, she'll beg to get out. She'll do anything to avoid being put back in. And I mean… anything."

"Like the trunk of a car?"

"No, I mean the type trunk grandma keeps in the attic for old sweaters."

"She's pregnant, for God's sake!"

"Yeah, so what? I don't want to sound callous, but these guys are cold."

By this time, my speedometer hit 85, sweat dripping from my brow. I pulled off at an exit and stopped on the shoulder. Such cruelty was unimaginable. "Are they trying to break her?"

"You get the picture. Like a horse."

"How do we free her?"

"I've told Madison to stay calm and keep Nash under control. If she can do that and raise enough cash, we might have Cinderella back soon." A radio played in the background, mixed with the staccato sound of an occasional blinker.

"Does that mean you've talked to Graveno?"

"Don't be an idiot. In a situation like this, Graveno doesn't talk to anyone directly. I got one of his lackeys a get-out-of-jail pass a couple of years ago, so he's my contact. Things are fluid, Willi. Graveno might do cash, or he might do a trade."

"Trade for what?"

"Something about artwork your girlfriend has. Graveno might take it in trade."

"How the hell does Graveno know about Styles?" I bit my lip for saying too much.

"Listen, Willi, the mob world has connections you and I only dream of. I've set up a meeting with Madison for tomorrow. We'll talk then. I've got another call coming in, so I gotta go. By the way, when we meet, I'm gonna need another down payment to keep me on this case."

"How much?"

"This is far more complicated than I expected. At least ten grand. Cash."

He hung up. I gasped.

•

AS I PULLED IN FRONT of the house, Madison was rolling a suitcase to her Camry. The car was fifteen years old with a slightly bent hood and the front headlight taped into place after an accident. She hardly looked up when I swung out of the van.

"Hey, you seem upset."

"I am upset, Willi. I think my son will kill himself to get his kidnapped girlfriend and my husband slept with my ex-lover. That's upsetting." She threw her suitcase in the trunk.

"Where are you going?"

"Chicago. That's where Graveno has Cinderella." Tears welled from the corner of her eyes. I stepped over and opened my arms.

Her icy glare froze my raised arms. "How could you do it? I warned you what she was after."

"It wasn't exactly what you think. Can we talk?"

She stepped forward with fists clenched and pounded on my chest. "No! I'm going to find Nash before he does something stupid. He's not answering his cell." She pounded again and wept. "You're so damn stupid," she choked out, hitting my chest. When I put my arms around her, she pushed away, pounding some more. Finally, I caught her wrists.

"Madison. Stop! Nash's probably already done something stupid. So did I, and a third stupid isn't going to fix anything. Okay? Let's talk!"

She twisted her wrists from my grip and let out a deep sigh. "I'll give you five minutes."

"How about an Irish coffee?" Her turquoise irises had turned to sharp stone grey. Fists balled. There's a moment in the ring every fighter faces. It's not the power of a punch that saves the fight, but dragging oneself off the floor after the knockdown. We were both on the floor.

I extracted her suitcase from the Camry and followed her in. When I entered the kitchen, she brought her sketchbook to the table. "How did Ann Arbor go?"

"It was good. Made money."

She nodded, uninterested. I fixed two coffees with a shot of whiskey, set a mug in front of her, and sat down. She opened her sketch pad. My head lay between Kim's breasts, one with a serpent tattooed around it, nipples erect.

I took a deep breath. "There was no serpent," I said, which wasn't smart.

"Yeah, well, that's because either you didn't have the lights on or were too drunk to notice."

"No, it's because I was drugged."

She flipped to the next drawing. There was Rolland on the floor with half his head missing. My chest vibrated, tears welled. Madison searched my face.

"I didn't know what this picture was about, Willi. I was afraid for you. Someone died?"

"Murdered," I responded.

She touched my hand. "Oh my god, Willi... what happened?"

The entire incident streamed out in tears and choked up words. From picking him up in a rainstorm to Rolland's killing, to the cowboy with maroon boots and the curving bullet, the dreamlike story became reality again. I told her about the drugs given by medics and pills Bid Ed gave me, then the chance meeting with Kim, and the whole debacle in bed. If ever there was a story to disbelieve, mine was it. But the next page in her sketchbook stunned me. She had captured the cowboy in pencil, his maroon boots in colored marker with his fingers forward and spread. My mouth dropped open.

She looked at the drawing. "I didn't know what this meant until your story. And the bullet curving away from you and hitting Rolland? I believe it happened just as you told me. Worlds are intersecting, and for unknown reasons, we are standing in the doorway of two realities. We were chosen, it's not chance."

"I totally don't believe that. But so much has happened... your drawings, Annabelle's story, the bullet, then meeting Kim after the murder was more than odd. I think she's part of this, too."

"I knew Kim was going to Ann Arbor, and I figured she'd find you. She's like a heat-seeking missile."

"Believe me, it wasn't a romantic interlude! In the morning, I wasn't sure what had happened. She left a note. Said we hadn't…" I raised my eyebrows.

"What? Fucked?"

"I was too drugged. I felt stupid, taken, and blamed myself. Even after scrubbing in the shower, I couldn't get all her perfume off me."

"You were raped." Madison downed the last of her Irish. "Plenty of women know exactly how you feel."

"In the morning, I slept in. When I woke, Kim had left. Here's the weird part. During the night, Kim got up and drew a bullet curving across open space. She placed the drawing on my suitcase. A note said she didn't understand what it meant." I unfolded the picture and laid it on the table. "I never told her about the curving bullet." Madison stared at the image.

"She always could draw…" She let out a breath. "I suspected she heard voices. She tried to hide it, but one night, after we made love, it slipped out. She told me the voices scared her. It bound us together… for a while. But back then, neither of us understood what was going on. Not that I do now, but it doesn't frighten me like it used to. When she drew me pregnant, I freaked. Little did I know that later in the summer I'd be in Paris with Peter, carrying his child." Madison placed Kim's drawing in her sketchbook. "Why didn't you call me?"

"Madison! I tried but couldn't get hold of you or Nash, so I finally called Jimmy. He filled me in about Cinderella missing."

"Well, it's gone beyond Cinderella. Nash isn't answering his cell. I think he went to find her."

No sooner had she finished her sentence when a car pulled into the drive. A moment later, Jimmy stood at the front door.

•

I OFFERED JIMMY AN IRISH, but he waved it off and said, "No coffee, just the whiskey." He wasted no time getting down to business.

"Before we start, we need to talk money. The retainer has run out. I don't do the hourly rate thing. The next couple of weeks will be intense, some of it dangerous. If I'm to stay on this case, it's gonna cost ten grand."

I held up two bottles. "Bourbon or Beam?"

"Bourbon." I poured one for him and one for myself.

Madison didn't flinch. "Five grand, Jimmy. The most you'll do is make a few calls. Not that they won't be important. We need you, but once things are in motion, the only service we'll need from you is advice."

"Well, advice costs. Six grand five. Final."

"Five grand five, cash." Madison's eyes never left his.

"Cash? It's a deal." Jimmy stared back.

I knew she didn't have the money. Madison lived like most artists do, month to month, week to week. Pushing back from the table, I opened my briefcase, which lay on the nearby couch. My money pouch from Ann Arbor lay on top. Returning to the table, I counted out five thousand five hundred, mostly in twenties, and slid the pile over to Madison. She pushed the stack in front of Jimmy, caught my hand, and squeezed. Tears welled.

Jimmy raised his eyebrows, gathered the bills, and stuffed them in his coat pocket.

"Where do we start?" Madison began again.

"There are a few things you don't know," he began. "Remember your nemesis, Reid Johnson?"

I could hear Madison grinding her teeth. "What about Reid?"

"You thought he stole two of Edgar Styles' drawings. You were right. Reid contacted a Chicago fence and tried to sell them for fifty grand each."

Madison went livid. "That son-of-a-bitch."

"The fence works for Graveno. He goes to Joey and tells him the pictures are part of a set, but two are missing. It's not rocket science. Each drawing is marked—set of four, Reid has one and two. He also tells Graveno that the entire set is worth in the area of nine hundred thousand dollars. Now Joey is interested."

Madison rose from the table and walked to the counter. She picked up an apple, rotated it in her hand, staring at it as if she'd never seen one before. I had seen that gaze before—turning so completely inside herself that the rest of the world seemed non-existent. I'm not sure she knew she was standing.

"Isn't Graveno going to need provenance? Some proof the sketches are authentic."

Jimmy looked up at me. "He's not head of the mob because he's stupid. Of course, he'll get someone to authenticate. But here's the point. The fence asked if Reid had the other two drawings. Reid told the fence he'd get them soon. After a few photos and consultation with an art expert, the fence contacted Reid for another meeting. She confirmed the drawings are authentic."

Madison snapped back from meandering through the universe somewhere. "Who's the expert?"

"How the hell am I supposed to know? Some woman," Jimmy retorted.

"Because it's important. I want to know."

"Okay, I'll see if I can find out." Jimmy slugged his drink and continued. "Here's the point. The fence does some investigation of his own. The whole deal is too good to be true, but the fence doesn't have two hundred thousand to buy the four drawings from Reid. He goes to Graveno, who is a good customer, and makes the pitch. The boss is interested. He'll finance the buy, give the fence a good commission, and still make a huge profit when he sells the set. But there's a catch; Graveno will finance the deal only if he can get all four drawings; and he wants to know who owns the other pictures.

"The fence contacts Reid and offers him twenty-five grand for each drawing, but the deal is on only if he can buy all four drawings. He also wants to know where the other two drawings are.

I closed my eyes and shook my head. Madison stomped her foot on the floor. "God damn Reid! I could kill him."

Jimmy turned. "Wouldn't do that just yet. And better watch your mouth. Reid told the fence a collector has them and wants to sell, that it'll take a few days to arrange everything. In the meantime, the fence studies the drawings and does a face search of the posing model. Guess whose face comes up…

yours. Not only does he know who you are, but also where you live—next to the deceased Styles. This is a windfall for Graveno. It's easy to connect you to Nash and to Cinderella. So, Graveno grabs Cinderella, who now becomes a pawn and, more than likely, icing on the cake, right?"

"Wrong!" Madison slammed a knife through the apple, like a guillotine slicing off a head.

Jimmy turned in his chair. "Look, Madison, Graveno knows you have the drawings. Maybe not here, but somewhere. He's got Cinderella, but if that doesn't work… Nash could be next. These guys get what they want. You've got to understand this."

"Who says he's going to give up Cinderella?" I asked. "How do you make the exchange?"

Jimmy twisted his lips into a pretzel and nodded. "There are ways. If Graveno gives his word, it's usually good. That's how things work in their world."

"Well, not in my world, Jimmy." Madison stabbed the knife into a cutting board. "How much are you making from this deal?"

"If I have to go to Chicago… I want the full ten grand. Danger pay."

I put my elbows on the table, resting my head in my hands. "We need to talk about this. How much time do we have?"

"Depends. I'd give Cinderella three days before she breaks, maybe four days. Tops. And a warning, Graveno doesn't like waiting." With a big blowout breath, Jimmy stood. "If you want me as your man, best call me by tomorrow with an answer. Time to get this thing settled and everybody safe." At the door, Jimmy stopped and turned. "Give Graveno the two god damn drawings and be done with this."

"Why doesn't Graveno send his goons here and get the drawings?" I asked.

"Because he's smart. Small town, doesn't know the layout, doesn't trust Reid, and doesn't like publicity. Cinderella was an easy target. And he'd rather make a deal on his own turf. This is only one conflict among many he's involved in. He's a fighter and experienced. I used to represent these guys all

the time in court. And he's dangerous. I saw a photo of that first drawing…
it's lewd and what Graveno likes. Madison should stay as far away from
Graveno as possible."

"Thanks, Jimmy." I wasn't sure what I thanked him for. He got into an old
Bronco and drove off.

Madison came up from behind me, holding her Glock. She aimed the gun
at a whirligig on top of the barn, two hands on the handle, and squeezed the
trigger. With a thunderous bang, the weapon fired, sending the metal rooster
twirling and my ears ringing. When the bird stopped, there was a hole in its
head. The shot was amazing.

"Where'd you learn to shoot like that?" I asked.

"There's plenty you don't know about me, Willi."

She tucked the gun into her belt and went into the house.

CHAPTER 26

ANOTHER CONFESSION

MADISON SPENT THE AFTERNOON ALONE in the studio drawing. She didn't want interruptions, and I stayed clear. She had returned the weapon to the kitchen drawer, which provided relief for me. There were lots of moving pieces, and she needed time to sort them out. I cleaned the van, then prepared soup. My next art fair was three weeks away in Uptown, Minneapolis. The show was always insane, hot weather, three hundred fifty artist booths, enormous crowds, long days, and exhausting, but the slog usually resulted in a payday way above average. With money made in Ann Arbor vanishing into Jimmy's hands and demands for more forthcoming, it was critical I do well.

Hours later, after I finished a cold gazpacho, Madison came in and put her arms around me. "Smells delicious. Are you preparing for another soup festivity?" It was a welcome change in mood.

I laughed. "I think the rules say one sexy soup fest per year. How about some nourishment? You've been at it for hours." The aroma of cumin and turmeric floated in the air. Madison pulled close.

"Let's make love."

"Now?"

"You stood up for me, Willi. That was a lot of hard-earned money."

"Repayment not required."

"I want to devour you and I want you to devour me. Let's wash away all these worries that swirl about."

I laughed. "So, clear-the-mind sex?"

"Exactly." She marched down the hallway to the bedroom, leaving a trail of clothing behind her.

We made slow grinding love that stopped churning thoughts, connecting with raw physical. Her kisses were deep and passionate, eyes sad and hungry. Arms and legs tangled together. I teased and was playful, which she liked. A mystical wind carried us into the hexagram of an unknown future, and we held each other like gravity holds the moon in orbit—our rhythmic movement a long and ancient dance. When she took control, she wanted warp speed. We blew by ignition and flew directly into the sun, flesh and bone returning to star dust. The heat stripped away our worries, bodies pounding against each other until exhausted and exhilarated. We laid, annihilated, sharing heartbeats and breaths.

She pushed herself up, breasts skimming over my chest, legs spread, long hair washing over my face, eyes gazing into mine.

"I love that connection with you when we cross the boundary line that separates our bodies. Such a lovely sensation. But now... I need something else."

"What's that?"

"Your deep attention."

She rolled over on her back. I pulled the covers over both of us.

"Can I catch my breath first?"

"There's another boundary line, Willi. One that I breached with Styles."

I turned on my side. "You slept with him?"

"No. He never touched me that way. Something deeper. There's another part of the story I haven't told you... or anyone."

My brain hurtled from space to earth. "Of course," I said, surprised and not surprised simultaneously. "I'm listening."

"Styles didn't draw those pictures."

"What?"

"I drew them." She stared at the ceiling.

"One of the most famous painters in the country signed your work?"

"He took photos of me, enlarged them, then gave precise instructions about his style, accuracy, weight and value of line. He scrutinized every stroke I laid on paper and made corrections. The idea for the four drawings was his."

"Why didn't he draw them himself?"

"It's that… his hands shook too much. Parkinson's diminished his talents. My work had impressed him, so he gave me the assignment of a lifetime— draw out his ideas. I agreed to the plan, and believe me, it wasn't easy. It took weeks. When we finished, he said no matter how hard I tried to copy his style, the work was really mine. There were insuppressible nuances that came out as me. He surprised me and signed the drawings, not to diminish what I did, but because of the money they would bring. He said he couldn't have done better, and I think he fell in love with me. In the third study, when he shaved my head, I knitted my initials into locks piled on the floor."

"He shaved your head?"

"Not just my head, Willi."

"You were naked in all the drawings?"

"Yes. But before starting number three, Styles and I took off our clothes. We stared into each other's eyes for thirty minutes. Maybe longer. He cried. Admitted to hating his body and what Parkinson's had done to it. And I cried because of the way I had let my body be used. The completed series was a visual description of how innocence is stripped away. That's when he tied that key around my waist. He said the key was a metaphor, but also to a metal box. It shows up in the fourth and final drawing. When he died, he wanted me to have that box."

"And you have that box?"

"Yes."

"The one you haven't opened?"

"Correct."

A silent breath escaped from my lips. "Madison, why?"

"I was tempted but the voice told me not to touch it."

"Where is the box?"

"It's buried."

"Buried? How long is it to remain hidden?"

"Until you dig it up, Willi."

"This is a bit confusing. How am I to dig up a buried box when I don't know where it is?"

"There will be a time when I will tell you. You may not understand what's inside, but its contents will save my life."

"Do you know what's inside?"

"No."

"Madison! Do you know how crazy this sounds?" I rolled my eyes. "Okay, so much for the metal box. Who owned the drawings, you or Styles?"

"He said the high prices the drawings could bring weren't about art. That was the business of selling art. He knew I needed money. He gave them to me."

"An expert would know, right?"

"Experts scrutinize the signature first. Once established as real, the rest of the piece is examined summarily. No one would suspect... that is almost no one."

"What does that mean?"

"There is one expert...." Her lips tightened.

One name blew across my mind. "Kim, right?"

"She's become the darling of the Art Institute and upscale Chicago galleries for authentication of contemporary art. Peter taught the importance of signature and provenance in school. If anyone knows my style, the ins and outs of my work, and me, it's Kim."

"You don't think she's the 'expert' the fence brought in?"

"It's possible. I should talk to her."

My heart sank. "Not a good idea."

"Look, Willi, if she sees those drawings, she'll know something's up. That will raise every red flag in her assessment tool kit. I want to talk with her." Madison swung out of bed and shimmied into her jeans. "Let's eat. I'm famished."

Somewhere between the bedroom and the kitchen, a plan had formed in her mind. As we slurped soup, she explained her strategy. "I want you to find Nash. Start at his apartment. I know places where a few of his Asian gang-banger friends hang out. I'll talk to Kim. We'll meet back here."

"She's going to exact a price, Madison, which might include part of the proceeds if the drawings are sold at auction."

"It's not money she would want, Willi... it's me. And if sleeping with her means saving Nash, I'll do it." We stood facing each other, her hands trembling but eyes steely cold. A pang shot through my gut. She wasn't kidding.

•

AN HOUR LATER, AS I crossed over the Mississippi into downtown Minneapolis, my cell rang. It was Madison.

"Willi, I just talked to Kim."

"Already?" I banged the steering wheel with my hand. "Okay. Spit it out."

"She saw the drawings. Some guy calling himself Don Johnson showed up at her studio carrying them."

"Don Johnson, the movie star? That's so stupid it must have been Reid."

"Yeah, it was. She drew a quick sketch of his face and texted it to me. It was him."

"Wait. She sees Reid once and draws his face?"

"She even got the stitches laced in his eyebrow. I'm not the only one with an Eidetic memory, Willi. She's brilliant. I'm sure she could draw you with no problem."

That was unsettling. Who knows what she'd put up on social media? My heavy foot pushed the van to eighty in a fifty-five zone.

As if she could read the speedometer, she said, "Calm down, Willi."

"What else?"

"Reid wanted a quick authentication, like she was a fast-food outlet for art. He didn't know it requires a photo microscopic analysis of the lines. An answer would take two days. She was shocked that I was the model in the drawings with Styles' signature… and suspicious. Reid paid three thousand cash upfront. He wanted a certified copy of the results. She didn't trust him."

"Reid brought cash? What the hell."

"He came prepared. There's a lot of money riding on her expertise."

"That's not all. If she gave the 'right' result, another ten grand would be forthcoming. She didn't know the deal involved a well-known gangster, but she suspected foul play."

"Are you saying that Kim has the two drawings in her possession?"

My foot had become a brick on the gas pedal again. I pulled off at the Riverside exit and parked at a service station. "What did she say?"

There was a long silence.

"Madison!"

"Not only does she have them, but she knew it was my drawing. What confused her was Styles' signature was authentic."

"I told her those drawings belonged to me. So-called 'Don Johnson' was a cop who had stolen them and murdered Styles to get them."

I bent my head till it touched the steering wheel. Pressure grew from the base of my throat, my teeth clenched. "What does Kim want?"

As if she could see me, Madison said, "Relax. Take a breath. We have some time. Kim invited me to stay at her place and we'd talk."

She must've heard me groan over the phone. "Willi, please, steady. I know who I am. You've got to find out where Nash is."

"Madison, promise you won't go to Chicago without me." I banged the wheel, letting go a sigh sounding like a windstorm.

"No promises, Willi. I'll keep you updated and call me as soon as you know anything. If you find Nash, we can work this out through Jimmy… maybe."

"Ya, that's a big maybe," I retorted. She hung up. I got back on the highway, multiple scenarios running through my mind, which made me think of Madison's drawings of flames. Were our lives about to go up in smoke? Every outcome spelled disaster.

I PULLED IN FRONT OF Nash's apartment and rang the bell. To my surprise, the door buzzed open, and I went up the long, dark stairway to the second floor. At the top, I knocked. The door drifted opened by itself. I stepped in. Off to one side was a short stocky man, wearing a leather jacket and bandana on his head. His eyes were slits in a round face, a fluff of hair on his chin. In his right hand, a Smith and Wesson pointed at the floor. I put my hands in the air. This guy wasn't kidding.

"Whoa, no problem. I'm a friend of Nash."

A second man stepped from behind. "Turn around," he commanded, "slowly." He held a magazine loaded semi-automatic, his finger on the trigger. He immediately recognized me. "I've seen this guy before, with Nash. He's okay." He closed the door behind me.

"No weapons. Just want to find Nash." I lowered my hands. "His mom and I think he's in trouble. I was told Seng might have some information."

The one with the short beard holstered his gun and tilted his head, giving a silent command to his partner.

He padded my legs, working their way up my torso. After a thorough search, he said, "Sit on the couch."

I sat and looked around. Cinderella's underwear wasn't hanging in the window, but the place was tidy. A new blue baby carriage parked in the corner. The two men stood in front of me. My heart beat like a doumbek at a belly dance competition.

"Do you know Nash?" I began.

The bearded one put out his hand. "I'm Chun, Seng's brother." Relief flooded over me.

"I'm Willi. I live with Madison, Nash's mother." We shook hands.

Chun's partner went into the kitchen and brought out three beers. They sat on stuffed chairs near me. We sipped in silence. No one seemed to know where to start. I came clean.

"We think Nash might be in Chicago to rescue his girlfriend, Cinderella."

They said nothing.

"Joey Graveno. Does that name mean anything to you?"

Their eyes were poker practiced blank stares. But Joey's name caused both of them to shift positions. They were listening.

"Madison and I want to help." That was the icebreaker.

"Too dangerous. Stay away. Someone will get hurt."

"Can I talk with Nash?"

"He's not here."

I went out on a limb. "We heard he and Seng went to Chicago."

The two of them looked at each other. "Time for you to go."

That confirmed Nash was on his way to rescue Cinderella. But her whereabout was still an unknown, and they weren't big at conversation. So I let go a sizeable piece of information to keep things on track.

"There are two drawings that might be helpful in a trade for Cinderella. Madison has them. No one needs to get hurt. We just want to get them to Graveno."

"What drawings?" Chun raised his eyebrows. He knew nothing about this.

"Something Graveno wants. They're safe in Chicago now. We need to give them to Nash for the trade. They're worth a lot of money and Graveno fences art, expensive art."

Chun got up from his seat, pulled out his cell, and walked into the kitchen. I could hear him chatting in Mung. A few minutes later, he returned. "Nash or Seng will contact you or his mother. Far too dangerous for you to get involved."

"I'll be there tomorrow by noon." That meant I'd have to drive most of the night. "Can I get a number to contact Nash?"

He shook his head. "He'll call you." Chun looked at me with cold eyes. "You amateur. Stay clear or someone gets hurt, maybe killed."

I nodded. His stare was discomforting, but what he said could be true. I backed out the door and almost tripped down the long stairway. Once in my van, I called Madison. No answer. Called again. The phone machine answered with a message— 'the geese have flown to the windy city.' My heart sank. I banged the steering wheel.

"Damn it, Madison! Why didn't you wait!"

•

WHEN I PULLED INTO THE drive, her old beater was gone. I threw open the studio door, but all the lights were off. In the kitchen there was no note, only empty ice trays in the sink. At her drawing table lay a new picture of a house in flames, drops of blood raining from the sky. The voice had spoken again. It was a frightening drawing, perhaps a tragic prediction. But my fearful reaction turned to terror. On closer inspection, the red drops weren't pigment. They were actual blood. An X-Acto knife lay on the tabletop. Madison had cut herself, then used her own blood as paint to draw with. A cold stone dropped into my gut. I ran into the bedroom, shoved some clothes in a bag and grabbed all the cash from my last two shows—six grand between me and destitution. As I rushed out of the house another alarming thought stopped me. I backtracked to the kitchen. Opening the pot holder drawer, I searched for the Glock. Way in the back, I found an empty box of tracer bullets. The gun was missing.

CHAPTER 27

RECONCILED

I'D DRIVEN THE ROUTE TO Chicago dozens of times, but I never saw an accident as gruesome as this one. Outside of Tomah, traffic snaked by the twisted remains of a vehicle hit by a tractor-trailer. Amidst the flashing red lights of fire engines and police waving at gawkers to move on, two bodies lay covered in sheets on the shoulder. In my rearview, an ambulance with sirens screaming wove its way toward the scene. Who knows how it happened, but it only took one regrettable mistake or miscalculation to end two lives. Madison's clairvoyance could see the future, but even she admitted not all of it. I feared Chun was correct. We were amateurs in a professional game.

When I made the tollway, I called Madison again. It was four a.m. Kim answered the phone.

"Hello, Willi." She must've seen the caller ID.

"Kim? Where's Madison?" I heard a groan in the background.

"She's here, asleep," Kim replied. Covers shuffled, a light switch clicked and a whisper, "It's Willi."

"Willi?" a sleepy voice responded.

"Are you in bed with Kim?"

A long silence ensued as I slowed through an I-pass toll booth.

"Madison!"

"We reached an agreement, Willi. Where are you?"

"I'm an hour out of Chicago." A cop flew by me with his lights flashing.

There was a deep sigh and another silence. Then more whispering. "Come over here, Willi. We'll have breakfast together."

"This is way beyond my comfort zone, Madison. How about you and I go out for breakfast and talk?"

"No! Meet here. Kim is part of this, whether we like it or not. I got your voice-mail late last night. Since then, I spoke with Nash. We have to work this out together before it explodes in our faces."

"Text the address," I said and hung up. I wasn't sure if she meant the situation with Cinderella or the one with Kim. She was the one who warned me about Kim, and now she's in bed with her? A pang shot through my heart. A moment later, Kim's address text-buzzed on my phone.

•

KIM RANG ME IN TO her apartment and greeted me at the door with an unwanted kiss on the cheek. When I stepped in, Madison threw her arms around me and kissed me on the lips.

"Oh, Willi!" she exclaimed. "You look exhausted. How about a coffee?"

I nodded. Madison wore Kim's safari pants.

I collapsed into a cushy armchair. Kim's art gallery living room had paintings covering the walls, others, wrapped and tagged for art dealers, leaned against furniture, a drawing table faced the front window. Small bronze sculptures on shelving book ended large cover art books—Pollack, Emily Carr, Richard Serra and others. Couch and chairs were vintage sixties, angular but comfortable. A metal sculpture suggesting a figure reaching for the sky stood in one corner.

A spare bedroom had the door removed. Inside, a large adjustable easel with a half-finished canvas stood in the center of the room, tubes of acrylics and cans of paint lined shelving. On the opposite wall was a magnificent four panel painting. A marble countertop separated the kitchen from the living room with stools in front of it. The place was eclectic, not cheap. Kim was doing well. Madison brought coffee, then sat on the couch. Kim settled in a chair next to me.

"We know where they're holding Cinderella," Madison began.

"Can we back up a bit? Am I the third party out here? I feel like I'm interrupting something between you two."

Madison got up and sat on the arm of the overstuffed chair, slid down, squishing me over to one side. "We finished something that ended badly years ago. Love is easily twisted into something it's not." Kim was solemn and said nothing. I gazed out the window.

The first rays of morning sunlight fell on the drawing table. Outside, the city awakened. Ten thousand arms stretching across ten thousand beds, people holding each other close, the wellspring of another day upon them, while in other beds there was no one there to reach out to, just another day, alone. Madison turned my head with her hand, exploring my eyes.

"Willi... look at me! When I wake in the morning, it's your arms, and your body I reach out to touch. You are my go-to, my rock... but most of all, you are my love." She looked at Kim. "It's not that my love for Kim has disappeared, there's no doubt it has roots, but it's not possessive and needs no action, yet it stirs me, but I don't want to run off and live with her." She reached across to Kim and squeezed her hand. "I... we... live out our choices." She gazed into my eyes. "I choose you, Willi, and I want you to choose me..."

"Is this what love does?" I asked. "Fling you off a cliff, then catch your broken heart mid-flight on the way to oblivion, only to lift you up again."

"It's the geese flying south, Willi. They can't do it by themselves. I can't do this by myself. We fly on gossamer wings. Come with me."

Kim quietly wiped a tear from her cheek. "How about I make some breakfast while you two talk?" She headed for the small kitchen.

Madison reached out and pulled me up from the chair. "Come. I want to show you something." On the way to the drawing table, I spun her around and we kissed. Soft, passionate lips expressed the deep feeling between us. Love is such a risk, there's no center line, you're in or you're out. And I was in. Over my head in.

"The voice was back," she explained. "In the middle of the night, I found myself at Kim's drawing table. She saw me get up and followed. As I sketched, Kim talked me through it, asking questions, fleshing out details like the house number, 41465. The image was clear, like a mirage we could both see. My hand felt guided, and before returning to bed, we both knew this was where we had to go."

The drawing was a clapboard house, low unkempt shrubbery extended along a front porch, a cracked cement walk led to wooden stairs, one riser in need of repair. A boarded third-floor window and peeling paint made the place look condemned.

"It was amazing, Willi," Kim said as she cracked eggs into a sizzling pan. "It seemed Madison was in a trance, yet I could see the mirage and ask questions. Have you done this?"

"Not so gifted," I replied. "I've only seen finished pictures. But I saw one," my eyes shifted to Madison, "drawn in blood."

Kim set dishes on the counter and looked up. "Blood? Madds, you painted with your own blood? Awesome!"

But Madison turned away.

"Why blood?" I asked.

Tears flooded her eyes. She leaned against my chest and sobbed. The reservoir of sorrow and pain spilled onto my shirt, and her body shuddered and shivered. Kim came around the counter and we cradled her in our arms as she trembled.

"Madison... what did you see?" Kim asked.

"If there is mercy in this world, what I saw will never happen." She pushed back from my chest, turned and kissed Kim on the lips. "Thank you," she sniffled. "Thank you both... hey, the bacon's burning."

Kim rushed back to the kitchen. Madison wiped tears from her cheeks. "I'm afraid, Willi, for all of us."

Before she could explain, her cell buzzed. When she said, "Nash," Kim and I froze, listening without saying a word. Madison turned suddenly, slamming her hand on the drawing table. "Damn you, Nash!" She disappeared into the painting studio. Kim waved me over and poured another coffee. "She needs space."

I was coming to a new understanding of Kim. Her relationship with Madison had deeply touched both of them. It didn't explain all her other love affairs, but it explained her jealousy of me. Without her seductive demeanor, she seemed softer, very human, and vulnerable.

"Listen, Willi, I realize I did some…" She took a deep breath.

I put my finger to her lips. "There are no winners or losers here, Kim… only survivors and..." my eyes drifted, "lovers."

"I want you to know… I love Madison and I ruined a beautiful relationship. I hope I haven't done the same with you."

Before I could answer, Madison stomped out of the painting studio, furious. "I will not let him kill himself over Cinderella." Her face was flush, fists clenched.

"Madison, wait! What did Nash want?"

"He knew little about the drawings, said it was a ploy to get me involved, and wants—no, demanded—I stay away. He and Seng can handle it."

"What does Nash plan to do?" I asked.

"He didn't say… but I think he's planning to storm the house and rescue Cinderella. A carload of 'friends' is on their way from Minneapolis. I'm calling Jimmy!"

"Oh my god," Kim cried out. Silverware crashed on the countertop.

"Madison, slow down," I yelled. But she ran past me into the bedroom and slammed the door. When I went to follow, Kim grabbed my arm.

"She's in charge, Willi. When she comes out, she'll have calmed. Then we can all talk."

Kim was right. We both knew Madison needed space. I sat at the counter. After serving burnt bacon and eggs on a cold English muffin, Kim perched across from me. She slowly pressed the plunger on a French press coffee maker.

"Both of you were young when you met, weren't you?" I picked at the bacon.

"When I met Madison, she was a virgin."

"A virgin? She had a six-year-old kid."

"Because you get fucked, Willi, doesn't mean you're not a virgin. She knew nothing about a relationship with another woman." Kim poured coffee, eyes drifting upwards, catching my stare.

"If you were so concerned about Madison, why did you betray us at the Des Moines show?"

"What you did wasn't right." Kim squeezed her lips together but didn't avoid my eyes. "The real reason, I was jealous. Not only of you, but her talent. I was furious when Peter would swoon over her work. She was a true genius. Imagine Edgar Styles signing one *of my* paintings. Inconceivable. Yet, he signed all four of her drawings."

"And what did you say to Evelyn Hirshhorn?"

"After I notified the show directors, Evelyn came to my booth and announced I was the winner. I don't think she knew what I had done. I told her that Madison should get the award." Kim grabbed the coffee pot and filled my cup.

"And?"

"Evelyn said she already knew that… that Madison was exceptional, but the circumstances were devious." Kim's sad eyes returned to mine. "You're also exceptional, Willi. It's difficult for an artist to see their own work, but those giant platters you throw are amazing. You make it look easy, as though anyone could do it. People come into my booth all the time and tell me they could splash paint too. What a joke! To you and me, talent doesn't feel special, it's just part of us. But Madison is in a category that borders somewhere on the edge of the universe…. She makes surrounding work seem… common. I told Evelyn she should follow up with Madison."

"Evelyn followed up. She's offered Madison a show in New York."

"How not surprising and so Madison. She probably turned it down."

"Close… she accepted the invite, but there are complications."

"Tell me about it." Kim laughed, reached across the countertop, and squeezed my hand. "You're a good man, Willi. I'm glad you found each other."

Her words seemed genuine, and so did her affection.

A moment later, Madison charged into the room. "Hope you don't mind. I borrowed some clothes." She wore a pants suit that would be perfect for working in a corporate insurance office. She stopped mid-step. "Wait a minute. I need cash. As much as you two can muster." She ran into Kim's painting studio. Kim shrugged her shoulders and retreated to her bedroom. I pulled a cloth sack from my backpack. Five minutes later, Kim returned dressed like a museum docent. Madison carried in a small paper bag with handles and clunked it on the countertop.

"I want to make it look like it's overflowing with twenties." Two metal cans and Kleenex tissue took up the bottom half. Kim threw in a handful of bills. By the time I finished, five of the six thousand I brought was part of the stash. Madison crumpled up the money, adding three hundred of her own. It all happened so fast I hardly had time to think about what I was doing. When we finished, cash leveled with the top edge.

"Thank you," she said. "You'll get it all back. I promise."

"Why a sack of cash?" I asked.

"We'll need something to get in the door." Madison seemed nervous. "If we don't need it, all the better, but I want to be prepared. I talked to Graveno, and he assured me it would be a business meeting. He was definitely interested in Styles' drawings."

"Wait! You talked to Graveno? When did this happen?"

A knock on the door startled us. Madison glanced at Kim. I looked at Madison. Kim stared at me.

"Willi, look through the peep. See who's there."

I soft-stepped across the room and peered out.

My face turned ashen. "We're fucked," I whispered. "Reid Johnson is in the hallway, wearing a suit coat and tie." He looked like a salesman... or hitman.

"How did he get in without buzzing you?" Madison whispered.

"No matter now. Back door." Kim waved her arm.

"Willi, take the cash bag!"

So much for my question about Graveno. Madison grabbed four long packing tubes leaning against the drawing table. I assumed they contained the drawings with Styles' signature on them.

"Are you giving those to Graveno?" Kim's eyes panicked.

"Not all at once," she replied. "We need something to get him interested."

We ran down the back stairs to the underground parking lot. I puffed, sprinting behind the two women. I felt like a desperado running from a crime scene. Except, I wasn't sure what crime we committed.

"Willi, let Kim drive. She knows Chicago." I threw her the keys and took the back seat.

Everyone in the art fair world knows how to drive a van. Kim slammed the pedal to the floor, and with tires squealing, we roared out of the parking ramp.

CHAPTER 28

FIRESTORM

"HOW DO YOU KNOW WHERE you're going?" I asked.

"Traced the house number," Madison answered. "Then made sure by referencing it using Google earth street view... Kim, watch out!" A pedestrian barely made it to the sidewalk as she raced down the street.

"41465," Kim said. "Same date Booth shot Lincoln."

"TMI," I said. "Didn't need to know that."

Kim laughed. "I agree." She sped through yellow lights, cut through traffic like a knife slices soft cheese. When she turned onto Lake Shore Drive, lines of cars snaked in fits of stop and go.

Madison's eyes were all over her cell map. "Turn off on South Loop head for Roosevelt," Madison yelled. "If Reid calls Graveno, we're..." her eyes flipped back to her phone.

"Fucked," Kim finished the sentence as she cut over three lanes and engineered her way onto South Loop.

"Your driving is unbelievably... bad."

"Opportunistic. It's how I paint, Willi. Between the cracks of thought, between the time it takes to load the brush till it strikes the canvas, there is a world of opportunity."

"Bullshit," Madison laughed. "No brush, no painter, just paint."

"See," Kim smiled, "it takes talent to know talent. Art is a fundamental force in the universe, like gravity. And, by the way, so is love." She glanced at Madison.

I chimed in. "My teacher once said my problem was that I'm always looking with my eyes."

Both Kim and Madison laughed.

"He was right, Willi," Kim said. "Unless those eyes are windows into the heart." She turned her head, "Eyes open or closed, I love both of you."

At that moment, I fell in love with Kim.

WE TURNED ON SOUTH LOOP, which melded into Roosevelt, and headed to the outer edges of Chicago proper. Traffic in the opposite direction jammed the street, but Kim lost no time taking advantage of fewer cars heading west. Anxiety driven by adrenaline overloaded my visceral senses, fingers tingled, pulse thumping. There were so many unknowns in front of us, it felt like we had entered a tunnel with no exit in sight. She drove wild, as though chased, and maybe we were, by time, by destiny, or something worse, fate. Everyone sat subdued till we reached Jackson, six blocks from the target address. Kim pulled over.

"What's the plan?"

Madison gripped the door handle. "Before this begins, I want to say how much this means to me. I love both of you so dearly. If I lose Nash, part of me dies with him. Our efforts are about saving him. This is a performance, and everyone has a part."

"Okay," I said. "And my part is…?"

"First, we'll switch drivers, then scout the block a couple of times. You'll drop us in front of the house, circle around the block, and park by the corner."

"Sit in the car? No way." I shook my head.

Madison paid no attention to my protest. "Two drawings will remain with you. When I call, get out of the car and walk to the front door. Bring the other two tubes with you. Do nothing till I call." She ran her hand over her face as if to clear her thoughts. "Kim and I will head in, meet Graveno, show him the first two drawings, and make the deal."

"What's my part, Madison? Why take me in?" Kim asked.

"You're the authenticator. You'll give the proof these drawings are real. Graveno might know you by reputation and will want proof directly from the expert. And, you've got to tell him the set is worth far more than just two."

"Then what?" I asked.

"Either he accepts the deal, or he doesn't. If he does, we walk out with Cinderella, and hand over the other two drawings."

"Why the paper bag full of money?"

"We'll need an in. Guards at the door will think we're there to buy meth. Not only that, it will sweeten the deal and add insurance with Graveno."

I got out of the vehicle and met Kim halfway around. We passed without looking each other in the eyes. Her face looked pale. I swung behind the wheel.

Madison's cell buzzed—it was Nash.

"I'm in front of Graveno's house now," her first words. There was some garbled yelling, which Madison interrupted. "I'm doing the trade. We'll have Cinderella within the hour." More yelling from the other end. "I'll call you when we have her. Don't do anything stupid!" She hung up and turned to us. "No matter what, he'll be here in thirty minutes. Let's go."

She looked into my eyes with that same intense stare as when she worked, except there was no love, only determination. I started up the street.

Three-story row houses built in the twenties and thirties lined both sides of the street. The neighborhood was in disrepair: Large front porches, steep roof angles, and tiny yards, a forgotten section of the city, where lower middle-class working people eked out a living. Kids playing street soccer cleared out as we drove up the block. We drove past Graveno's house. The front steps were in need of repair, paint peeling from the first floor up, third-floor dormer windows boarded, exactly as drawn. Two tall, skinny men sat on chairs on the porch, feet up on the railing, smoking something, not tobacco. A car parked curbside looked suspicious, four young guys inside, windows open, head scarfs and tattooed arms, radio blaring—gang-bangers buying dope. I tried not to stare at the house, but Kim and Madison absorbed the entire scene. At the end of the block, I turned to make another pass-by.

"Narrow sidewalk between houses led to a back alley. Did you catch that?"

Kim nodded, yes. "There was a side door, slightly open."

"Same on the second floor, right side window open about an inch, curtains partially drawn."

"Did you notice something strange on the roof?" Madison continued.

"Yeah, a small platform next to the third-floor dormer, where someone could stand lookout. But no one was there."

"They didn't need a person; a camera mounted under the peak. And another one above the front door."

"I saw that too," Kim said. "Did you notice the front window curtains?"

"The windows were original to the house, leaded. The curtains, raggy, ancient," Madison answered. "The place is a firetrap."

Their description was so amazing I wondered if I missed the entire house. "But isn't the most important part the layout inside?" I said.

"I saw a fireplace through the front door window. One of those early coal burners with a cast iron front," Madison continued.

"Yeah," Kim nodded, "that usually means a staircase on the right and the living room on the left. Victorian leftovers."

"I'd guess that behind the living room is a meth lab and Graveno's main office. A quick exit would be out his office door, by-passing the kitchen and to the side entrance."

Kim nodded. "I agree." It's as if the two of them had constructed the interior of the downstairs with one pass by.

"Should I drive by again?" I asked.

"No." Kim and Madison spoke at the same time.

I drove around the block and parked in front of the house. The gang-bangers had left. As Madison got out, I said, "They'll never let you in with a Glock stuck in your pants."

"I know, Willi. They'll disarm the gun, take the magazine."

"Then what?"

She got out, closed the door, and tapped on my window. "Give me your hand." I stuck it through the window. She placed a single bullet on my palm. "When you come to Graveno's office, hand me this. It's a tracer bullet. Don't let anyone see it."

"This is crazy."

"It's extreme but may be our only way out." She held up her cell. "If I don't call in thirty minutes, you phone me. If I don't answer, call the cops."

I couldn't believe that was her backup plan. In thirty minutes, she could be dead. The weird butterfly feeling in my stomach was more like a prelude to puking. *Get over it, Willi*, I told myself. I put the bullet in my pocket and watched the two of them march up the front walk.

They looked like a lawyer and client headed for court. As they approached the stairs, the two skinny men sitting on the front porch jumped up. After a brief conversation, Madison unpacked her gun from the back of her pants, snapped the clip out, and gave it over. One man pulled back the carriage, a live bullet ejected. Madison smiled. He returned the gun with a stern look. After a thorough pat down, including groping under her shirt, she slipped the weapon into her pant's pocket. The two guards turned their attention to Kim. She opened the paper bag full of money, which produced big smiles. After the pat down, the two women disappeared inside. I pulled away, a river of sweat running down my armpits. If I could take back one moment of my life, it would be letting the two of them walk alone into that house.

I swung around the block and parked behind an Amazon delivery truck. When he pulled away, I had a clear view of the house. I was just another car on the street.

A group of kids playing soccer thumped the ball against my van. I rolled down the window. "Hey," I shouted, "be careful." One kid came over. Maybe he was nine years old.

"What's your problem, mister?"

"Don't hit the vehicle."

"Maybe your van is in the goal line." He put his hands on his hips and stared me in the eye. Two other boys joined him. They reminded me of a pack of hyenas.

"Maybe you should move your goal lines. There's a lot of cars parked here."

"Maybe you don't belong here. Never saw you before." The kids disappeared back into the street and continued playing. But he was right. I didn't belong here. I knew nothing about the neighborhood, the people who lived here, nothing about meth houses or the people who run them. Before another thought could drip out of my hyperactive mind, my cell rang. It was Madison.

"Willi, bring in two tubes." She hung up.

It looked like negotiations were going as planned. Part of me wanted to call the cops now, but the part that prevailed got me out of the vehicle walking up the street carrying the drawings. Who would suspect their value in the hundreds of thousands of dollars? If I hadn't checked out Styles' work on the internet, I wouldn't have believed it myself. One of his paintings sold in Europe for two point six million.

When I reached the front porch, one of the skinny men frisked me, the other punched a number into his cell. "Ya, he's here… yes, he's clean." He opened the door and I walked in. As Madison described, the coal fireplace was directly in front of me, with a stairway on the right side. A big burly man with a gun holstered in a shoulder strap escorted me through the living room to the back of the house. Ragged furniture stunk of cigar smoke and mildew, cigarette burns on the cushions, stuffing popping out of two recliners, a large flat screen tv was the only thing hung on the walls. Bleak would be too kind of a description.

The burly man left me in front of a closed door. "Wait until you're called in," he said, then retreated to the living room. I assumed the door was to Graveno's office. How many others had waited nervously to meet 'the boss', either buying dope or dealers settling up, some pleading for their lives.

Madison opened the door, her face ashen, but eyes determined. "He wants to see all four drawings," she whispered. She put out her hand. As I reached for the bullet, the tubes slipped from my grasp and crashed to the floor. While I gathered them together, Madison slid the Glock from her pocket, opened the carriage, jammed the bullet in, and snapped the carriage shut in the time it took me to collect the scattered drawings. Without another word, we entered a room reeking of acetone, lantern fluid, and ether. It could've been a hospital and painting studio mixed together. But it wasn't, it was a meth lab, and the odor burned my nose. In the back of the room, large containers of kerosene sat on the table near a lit Bunsen burner tended by an assistant cooking meth. A large, open bag of white powder flopped on the table. I knew little about this operation, but it looked careless and dangerous. That Graveno would have his office in a meth lab surprised me.

Graveno sat behind a cluttered oak desk. He wore a sports jacket over a thin Hawaiian shirt, bushy eyebrows, clean-shaven, hair greased back. Under his jacket, a shoulder holster strapped across his chest, the gun, a Colt forty-five, lay on his desk, near his hand.

He looked up. "The boyfriend?" Graveno laughed. "Pathetic." His voice was gravelly, eyes hawklike.

I handed the tubes to Madison. "Mr. Graveno…" Kim began, but he held up his hand.

"Wait a minute girlfriend or whoever you say you are. You said you snort, right?"

Kim nodded. "Yeah, so what?"

"So maybe you and me do a line."

He snapped his fingers and the man working behind him poured some white powder on a sheet of paper. Graveno formed it into a line and laid it on his desk, offering Kim a short straw. There was no choice but to take it.

"That's a heavy line." She smiled at Graveno and pulled a credit card from her purse, dividing the line in two. "Half for you, half for me." She bent over Graveno's desk and sucked the powder up her nose. Graveno watched but didn't snort in the other half. Kim's eyes dilated; forehead raised. "This stuff is as pure as Snow White on her wedding day," she exclaimed. She took a step back, pinching her nose.

Graveno watched Kim closely. "You don't snort much, do you?"

"Been awhile," Kim answered. "Your turn."

"I don't snort and do business," he leaned back, "and I assume you came to do business, right?" It was a trick, and I hoped Kim could still function. "Let's see the drawings."

Madison pulled a drawing out of the tube and unrolled it. The pose was her leaning naked over a desk. It was erotic as hell. Graveno looked at the picture, then at Madison. She turned the paper around and pointed to the bottom. His lip curled, eyes blank. He looked at the picture as if it was yesterday's news. He grabbed a magnifying glass from his desk drawer and inspected the signature.

"You see, Mr. Graveno, that's Edgar Styles' signature. Kim is a curator for many local galleries and museums here in Chicago. She'll vouch that it's authentic."

Graveno looked at Kim, whose eyes were now moons. She covered a giggle.

"I rarely do business at this location," he said. "You're lucky I'm in town, but that doesn't mean I'm not busy. Okay, doll, what's your pitch?"

"The two over four means it's a series of four drawings altogether," Kim said. "These two are worth a bundle by themselves. The set of four is worth ten times more." Madison went to step forward, but Kim stepped in front of her, eyes dilated.

"Listen, I think you and I are on the same channel." Kim seemed confident. "So I'll tell you my part in this."

At this point, my forehead was glistening. What the hell was Kim doing?

"A man shows up at my front door. Right away I smell a cop or ex-cop or something law enforcement. Anyway, he wants these two drawings appraised. I've appraised a lot of paintings, but I know right away something's not right. The drawings look like the work of Edgar Styles, but this guy is too stupid to know what he's got, and he wants a letter of authenticity…" Kim stopped, her eyes rolled up, obviously having a hard time with her next thought. She was one hundred percent stoned. "And he wants it in a hurry."

"Authentication is not like a fast-food restaurant, Mr. Graveno," Madison jumped in. "It's a process that takes time."

"Meticulous work," Kim collected herself. "I had to look close to make sure it's the real thing."

Graveno looked amused. "Tell me, doll, how do you authenticate?"

"First a PH test on the paper, then microscopic evaluation of the pencil lines, making sure it's not a copy. Fingerprints of some sort are on the piece…" Kim paused as if trying to remember why she was here. "Then line comparison with other drawings. An artist this famous has an archive on the internet so it's easy to find and compare."

Graveno shook his head. "Okay," he says, "what did you conclude?"

"A detailed study confirmed my suspicions. The drawings are originals from Edgar Styles, a famous painter, contemporary, well collected. These Edgar Styles pencil drawings are rare, and, as you may or may not know, Mr. Graveno, worth a lot of money."

"How much?" Graveno lit a cigarette, which seemed pretty brazen in a lab filled with flammables. He was enjoying Kim's skyrocketing meth high.

"I'll get to that." Kim stopped again, covering a smile, her fingers restless by her side, her forehead sweating. "I found the model for the drawings on Facebook. It's this woman," she points to Madison, "and I contacted her."

"Why'd you do that?"

"Because the markings on the drawings indicate a series of four, the cop only gave me two."

"And these are two here, right?" Graveno points at the tubes.

"Correct. We've brought the set." Madison also noticed Kim having difficulty keeping it together. "And they're all authentic."

"How do I know that?" Graveno's eyes shift to his gun.

"I'm an expert at authentication, Mr. Graveno," Kim said. "Authentication is what I do."

Graveno's attention shifted to Madison. "Do you two know each other?"

This was an odd question. The conversation was like a ping-pong match.

"We met a few days ago," Madison answered. "Before I called you about a… a deal. You said you wanted authentication, then you'd meet with me, remember?"

"Ya. You're the girl who wants to trade these drawings for Cinderella someone, right?"

"We think you… you might know where she's located." Madison's voice wavered. "Perhaps we can trade these drawings for Cinderella, or you can help us find her."

Graveno leaned forward. "Cinderella and her boyfriend got themselves in some trouble. Cost me a shit-load of money."

"We want to make that up to you and more. In good faith, we brought this." She placed the bag of money on the desk in front of Graveno. He opened the bag and looked in. Deadpan eyes said he was unimpressed.

"What's your relationship with Cinderella?" Graveno blew a cloud of smoke into the air, leaned forward.

"She's a… a best friend," Madison replied. "She's pregnant."

"Really?" Graveno said, brushing pregnancy aside like dust on the floor. "I understand you're a pretty talented artist yourself."

Graveno was leading the conversation somewhere. I was getting nervous.

"I'm a part-time instructor at MCAD in Minneapolis."

"Hmmm. Yeah, I found your picture on Facebook. Came all the way from the twin cities. Long drive."

"Mr. Graveno, we want to trade these drawings as payment for any damage Cinderella might have caused you. They're precious." Madison's voice was desperate.

At that point, something changed in the room. Graveno waved to the man cooking meth behind him. "Charlie, girlfriend over there is going to give you those tubes she's holding. Take them upstairs."

"Yes sir, Mr. Graveno." Charlie moved around the desk. Madison put up her hand.

"You gave me your word you wouldn't steal these from me. We have an honest deal to make here." Her voice desperate. "You said you'd listen."

"Sure, doll, I have listened. But you've come in here and wasted my time with lies. I think all three of you know each other. Maybe you all sleep in the same bed. I don't know, I don't care. But what I know is that you cooked up a scheme with phony drawings to get Cinderella... and your son out of trouble."

At that point, I knew we had a problem. He was no fool. I hadn't considered that Madison would bring copies of the originals or that Graveno would connect Nash to Madison.

He put both arms on his desk and leaned forward. "I'm not very good at art," he continued, "but I'm real good at spotting liars." Graveno picked up the gun and waved it in front of us. Color drained from Madison's face. I gasped. We all stiffened.

Graveno smiled and tilted his head. "Normally, I'd shoot all three of you, stuff your bodies in fifty-five-gallon drums and drop you in the lake. But I'm not going to do that. I got a call from Reid, the cop who says he's got the originals and a letter to prove it. Now, who am I to believe? A couple of lying amateurs who prance in here to make a deal or a crooked cop who wants to make a dime?"

"Reid's such a liar. He murdered Styles to get those paintings," Madison blurted out.

"If he murdered Styles, which really makes no difference to me, then he's most likely got the authentic drawings, right?"

"Not true," Kim piped in. "I saw the two he brought over. Clever fakes."

"And who could make clever fakes?" Graveno's eyes drilled into Madison. "Perhaps a clever model and talented artist who works at MCAD, a famous art school, a woman attempting to get her son out of trouble. You see what I'm getting at?"

I thought I could hear my heart beating. Graveno wasn't buying anything.

"So, I'm going to do you a favor. I'm only going to shoot one of you right now. We'll wait and see about the drawings Reid's got, and maybe I shoot another one of you later or both at the same time." He pointed the gun at Madison. "I've got a stone-walled potato cellar here under the house. Not too comfortable, but I think with a little persuasion you'd make a good whore or maybe we do something else. I'm not sure." He pointed the weapon at me. "There's a gay joint down the block who'd pay a lot for a handsome body like yours." He paused. "Any volunteers?"

Before I could twitch a muscle or Madison could say another word, Kim stepped forward. "Then shoot me." The silence that followed was deafening.

Graveno swung the barrel at Kim and squeezed the trigger. The sound shook every nerve in my body. My head turned like a robot as I watched the bullet slowly tear through the air, whistling like a supersonic jet, an impartial missile, following the laws of physics. The chunk of smooth steel ripped into Kim's chest. The projectile went through her body, blood spurting out from her backside.

Kim fell backward on the floor. I wanted to scream, but found my breathing paralyzed. Madison had already pulled the Glock from her pocket— a single round in the firing chamber. She raised her arm and fired, not at Graveno, but at the bag of money sitting on the desk in front of him. The tracer bullet floated through the air, tore into the bottom of the bag, striking two cans of highly flammable liquid acetone. Exiting the other side, the bullet left a massive fireball in its wake. The pressure wave from the explosion knocked me over. Graveno's clothing instantly burst into flames. His body blown backwards off his chair. The tracer bullet left a vapor trail and smashed into a two-gallon container of kerosene on the table behind the desk. The can exploded into flames. His assistant flew off his feet, knocking over other highly flammable liquids. The meth lab ignited into a fireball, and the ragged curtains instantly dissolved into flames billowing up the wall.

The explosion lifted Madison off her feet. She fell next to me, unconscious. Flames licked the ceiling, shooting over our heads. I quickly smothered Madison's smoldering hair. She bled from a gash above her eye. Kim moaned, bleeding profusely, body writhing, knees rising and falling.

The office door swung open. Curling flames greeted two henchmen, blasting them in the face. I collected Madison in my arms, ran past the kitchen and out the side door. Flames were already leaping out Graveno's office window. I laid her on the grass. Madison's eyes blinked open. Her hand reached out and touched my face.

"Willi, you've got to get Kim. She's not dead."

My blood turned to ice. "Not dead?"

"Get her out!" she screamed. When she attempted to push herself up, I pressed back.

"Don't move. I'll get her."

As I pulled myself up, Nash and two carloads of the Asian dragons squealed up the street, bumped over the curb, drove into the front yard, windows rolled down, gunfire raining down on the house.

My feet hardly touched the ground as I ran to the side door, my chest so tight I could hardly draw a breath. Sweat dripped into my eyes. I grabbed a garden hose and doused myself with water, then ran back into a flaming house.

The kitchen hadn't caught fire yet, but the living room was turning into an inferno. A barrage of return fire from the second floor peppered the air. I crawled on my knees, under a river of smoke and into Graveno's office. Kim had crawled to a corner. I scurried to her side. Her eyes were open.

"I knew you'd come back," she said, blood gurgled from her mouth. I curled her into my arms.

"Shh. We're getting out of here."

My clothing turned into a steaming cloud. As I ran out of the office, my shirt began smoldering. In the kitchen, a body lay on a table, another man stood over him, trying to patch a bloody mess. Kim's synthetic pants were blistered like chicken on a grill.

I laid her next to Madison, who ripped off a corner of cloth from her blouse.

"Kim...." she cradled her head in her arms, tears streaming down her cheeks. Kim's shirt was a bloody graveyard. Her eyes flickered open, managed a slight smile, then closed once again. She was barely breathing. Sirens blared in the distance. Bursts of gunfire came from the second floor and returned from the vehicles.

Madison took my hand. "Willi..." she puffed, "I need you to do one more thing." The top of her head was a bloody mess of burnt hair and blistered skin, turquoise eyes dulled, voice desperate. "Nash went into the house. Cinderella is on the third floor. You've got to get them out."

There was an explosion through the kitchen that blew out the side door. The only way in was through the front door. I zigzagged down the front walk, sprinted up wooden front stairs, dodging bullets. The two skinny guards lay dead on the front porch. Sirens were coming closer. To the left, the living room was a flaming hell, the stairs on the right still intact. I knew I had only minutes to find Nash before flash point consumed the entire house. A few of Graveno's men shot from bedroom windows, not noticing as I ran past. The third-floor attic door was partially open. I took the narrow staircase three at a time. On the top stair, Nash swung around, a luger in his hand.

I put up my hands. "Whoa, Nash, it's me."

"Willi," he shouted, "give me a hand." He banged on the trunk lock with the butt of his gun. "Cinderella is inside."

"We've got to get out here," I yelled. "This place is about to explode."

Nash pointed the weapon and fired. The metal padlock shattered, pieces flying in all directions. He threw the lid back. The odor was shocking. Cinderella laid in a fetal position, unconscious. The crackling burning wood below us sounded like the jaws of hell reaching out of its lair. Smoke billowed up the stairs, flames not far behind. With the windows boarded, the fire had us trapped.

Nash pulled Cinderella from the trunk and laid her on an old brass bed. Her body bent backwards like a ragdoll, clothing soaked in putrid urine and blood. Nash wrapped her in a blanket and wiped vomit dribbling from her mouth. I found a metal bar and attempted to pry boards off the window. Swirling smoke forced me to my knees. My eyes stung. Breathing became difficult. Nash covered his nose with a pillowcase, grabbed the bar from me, and whacked furiously at the covered window. When a flash of red leaped up the stairways, I knew the flames had found us.

Out of that red flame, a fireman came tromping up the stairs, looking like someone had wrapped him in aluminum foil. He had a helmet and face shield over his head and an oxygen pack on his back. When I saw him, my entire body began to shake.

He took off his helmet and swung the oxygen tank off his back. Nash grabbed the tank and covered Cinderella's mouth with a clear plastic mask. Almost instantly, she began coughing. The fireman said nothing, grabbed my arm and threw me over his shoulder in a fireman's carry.

"No!" I screamed. "Not me, them." I pointed at Nash and Cinderella. His grip was iron tight as he stepped toward the stairway. With fire now leaping over his head, he turned, raised his palm to the flames. The fire obeyed, backing down the stairway. Bending my head upward, I looked into eyes as white as pure porcelain, reflecting only the flames below. "You've got to save them," I pleaded.

Stretching his arm out, he pointed at the wood plank covered window we had been beating at. Instantly, thick boards exploded, debris and dust flying outward. But the new opening caused a horrific wind to course through the room. The fire roared up the stairs once again. Without oxygen or headgear, with me over his shoulder, he headed into the inferno. I opened my mouth to scream, but no sound would come out. Surrounded by roaring flame, the fireman walked unhurried down the stairs, as though pushing through a fog. My body should have become an ember, but I felt no heat, no pain. I was inside the kiln, the devil's tridents leaping around me, transforming everything they touched, consuming walls, ceiling, a swirling storm of destruction. His arms kept a firm grip as he trudged through a torch-lit living room. The TV dripped melted plastic and scarlet flashes leapt from polyester covered furniture. Graveno's office was a firestorm. In the kitchen, the man lying on the table burnt like a log in a fireplace, his companion on the floor curled up in flame. The fireman kicked down the back door and marched out into the yard. He crossed into the alley and laid me on the cement. For a moment, we stared at each other, like aliens from different worlds meeting for the first time. His mirror-like eyes reflected my image, and when I raised my hand to touch him, he backed off, looked up at a flock of birds honking overhead. "The geese are flying south," he said.

Voices from the end of alley shouted, "Hey! Get away from that man!" Two cops ran toward us. Boots scuffed on cement, "Stop or I'll shoot!" Gunshots rang in the air. When I blinked, he was no longer a fireman. He wore an old sport coat and dirty slacks. His face unshaven, with deep-set eyes and bushy eyebrows.

"It's your turn, Willi." He pressed something metal into my palm and closed my fingers around it.

"Get away from him!" one cop yelled, waving his gun, not more than twenty yards from us. Another gunshot rang out. Orlando took off, running down the alley. The cop shot again, this time aiming at the fleeing figure. The second bullet struck its mark. Orlando wobbled between two garages and disappeared. A second cop jumped over me in pursuit.

Tears erupted from my eyes. A headache from hell overwhelmed me.

"I nicked him." The cop stooped by my side. The acrid odor from the discharged weapon preceded him. "You okay, mister?"

"No, no, don't shoot," I cried out. "That guy saved my life."

"You got it wrong, mister. He was one of Graveno's thugs."

I tried to push myself off the pavement but couldn't move. "Take it easy, bud," he said. "You're hurt."

The second cop ran back from the alley. "Meisner, I think you killed him. He's lying between garages."

In the ensuing silence, the day turned dark. A lightning bolt tore across the sky. My body racked with pain, lungs stung with every breath. I laid my palm on my heart. It bled for reasons that cop would never understand.

The officer yelled, "Get medics over here, this guy's injured." He holstered his gun and talked sideways into a mini-microphone. "Two down. We need an ambulance to the back alley, asap."

I squeezed the odd shaped metal coin into my palm, still warm from the heat of his hand. Tears streamed from the corners of my eyes.

Sirens blared from every direction. More running footsteps. Medics loaded me on a stretcher as raindrops pinged my face and by the time they slid the gurney in, rain came down in sheets. I was suffocating from grief.

"What's your name?" The medic asked as he pushed two plastic tubes up my nose. Pure oxygen filled my lungs, but every breath was a painful effort.

"Willi," I replied.

"Listen, Willi, you're suffering from smoke inhalation and shock. I'm going to give you something to relax." He opened a box and took out a needle.

All I could think about was a man who had touched my life so profoundly now lying dead in an alley between two garages. My thoughts were so confused I kept squeezing my temples with my fingers. A warm hand pressed on my chest, and I looked down. There was Kim, sitting by my side. I attempted to sit up, but she gently held me still.

"Hold on, Willi."

"Oh my god, Kim. I thought you were dead. How did you…"

"Shh… just breathe." She put her forehead on my chest and her tears wet my shirt. Her back was cold and bloody, yet how comforting to have her next to me. The medic gave no notice of Kim's presence. She raised her head.

"They shot him." My breathing quickened. I was on the verge of passing out.

"Shh… I know, Willi. I know." She placed her hand on my chest. "But now we have another life to save."

At that moment, I sank into the earth. She meant Madison. When I raised my hand, Kim's blood dripped from my fingers. The sound between my ears was horrific. It was my own scream.

"He's delirious. Step on it," The medic yelled to the driver. Sirens blared as the vehicle lurched between lanes and away from the burning house.

CHAPTER 29

SORROW

MY EYES OPENED TO A nasty headache. A nurse nearby changed an IV bag above my head and inspected a needle stuck into my forearm. I returned, but not sure where from. Was the nightmare over? If someone declared me dead, I would have believed them. But life came back, kicking and screaming, presenting itself with a choice. Take me now or my nemesis will take you instead. A tall man in a long black coat stood next to the bed. He had no face. I shrieked.

"It's okay, Willi," a nurse leaned over the bed. She wore a white cap pinned to her hair and a stiff white uniform that smelled clean and antiseptic. "You're safe."

The apparition vanished.

I closed my eyes and waved at the window. "Can you close those blinds?"

"Certainly," she said. "I'll give you a few minutes to wake up. Would you like something to drink?"

"How about Jim Beam on the rocks?"

"How about an orange juice… no vodka?"

"Sounds good." I pushed up on my elbows as she raised the bed. My body ached, stomach nauseous, head pounding.

"Where am I?"

"Cook Country Hospital."

"How long have I been in here?"

"You were admitted yesterday."

"Why am I here?"

"Delirium and extreme shock. Doctors thought it best you spend the night. Your vitals have returned to normal. Outside of bruises and a bump on your head, you're fine, but the docs want to make sure you have no concussion. Would you like to contact someone?"

I want to talk with… Madison Ayana."

I went to grab my cell off the nightstand. To my surprise, I found my right hand stiff. "Why can't I move my fingers?" I asked.

"You held a metal object in your palm when you were admitted. We couldn't pry it out. The night nurse finally removed it. It's in a drawer by the bed. Let me help." She wrapped my hand in a warm towel and massaged my fingers. "You should do this every day, at least for a while."

Her massage was divine, and my fingers came back to life. She squeezed each one individually, pulling and stretching them, then handed the coin to me. The piece was hexagonal, made of bronze, with bird wings embossed on one side, a lit torch on the other. The fireman's face flashed before me, his words still fresh. 'It's your turn, Willi.'

"Are you okay?" the nurse said.

"Déjà vu."

"Of course. What happened was dreadful."

"The cops shot the man who gave me this coin. It was a terrible mistake."

"I hadn't heard about that," the nurse said. Her face was pale, lips faded red, cheeks puffed out when she smiled. "You were one of the lucky ones. The papers reported eight people dead, including one woman."

"One woman?"

"A bullet through her heart. She didn't make it."

I couldn't help choking up. Fantasy crashed into reality—the fire, Graveno's office, Kim stepping forward… a shot, Orlando hovering over me. Then Kim in the ambulance, which brought tears. It all came at once as the floodgates of memory opened. My world collapsed.

WHEN I WOKE, IT WAS morning. Hours had melted into minutes, time fluid like liquid mercury. A message came tumbling into my brain… 'Willi. Come.' A voice so clear I thought the nurse was talking to me.

"Did you say something?" I asked.

The nurse had her back to me, writing her name on a plastic board hanging on the wall.

"Hello, Willi. I'm your day nurse, Sandy. No, I didn't say a thing."

"Sandy. Right. What time is it? I have to see my…um, where is… Madison Ayana, do you know which floor?" Words fumbled from my mouth.

"Your wife's on a floor above us, Willi. In a burn unit."

"My wife… of course. I want to see her."

"She's been asking for you, too. I'll see if she's available."

"My wife!" I cried out. Oh my god, yes.

The nurse called upstairs, asked about Madison, then turned to the bed. "She's awake. Let's get this needle out. You don't need it anymore." She removed the IV and the port. I swung my legs over the bed, ready to run upstairs.

"Wait a minute, Willi." She set a wheelchair by the bed. "I'll drive." At the elevator she said, "Prepare yourself. She's in a burn unit. Don't expect too much and let's make this first meeting short."

She rolled me off the elevator and down the hallway to a room with Ayana on a nameplate. I gently pushed the door open. "I can walk from here."

"Ten minutes, Willi. I'll wait at the nurses' station. Just push her call button and I'll come if there are problems."

"I'll be fine."

I closed the door behind me and glided to her bedside. The room lit dimly, machines beeped, graphs displayed moving lines on a computer screen, numbers constantly changing. Madison lay still, IVs in both arms, a white bandana-like bandage around her head, the top exposed, raw and meat-like, difficult to look at. An oxygen mask covered her mouth. When I touched her hand, a smile formed and then tears dripped down the side of her face. I laid my head on her stomach and we wept together. A no-word prayer of thankfulness between us.

Raising my head, I found Madison staring into my eyes. She removed her oxygen mask and pointed to a cup of ice water. I put the straw in her mouth, and she gulped. Setting the water aside, her first words were barely audible. "Willi... I've never been so scared."

"Yeah, me too. You're gonna be alright. Your hair will grow back. That you're alive is a miracle."

"You're the miracle, Willi. You saved Nash."

That was so untrue, but now wasn't the time for explanation. It was the first I knew Nash had made it. "Where is Nash?"

"He and Cinderella are at Mercy Hospital. Nash broke both legs when he jumped, third-degree burns on his back when his shirt caught fire."

"And Cinderella?"

"Severe malnutrition, minor fractures. She fell on Nash."

"I told the doctors you're my husband." She drew me close, then bit my ear.

"Ouch!" I laughed. "I told them you're my vampire wife."

Her eyes danced over mine. "I am carrying your child."

"And?"

"On time and fine." She pulled me close again, lips touched, lightly. "I love you, William August Moses Steuben."

"And I love you, Madison Ayana."

"Madison Bright Eyes Ayana."

"There's always something to learn about you, isn't there?"

"Always." She placed her hand over mine. Tears formed once again and ran down her cheeks.

"Kim... they said she didn't make it."

I nodded. "Kim died on the way to the hospital."

Saying the words opened a spigot of grief for both of us, but Madison made no sound. Her hand crushed mine and her body shook. The memory of Graveno pointing the gun, and Kim saying, 'then shoot me,' was a fresh wound. I climbed on top of the covers and put my arm around Madison's waist. The gravity of deep heartache glued us together.

"I'm not supposed to tense my face," she wept. "It'll upset the skin grafts."

"Grief will have its own way, Madds."

"Kim used to call me Madds." Tears flowed again.

"She's sitting right here, in this room." My eyes were blurry. "I know it."

"I've felt her arms around me… just like in the apartment before we left," she spoke between spasms of deep breath.

I had no doubt that she had. The unknown had pierced both of our lives. It was either acceptance or insanity.

Her hand squeezed mine. I kissed her wet cheeks and tender lips, her bandage-covered forehead and eyelids, and our tears mixed in a cocktail of sorrow.

Madison placed the oxygen mask over her mouth and gulped air. I swung off the bed, held her hand for what seemed like hours, sweaty fingers interlocked, molecules and atoms giving and receiving strength. She closed her eyes and fell silent. Kim was right. You can't see love, can't measure it, or possess it, yet it's as real as any force in the universe. After a few minutes, I adjusted Madison's mask, pulled the covers to her shoulders. She had fallen asleep. I tiptoed out the door. Nurse Sandy came down the hallway.

"Is she going to be… alright?" I asked.

"It's not easy to have your hair burned off the top of your head. It'll be a week before she's released and several weeks before she recovers. She's lucky to be alive. It was quite the fire." She rolled me down to the elevator.

"Fire? You know about the fire?"

"It was all over the news."

I let out a deep breath. What lay in front of us seemed as complicated as what we'd just come out of, a thought that proved prophetic. When I returned to my room, two detectives were waiting.

CHAPTER 30

QUESTIONS

"MR STEUBEN, I'M LIEUTENANT INSPECTOR Charles Woods, Chicago police, fourth precinct, this is my partner, Sergeant John Sty." He held up a badge that looked official. The lieutenant wore a fedora and an overcoat with big pockets. He was clean-shaven, with beady eyes and a big chin. His partner wore the same brand coat. They must've shopped at the same Goodwill.

"We'd like to ask you a few questions," the lieutenant began. Nurse Sandy rolled me to the bed.

"Your breakfast is waiting." She eyed the cops. "He hasn't had a meal since yesterday."

"We understand," the lieutenant answered. "This shouldn't take long."

I settled between the covers. The light above my bed shone like a single bulb in an interrogation room. But the conversation started with a surprise.

"Congratulations, Mr. Steuben. You brought down a gangster we've been trying to nail for years."

I raised my eyebrows. "Graveno?" I said.

The cops looked at each other. "So, you knew Joey Graveno?"

"Not really."

"Were you in his house during the fire, Mr. Steuben?"

"Yes, I was."

"Were you hired to take out Joey Graveno?"

~ 224 ~

The question was so ridiculous I almost laughed.

"Mr. Steuben, your answer."

I was about to respond when a voice from the doorway said, "You don't have to answer that." Jimmy walked into the room.

The lieutenant swung around. "And who are you?"

"I'm his counsel." Jimmy strode bedside. "And you?"

The cops flashed their badges. "Why would you need a lawyer, Mr. Steuben?"

"You don't have to answer that either, Willi. Whenever cops ask questions, you have a right to counsel."

"Cooperation now will save you a lot of time later, Mr. Steuben." The cops pushed back.

"Okay," I said. "I've nothing to hide. Ask away."

Jimmy leaned over the bed and whispered, "You've plenty to hide. Make your answers short and vague."

"Why were you in Graveno's house?" The lieutenant took the lead.

"We believed he had kidnapped a friend. We wanted to make a deal."

"What kind of deal?"

Jimmy looked over at me. His sharp eyes told me to be careful.

"We had brought cash. We were trying to buy her back."

"Buy who back?"

"Her name is Cinderella."

The cops looked at each other. "Was she a hooker?"

"Look it… fuck you." The words popped out before I could stop them.

"Okay, sorry. She's your friend. We got it. Did Graveno take the deal?"

"No. He thought we were amateurs trying to scam him. The money we brought was pocket change to him. He got angry, threatened to shoot us."

"Do you know Kim West?"

My eyes drooped. The entire scene of her murder appeared before me. "Graveno shot her."

"You saw this?"

"Yes."

"Why did he shoot her?"

"Because he's a crazy son-of-a-bitch, and yes. I'll testify against him."

"He's dead."

"I know."

"You saw him die?"

"Discharging a firearm in a meth lab? That was insane. The whole place exploded."

Sandy came into the room carrying my food tray. "Time to eat, Willi." She turned to the cops. "You'll have to continue this some other time."

The lieutenant pursed his lips. "Thank you, Mr. Steuben." His piercing glare said this was not anywhere near over. "We'll be back in the morning." But as they left the room, his partner turned and asked, "By the way, do you know Madison Ayana?"

"Of course, she's my wife."

"There's no record that shows you're married."

Apparently, the cops had done some homework. "So what?"

"So, I'm wondering what was your role in all this mayhem?"

"If your wife was in trouble, wouldn't you help her?"

The sergeant shrugged. When he turned toward the door, I asked again.

"Wouldn't you help your wife, Sergeant?"

He turned and looked at me with blank eyes. "I'd call the cops, that's what I'd do."

Jimmy broke in. "Gentlemen, his eggs are getting cold. Let's leave this for another time."

The police left.

"Look it, Willi, I'm sure you were helping Madison, but things are complicated enough. There's lots of collateral damage here, and we may need the cops on our side, so let's not antagonize them." His words bounced off me like an arrow hitting a metal shield.

Jimmy sat on the edge of the bed. "You did good. Saying nothing about the drawings couldn't have been better. It's a complication the police don't need to know about. You kept it simple, didn't incriminate anyone. And remember, you don't have to answer questions without me by your side."

Sandy placed breakfast on a tray that swung over the bed. The bacon looked like sliced leather. The eggs covered in white slop with a side of white paste I think were grits. "I'll have coffee," I said, and pushed the tray away.

"Yeah, thanks for the advice, Jimmy." The meal came with a dessert that looked like a brown slurry I use for glazing the inside of pots. "Listen, we're out of money. You don't work for free, so what's in this mess for you?"

"Satisfaction. Graveno was a mean son-of-a-bitch. There's another part to the story you don't know about, but first I've got to talk with Madison before the cops get to her." He kicked off the bed, grabbed a piece of cold toast from my tray. "Tell them as little as possible and keep quiet about the drawings." He strode out of the room.

I doubted he worked only for 'satisfaction'.

•

THAT NIGHT, I DREAMED OF Kim standing in Graveno's office. The gun had just fired, and I watched the bullet float toward her. She looked over at me.

"It's your turn, Willi," she said. "The final brush strokes will be in your blood."

Madison appeared out of nowhere, eyes blazing, "I need you, Willi, now!"

I woke sitting up, puffing and sweating. A nurse rushed into the room.

"Is something wrong?"

My thumb still pressed the call-button. "A nightmare, that's all. Sorry."

"Would you like something to help you rest?"

I shook my head. "What time is it?"

"Two a.m. I have sleep-aids, if you need them."

"I'll pass for now."

"Okay, your call. Just let me know." She turned down the lights and left.

I crashed back on the pillow, tossing and turning. Madison's cry for help churned in my thoughts. Finally, I climbed out of bed, put on a robe so thin it was almost a negligee, and made my way through empty corridors to the elevators and up to Madison's floor. The flurry of activity in her room surprised me. Nurses scurried in and out, a medic wheeled equipment through the doorway. At 2:00 a.m., something was not right.

"What's going on?" I asked.

"Are you a patient here?" the nurse asked.

"Yes, and I'm Madison's husband."

"You should go back to your room."

"Listen, if something's wrong, I want to see her."

She stood blocking the doorway. "You can't see her. Maybe later. Her condition has turned from serious to critical. Sepsis. She's fighting for her life."

A cement block fell into my heart, tears washed my face, my body shook. I slid onto a bench by the wall, holding my head up by my arms. That Madison wouldn't make it was unimaginable. Cursing and making impossible promises, I reached into my pocket, squeezing that coin as if it were a magical amulet. A medic sat on the bench next to me.

"I understand you're Madison's husband?" he said.

I nodded, staring at the floor.

"I'm sorry," he said. "She's a very sick woman."

"Sick? She was fine last night!" My fists clenched. "Aren't you supposed to be helping her? I don't get it. This is a hospital, isn't it?"

"It's not that simple. But you can help."

"How?"

Your Willi August Moses Steuben, right?"

"Yes, sir."

"She needs a transfusion, Willi. Both you and Madison have the same rare blood type."

My eyes blurred. "Take all of it," I said. "I'll give you every drop."

Medics laid me on a gurney and brought me into Madison's room. She looked dead under muted lights, her eyes closed, an oxygen mask over her nose and mouth. Machines beeped like an out of sync orchestra. Numbers I didn't understand ran across their screens, bags hanging above her dripped clear liquids into her arms. A nurse swabbed my forearm and stuck a needle in. Red liquid flowed through a thin tube into a grey box between our beds. From the other side of the appliance, blood flowed through a tube connected to Madison's arm. In between, numbers tumbled like a slot machine. I remember a nurse saying, "We've lost her."

The bed vibrated, like a seat in a rocket launch. The room darkened, and all beeping ceased. I drifted for a moment in a dark universe until a hand shook me.

"Willi, you can open your eyes." It was Madison's voice.

I stood in her painting studio, looking at myself in the mirror, half my body painted. She was laughing. "You look beautiful."

"What the hell?"

"That's you, Willi. The part you don't see."

"Madison? Is this a dream? What's happening?" The trapeze hung overhead, the large canvas with my outline behind me, cans of paint everywhere. Was I drugged, or were we both dead?

"What am I to do?" I asked.

She stood before me, head shaved clean, clothes scattered on the floor. "Paint me, Willi. I want every bright color in the universe on my body." She handed me the brush. "It's up to you."

I splashed and splattered, threw cupfuls, then cans full of glowing paint over her front side. She laughed and demanded more, then turned around. I went at her backside with the same ferociousness. Paint splattered everywhere. She turned again, bent her head down and I poured paint over her hairless scalp. The canvas behind her splashed with color, camouflaging her body. She began blending into background pigment until I couldn't tell her from the canvas. Her three-dimensional body faded into a two-dimensional painting. I was losing her.

A voice from behind me said, "Try this." Kim appeared out of nowhere. With an iron grip, she grabbed my arm and slashed my wrist with a knife.

"The final strokes are in your blood," she said. Thick red liquid spurted like a fountain from my vein. Kim held my wrist to Madison's open mouth, blood splashing over her face and dripped from her lips. Madison stepped out of the painting. Kim spread the viscous liquid over Madison's body using her hands, transforming her into a blood-soaked goddess, ember red, porcelain white eyes surrounding deep turquoise irises. Kim kissed her on the lips, smearing blood across her mouth.

"It's not over," Kim said. She faded away like smoke rising from a fire. A blinding light burst throughout the room, and I fell to my knees in a pool of blood. My blood.

I woke with a deep gasp. Machines beeped, an oxygen pump swished, and lights from computer screens created a dull pall over the darkened room. I wasn't sure what world I lived in or if I was dead. Madison lay still in the bed next to mine, her chest rising and falling rhythmically. Everyone was gone except one nurse, changing an IV bag.

"You're awake?" She walked to my bedside. "Congratulations. You literally brought her back from the dead."

A tidal wave of sorrow and relief released a flood of tears, and I wept silently in the darkness, as Madison's machines piped out a symphony of sounds. The nurse dabbed my cheeks and gave a sweet smile. "She'll be fine," she said. "And so will you."

I raised my pulsing arm where the needle had been stuck in. On my wrist was a thick scar where Kim had sliced me. I couldn't believe it.

·

A WHIFF OF SCRAMBLED EGGS and bacon sifted into my consciousness. But it was the aroma of hot coffee that opened my eyes. I was back in my room. The morning nurse was new yet seemed aware of my 'situation'. She removed the cover from my breakfast plate. Her eyes found mine. "The police are checking in at the nurses' station, Willi. They'll be here in ten minutes. I wanted to give you a heads up."

"Thanks," I replied. I wasn't sure where to start the day. When I went to grab my phone, she gently put her hand on my arm. "Eat first. It's been a while since you've had nutrition. I began by nibbling, then cleaned the plate. I was hungry. Jimmy answered when I rang Madison's cell.

"What are you doing in Madison's room?" I asked.

"I told them I was her brother."

"She doesn't have a brother."

"Are you sure about that? Listen, Willi, I knew nothing about what happened up here last night. You're a hero."

"Hardly." The scar on my wrist looked like attempted suicide. "What are you doing there?"

"I thought I'd coach Madison before the cops came up—but she's not fully awake yet."

"I hear voices, Jimmy. Who's there with you?"

"A group of doctors are trying to figure out what happened last night. Apparently, they're pretty amazed at Madison's recovery. Uh oh, they're kicking me out. She's safe, Willi, for the time being."

"Jimmy wait. I need your help. The police are already on my floor. They'll be here any minute."

"I know this is callous, but I can't come right now. Blame as much as you can on Kim. Her idea, her cash, a plan gone bad, understand? Say nothing about the drawings or Styles. And there's a twist that's not good. Graveno's son has taken over the gang. Things are still a mess in the gang world, but Madison's name has been in the news, so I'm bringing in some protection. I'll be in touch."

"What the…!" but Jimmy disconnected without an answer. When the cops came in for another interview, I was mostly silent. Telling them about Graveno's son would be a complication that would only raise more questions about my involvement with Graveno. My silence frustrated them. All I wanted was to see Madison. They told me not to leave Chicago until I gave a full statement at the station.

After they left, my cell buzzed. It was the nurse. Madison was awake. I slugged down bitter coffee and headed upstairs.

WHEN I ENTERED THE ROOM, Madison sat in a bed, jacked in a sitting position, a pencil in her hand and a sketch pad by her fingertips. She smiled but kept the oxygen mask on. I took her free hand and squeezed. She squeezed back and wrote, 'Thank you'.

"Every vampire needs blood," I said. She touched my ear and smiled.

There was so much I wanted to say, but words log-jammed in my throat. She ran her fingers over my scarred wrist, then opened her sketch pad. There was Kim, slashing my wrist with a knife, a fountain of blood drawn like the petals of a flower.

I let out a deep sigh. Bolts of energy surged down my legs. "Madison... how did you..." She stopped my words with a finger to my lips, turquoise eyes as intense as ever. Words rang in my head, "Yes, I feel it too."

My forehead wrinkled. We'd been through this before.

She pointed to the water glass. While I fetched it, she wrote a note and folded it. On the cover was a doodle of two people screwing doggy style. I laughed. Under it she wrote, don't read till tonight. I put it in my pocket. My eyes filled with tears. The geese were flying south again. The attending nurse told me her fever was under control and the skin grafts were healing. She was progressing at an astounding pace. Doctors said no interviews by cops, at least for a while. And, yes, her cell phone would remain charged. When I looked back at Madison, she'd fallen asleep. I kissed her on the forehead and tiptoed out.

I've lived life in a single dimension. That other dimensions exist were beyond comprehension. Acceptance of such a possibility demanded I let go of reasonable explanations. Connecting to a portal that passed between realities was the stuff of fantasy. The more I thought about Madison's visions and my encounters with Orlando Rock, the more my brain burned. I had attempted to lock it up, push it aside as crazy thinking, even deny all that has happened. No matter what I did, these experiences surfaced as part of my body and deep memory. Madison's words reverberated in my head — 'Willi, let it be.' Acceptance isn't easy. It comes from the heart, not the brain.

AN HOUR LATER, MY DOCTOR released me from the hospital. I called an Uber for a ride to my van, still parked down the street from Graveno's burned-out house. Yellow tape marked 'stay out police' surrounded blackened walls, the roof had collapsed. I wondered if they had found all the charred and bullet-ridden bodies. The house was a burned-out carcass and my stomach churned. The thought of carrying Kim out in my arms sliced through my heart.

Vandals had broken into my van using a wide metal bar. Windows were intact. A box of vases was missing—hopefully a few were sitting on someone's table with flowers in them. Luckily, the tires were still there, and the van started. I drove to Kim's apartment. Money was short and Chicago hotels were expensive. Settling there wasn't the best situation, but circumstance left little choice.

CHAPTER 31

STUNNED

AN EERIE EMPTINESS PERMEATED THE apartment. Everything that gave the place life had left. Dishes from a few days ago lay in the sink, burnt bacon on the counter, my shadow talking with Kim about Madison and love. I dropped my bag on the couch. Death creates heartache that drills into the soul. Her laugh, her voice, those marvelous green irises made her presence palpable. So many memories and so much left unsaid. Her vibrancy echoed within me. I forced myself from the couch and dragged a few blankets from the bedroom. Kim's fragrance permeated the bed. Silence turned to graveyard stillness. She had profoundly touched me and now a crater remained, yet I expected her to walk in at any moment and say, "Hey, Willi, how's it going?" I wiped away tears. On the fridge was a note: 'without a reference point, you are nowhere'. For both of us, Madison had been our reference point. There was so much about her I did not understand.

In the spare bedroom-turned-painting-studio, brushes lay meticulously cleaned, some sorted in cans according to size or type. Multiple tubes of acrylics in various colors filled shelves. Four canvases hung in a row on the wall, a progression of form and color dissolving into chaos. What caught my eye was a sketchbook laying on a side table, 'Book of Love' printed on the front. I opened the cover—an amazing drawing of Madison, in pencil, more like a colored photograph, capturing her fervent turquoise eyes. Several pages were pictures of Madison's body, done in sensual velvety lines and perfect dimensions. Kim's talent was enormous. As I flipped through the book, I found sketches of Peter, and a woman I assumed was his spouse. A page included a nude of Josie Wallflower, and many others. She had drawn the people she'd slept with, including a backside view of me sitting on a bed, a picture so perfect you'd think I'd sat as a model. But on the last page was an image I never expected—Reid Johnson. She had him with a mustache and dark incriminating eyes, jet black hair and thick lips, a handsome face. My mouth dropped open. Had she slept with Reid? I didn't think so, but… why did he show up in her Book of Love?

I closed the cover and browsed the room. Her latest work set on an easel—Graveno's house in flames. I sat and stared at her painting. There was no doubt Kim also had visions. It certainly wasn't Madison's style. As I scrutinized the painting further, I recognized a bloody body lying on the front lawn. A tiny cry escaped from my throat. I backed away and perched on the swivel stool. Shivers ran down my spine. Had she drawn her own death scene? I took out Madison's note and read it. 'There's more, Willi. A lot more than you think.'

I needed air.

CHICAGO STREETS WERE WET. A drizzly rain fell, casting a dreary pall over the neighborhood. I didn't care. I just walked. Nothing felt normal. My feet moved, but my mind and heart were somewhere else. Internally, I paddled up a raging river. Madison's note suggested she knew all of this. As I stood in a doorway watching water fall from the stoop above me, my cell rang. I slid the button across its face. Madison's voice burst from the speaker.

"I love you, Willi." She paused. "I hear thunder. You're outside, aren't you? I miss you so much," her words mixed with the pitter-patter of rain.

"Madison… did you know that Kim… Kim drew…?"

"Yes, I knew. She heard voices, too. But no one could predict such a tragic ending. What I draw is…" she let out a deep breath, "it's only a part. Willi, you've got to understand… the future is huge, ten thousand raindrops, remember? I can't see all of them. But I know this…" she paused again.

"What's that?"

"What's happening to you and me... it's not over."

My whole body shuddered, and a long breath escaped from my lips. "I love you, Madison Bright Eyes Ayana." An urge to kiss her face and her lips rose from within like a tidal wave ready to come ashore.

"Let you heart lead, Willi. Come to me tomorrow, okay?"

I nodded my head. "Of course, I'll be there."

"Willi, gotta go. Thank God! They're finally taking out my catheter." She hung up. I stepped off the stoop and put my hands out, catching ten thousand cold rain drops. Traffic snaked through the drizzle. People scurried past holding umbrellas. Rain washes the streets, but never really leaves them clean.

I DRAPED MY DRENCHED CLOTHING over the kitchen counter, found some trazodone in the bathroom, took two pills with a shot of Jack, and fell asleep on the couch.

Sunlight bathed Kim's drawing table in the early morning. After coffee, I wandered over to the windows and looked out. The world was beginning again, giving everyone another chance to straighten out messy lives. I shook my head and smiled. Thank God for the sun! My eyes drifted to a sketch pad on the table. At first, I didn't understand what I saw, and setting my coffee mug down, took a closer look. The note was simple, written neatly in the center of the page — 'Willi, the number is 4141.' It wasn't there the night before. A shiver rocketed through my body. The handwriting was Kim's— unmistakably Kim's. Crossed fours and big Ws were in her style. I sank down into the seat at the desk. Light circled the note like a spotlight from the sun. It was unbelievable.

CHAPTER 32

SAVED

MY APPOINTMENT AT THE FOURTH precinct police station was at 9:00 a.m. After a half hour wait in the reception room, Sergeant Sty led me to an interview room where I waited another half hour. The room was comfortable, a modern table with padded chairs, a bookcase, water cooler and coffee maker. A painting on the wall was most likely from a bin at Wal Mart. I poured myself a coffee and sat nursing a cup of bitter Joe until Lieutenant Woods came in with the sergeant. Without a good morning greeting, he flopped a folder on the table and opened it up. He picked out a picture and pushed it in front of me.

"Is that you?"

I was totally unprepared. There I was, walking up Graveno's walkway with four tubes under my arms. "Yes, that's me. Where did you get that picture?"

"Security camera across the street," the sergeant answered. "We've been surveilling the house for some time."

"What was in the tubes?" the lieutenant continued.

"I don't know."

"Maybe paintings?"

"It's possible. That's how artists transport paintings... sometimes."

"Why would you bring paintings into Joey Graveno's house?"

"I got a call from Kim to bring the tubes in."

"Were they part of the deal for Cinderella?"

I tried to relax my face. "Kim West was a well-known authenticator of paintings. It could have been work she did for Graveno."

"Graveno liked high-end art. What paintings would Kim be showing him?"

"I never opened the tubes." Which was true.

"Why would she be involved in a trade for a kidnapped victim?"

My armpits dripped sweat, forehead glistened.

There was a knock, which stopped the conversation. The sergeant pushed back from the desk and opened the door. There stood Jimmy.

"Hello, boys." He walked in with his hat on. "Just wondering why I wasn't invited to the party? Usually, the cops notify counsel when a client is being interviewed."

The lieutenant looked up. "Oh yeah. I was eating a donut over at the Dollhouse Bakery and forgot all about you. What's your excuse Sergeant?"

"I was on the crapper." He pulled up a chair. "Have a seat."

Jimmy scooted close to the table. "Please. Continue."

"Let's back up a little." The lieutenant shifted in his seat. "What's your relationship with Kim West?"

"She's a friend from the art fair circuit."

"What's her relationship with Madison Ayana?"

"School chums." I didn't like the way this was going.

"So, can we assume you all knew each other?"

"My client isn't agreeing or disagreeing to any of your assumptions," Jimmy jumped in. My heart lifted.

"Okay. Let's go back to that unanswered question. Why were you delivering tubes, with paintings in them, to Joey Graveno?"

Jimmy jumped in again. "He didn't know what was in those tubes. It could've been next year's swim suit calendars for all he knew."

"Look it, Willi. We know Graveno dealt in stolen art. He paid big bucks for heisted paintings, then resold them, usually abroad. You said yourself it could've been paintings. To your knowledge, were the paintings in those tubes stolen?"

"Listen, fellows," Jimmy broke in again. "My client brought in some tubes at the request of Kim West. He didn't know what was in the tubes. I think that's clear. Why don't you pick through the ashes and find out yourselves?"

Very clever, Jimmy, I thought. *Find out if they have the tubes.*

"We found no trace of those tubes anywhere."

Jimmy raised his eyebrows. "No kiddin'... incinerated. Too bad. Listen, my client has a busy schedule this morning. Why don't you write out your questions? He'll write the answers and mail them back?"

The lieutenant glanced at his watch. "Willi, we could finish this now and you'd be free to go."

I was about to say okay, when Jimmy jumped in again. "If you're going to charge my client with a crime, then do it. Otherwise, he's free to go. Send the questionnaire."

The lieutenant pursed his lips. "Okay, we'll send the questionnaire to your client and a copy to you. We want a signed, notarized hard copy returned right away... or we'll be calling you back in, which we might do anyway."

Jimmy stood, put out his hand, but neither cop shook it. "Let's go, Willi." I walked out unscathed. Jimmy was a genius. But when we reached the sidewalk he turned and said, "We gotta problem. A big problem."

"What's that?" I held my breath again.

"Reid Johnson. He doesn't believe the drawings were destroyed, and neither do I."

"What the hell? Then, where are they?"

"Madison knows, but she's clammed up. Reid is a killer, Willi."

"How much danger is she in?"

"Between Reid and Graveno's son, I'd call it a heavy risk."

"Why not inform the police?"

"After that interview, I don't think the cops are going to cooperate much. They're looking for connections, and I don't want this to get more complicated than it is. I've got muscle coming in to protect Madison."

"We should warn Madison," I said.

"Right now, she's in some sort of evaluation that will take all morning. I'm busy this afternoon." Jimmy had his hand in the air, trying to wave down a taxi.

"Busy?"

"I've got a client, interested in those drawings. Big money. And I mean big."

"So why doesn't this client talk to Madison?"

"Too much swirling about. She doesn't want to get caught in the updraft."

"She?"

"I've said too much. Be careful. Talk to Madison. Reid knows who you are, too."

A cab pulled over curbside, Jimmy got in and rolled down the window. "Be careful, Willi."

I phoned Madison, but the desk nurse said she was still in imaging, she wouldn't be back in her room till afternoon. My next stop was Nash and Cinderella.

•

FROM THE PRECINCT HEADQUARTERS TO Mercy Hospital was a ten-minute drive, plenty of time to mull over what Jimmy said. It fit that Madison wouldn't bring the originals and then use Kim's reputation to back up a claim of authenticity for reproductions. Graveno had listened to plenty of liars in his time, and also to those who were desperate. We were both.

Reid was also desperate, and those drawings were his ticket to the kind of wealth a cop's salary would never provide. With Graveno dead, Reid would put as much distance as he could between himself and the crack house. I was sure he'd ransack Madison's house looking for her two pictures. I called my own backup—Josie Wallflower.

"Josie? It's Willi."

"Hey, Willi, I was just thinking about you."

"I hope it was all good. Listen, I got a favor, a big favor."

"You in trouble?" I could hear the clomping of a horse's hooves. She must've been out riding.

"Madison and I are on the road at the moment, but I need you to come up to Madison's house for a few days. We think someone's planning a break in."

"A robbery? Are you sure?"

"It has to do with artwork. Not hers, but drawings signed by Edgar Styles."

"No way. She owns an Edgar Styles?"

"It's a long story."

"Well, it ain't my line of business, Willi. Why not call the police?"

"Our suspected robber is the police."

"Bad cop, I get it. Sounds complicated."

"It is. I'll explain more when we get back."

"When do you need me up there?"

I took a deep breath. "Tonight. We'll be home in two days or sooner."

"No way. I'll have to find someone to feed the animals. Tomorrow at the earliest."

"Perfect. Be careful about this."

"It ain't the first time I've dealt with vermin. Whoa… wait a minute, Willi. My horse is acting up." The clomping stopped… BANG! The phone jolted from my ear. Then silence.

"Josie? You okay?"

Again, silence.

"Josie?"

Laughter broke out over the phone. "Sorry about that, just a rattler in the middle of the trail. Well, now a dead rattler."

"What the…" I shook my head. "I'll text you where the key is. Call me when you get to the house."

"I'll be there, Willi… it's what friends are for. But right now, I gotta pay attention to my horse."

When she hung up, I pulled into the main parking lot at Mercy Hospital.

NASH WAS ON THE SIXTH floor, one leg in a raised sling-type contraption, the other in a cast to his knee. When I came in, he dumped a sketch pad on the tray and held out his arms. We hugged. Unbelievable.

"Did you bring a beer?" he smiled.

"No, but I brought this." I took out a couple of miniature bottles of Jack Daniels taken from Kim's voluminous liquor cabinet. I walked to the sink, grabbed two plastic cups, Nash filled them with ice from a bucket by the bed, and I poured.

"A toast to life." I held up my cup.

"To miracles," he retorted.

"If it wasn't for that fireman, we'd both be dead."

"What fireman?"

I furled my eyebrows. "The one who picked me up like a toothpick and threw me over his shoulder."

"Wait. You were up there too?"

"What? You don't remember me up there? We carried Cinderella to the bed after you shot the lock off the trunk."

"You're right, but... look, Willi, my memory is foggy. I don't remember you up there at all."

This stunned me. "We put Cinderella on that old brass bed. She was unconscious, not breathing, hands tied in front of her. The fireman tossed you an oxygen tank. Remember, we attempted to break the boards nailed over the window to escape the fire?"

Nash looked confused. "I'm... I'm not really sure what happened up there. The trunk, the brass bed, the window, I remember those..." His eyes brightened, "Oh yeah, the window blew out suddenly, not sure why. I grabbed Cinderella and jumped."

"Well, you're lucky. It could've been worse."

Who would believe some fireman carried me unscathed through an inferno and laid me out in an alley? I changed the subject.

"Hey, your mom's recovering."

"Ya, we talk most days. What she did was," he let out a deep sigh, "brave and stupid. I understand a friend of yours died?"

I nodded. "Her name was Kim."

"So sorry, Willi." He shook his head. "I caused the whole mess."

"I think the mess started long before Graveno, and long before Cinderella." A sad lump rose in my throat. I pushed it back down. "By the way, how is Cinderella doing? I understand she broke her arm."

"She landed on top of me. Her actual injuries were more psychological. They placed her in the psychiatric unit on nine. Drug addiction and PTSD. She's been down here twice for visits."

"And the baby?"

Nash closed his eyes. His silence spoke to the turmoil and grief packed inside. He didn't need to say it, but he did anyway. "She lost the baby. That's another thing we're both dealing with." I could see his eyes glisten, but he held back the tears. "Mom cried when I told her. Cinderella is a strong woman. We'll give it another try when we're settled."

"Oh God, Nash. I'm so sorry. Let's not lose anyone else."

Nash's eyes snapped to mine. "I'm worried about that. I called Seng. He told me Graveno's son took over the gang. That means revenge, so Seng and a couple of his boys are coming in to look after mom. She might be in danger."

"From the son?" I asked.

"Not only Graveno's son, but also from Reid."

"Reid?"

"Come on, Willi. You don't think she brought the originals into Graveno's house, do you?"

I puffed out a laugh. Seems I was the only one who had believed Madison's scheme. "Do you know Jimmy's also hired protection for your mom?"

"Street muscle is better than hired muscle," he responded. "Seng's driving up this afternoon. A few others will be on round-the-clock rotation starting tomorrow."

I wasn't sure this was good or bad and said nothing more about it. We chatted about his plans. He and Cinderella would move somewhere after his legs healed and start a new life.

"I've been sketching lately. Maybe I can find a job drawing comics or something like that. Take a look."

He turned the sketch pad on the tray, flipped open to the first page. The image was clear—he held Cinderella in his arms, her body limp, about to jump out a window, flames billowing into the room. It was exactly as I remembered it. Astounding. Except I wasn't in the picture. It would've made a great comic cover.

"Hey, what's that on the bed?" I held the picture close, inspecting details. "It looks like an oxygen tank and a fireman's helmet."

"I'll be dammed, you're right… didn't even notice that I included that."

"That's unbelievably good, Nash. You've got your mother's touch."

"Yeah, thanks. Can't wait to get out of here."

But Nash's fracture wasn't simple. And Cinderella's recovery wasn't easy either. She was still getting psych meds right and undergoing intensive counseling. Everything would take time. No doubt he had Madison's determination. And perhaps the fireman's hat and oxygen tank were a prelude to another talent. We parted with a big hug. I left with more questions than I came with.

IN THE LATE AFTERNOON, ON my way back to Cook County Hospital to see Madison, I got a call.

"Willi, you've got to get me out of here."

"Madison, slow down. What's going on?"

"When I woke up this morning, I drew something disturbing."

"Okay, what was it?"

"A bullet traveling toward your head."

I closed my eyes and took a deep breath. Thank God I was at a traffic signal. "Are you saying I'm a target?"

"Listen, Willi, I don't know the details. What I do know is that you're in danger. We've got to get out of Chicago."

"From who? Reid? Graveno's gang?"

"Damn it, Willi. I don't know the details, that's not how it works. But we've got to get out of here. The police were in my room this afternoon firing questions at me. They weren't pleased when I called the nurse and had them thrown out. Afterwards, they left a couple of cops patrolling the hallways. All seems quiet now, but something's going on. And I have a hunch Reid is still lurking around. Listen, visiting hours end around 11:00 p.m. tonight. Be here. I'll be ready to go. We're going home."

"Madison, I don't think leaving the…" She hung up before I could finish.

I rubbed my palms over my face, trying to take in this turn of events. Two nights ago, Madison's life was in jeopardy from sepsis. Now it's my life that's in danger. Adrenalin knotted my stomach as I headed for Kim's apartment.

IN BETWEEN THE TIME I left that morning and arrived back at Kim's, someone had been through the place. Kitchen and living room seemed untouched, but the intruder ransacked the painting studio. Four paintings depicting descent into chaos were missing. Her Book of Love laid on the floor, explicit drawings of Madison torn out. The rolltop desk ransacked. On the floor was a crushed-out cigarette. Kim didn't smoke cigarettes. Upon inspection, the remaining filter had Rothman printed in small letters. Reid's brand. He'd been here. Whatever he was looking for, he didn't find it in the studio, and left angry. A shelf of acrylics swept to the floor, the easel pushed over, and a hole punched in the wall attested to that.

I shoved clothes into my backpack and grabbed Madison's bag. I wanted to show the mysterious note to Madison, but I found the page missing, drawer contents dumped onto the tabletop. Reid stole the note. He also rifled through Kim's wallet, her license gone, leaving a few small bills. I wasn't sure what else he might have stolen. I grabbed a couple mini-bottles of Jack from Kim's liquor stash and headed out with the luggage in tow. In the hallway, the light above the elevator flashed. Someone was coming. Taking no chances about Reid coming back, I dodged down the exit staircase. I put the bags down and cracked open the door. Reid, in his police uniform, barreled toward Kim's apartment. At the door, he took out a key, unlocked the door, and went in. With my heart pounding, I double-timed down the stairs to the parking ramp, a bullet racing toward my head foremost in my mind. Next stop, Madison and getting out of town.

CHAPTER 33

ESCAPE

IT WAS FIVE TO ELEVEN when I reached the hospital. Exiting the elevator at the sixth floor, I skirted past the nurses' station. Two attendants drank coffee, faces glued to computer screens. The door to Madison's room cracked open. Inside was dark.

"Don't turn on the lights, Willi," she whispered, rolling herself back in a wheelchair.

"Can't you walk?"

"I can, but this will look more official if someone stops us. You're a transporter taking me down for an X-ray. There's a medic's uniform in the closet. Put it on."

Her bandaged head made me wonder if this was a good idea. "An X-ray at 11:00 p.m.?"

"Time has no meaning up here. If a patient needs an x-ray, the order is executed."

A clean shirt with a badge on the pocket hung together with white pants. "How did you get a medic's uniform?"

"Don't ask. Just put it on." Madison wheeled herself to the door and scanned the hallway. "Grab my bag, it's under the bed." Apparently, she had planned out her escape.

"Where's your sketchbook?" I asked.

"I'm sitting on it. Let's go!" Hallway lights seemed sunspot bright. The floor was silent, most doors closed. One room had the dull glow of a tv screen, the patient snoring—TV, better than a sleeping pill. Two cops were walking away from us at the other end of the long hallway. I rapid-walked by the nurses' station, turned right toward the elevators.

"I saw Reid entering Kim's apartment," I whispered.

"When was that?" Madison said.

"Just before I came up here. I think he was…"

"Shh… someone's coming."

A man wearing a housekeeper's blue uniform came toward us, pushing a cart stacked with towels and fresh sheets. The pants were short and his black Oxford shoes didn't fit the outfit. His gaze made me shiver.

"He's no room attendant," I said.

Madison turned her head and whispered. "He's got a gun between those towels. Get us out of here!"

"What gun?" I looked over my shoulder.

"The one with the long black barrel of a silencer sticking out slightly. I notice details, especially one like that."

I didn't doubt her power of observation and sped past the public elevators to the service ones. When the door slid open, a doctor stood in the rear, reading his digital clipboard. He raised his head. "Come on in, plenty of room." I wheeled Madison in. The attendant rounded the corner, still pushing the cart. I slammed the close button and pushed two.

As the elevator dropped, the doctor scrutinized me with a pointed gaze. "You're new here, aren't you?"

I smiled. "It's that obvious?"

"Your badge is upside down. Top button should be buttoned."

"Yes, sir. I am new. First night." I changed the badge and buttoned up.

"Where are you heading?" His tone was friendly.

"X-ray," I replied.

"Well, lucky you ran into me. We just passed the X-ray floor." He pushed the button for the next floor down.

"Thank you, Doctor. Yes, lucky." The elevator stopped, and I pushed Madison out. Two cops waited to go up. They paid no attention to us. When the elevator arrived, we all entered together. I pushed the button for X-ray on the next floor up. They pushed the button for Madison's floor. My palms were sweating.

"Looks like another problem on six." The officer puffed out a laugh.

"Yeah." His partner put his hand on the butt of his holstered gun. "Two of Graveno's lackies are up there with bullet wounds."

My heart stopped. Madison was assigned a room on the same floor as two wounded Graveno henchmen? How stupid can you get? At the third floor, the officers stepped aside, letting the wheelchair out. We waited nervously for the next ride down. When the elevator arrived, I held my breath as the doors opened... it was empty. On the way down, we stared at our distorted reflections in the polished metal.

"Halfway home, Willi." Madison forced out a smile. "Steady."

First floor reception was a large two-story atrium, bright lights, large glass windows, with an expansive granite interior. A bronze sculpture of a doctor and a nurse stood in the middle of the space with eyes cast upwards, their arms raised, pointing at a large blown glass chandelier, as if guidance descended from the ceiling. Two rent-a-cops stood nearby reception.

I had left the van parked in the circular drive by the front of the hospital. Fifty feet to freedom. Everything going smoothly, until I went to push her through the oversized revolving door. One cop waved us down. "Wait a minute, you've got to check out first." He pointed at the reception desk. My heart raced as I tried to control the panicked look on my face. Madison remained calm.

The clerk behind the desk never looked at us. "Name and room number?" The second cop meandered over, picked a candy out of a dish on the counter.

"Madison Steuben, room 916," she answered. "They didn't release me till late. I want to sleep in my own bed tonight."

"Don't blame you," he said as he typed in Steuben, 916. "Hmm, nothing entered for that room. Wait a minute, did you say Steuben? Willi Steuben checked out a few days ago."

"My husband," she answered. "I'm Mrs. Madison Steuben, same room. Terrible accident." I caught a glance from Madison, and she smiled. Mrs. Steuben had a ring to it.

"There are no release forms for a Madison Steuben. You'll have to wait while I contact the floor nurse." At that moment, a doctor came up behind us.

"Hello, Madison, what's the problem?" I stepped aside, too shocked to talk. The man was stocky, his white coat didn't fit, high-top sneakers for shoes, his hair cut short and spiked, a slight accent. His badge read 'Dr. Anthony Seng.'

"Oh, hello, Doctor Seng," Madison smiled, "my discharge papers seem to be amiss."

I looked at Seng, then at Madison. Unbelievable.

He looked over at the desk clerk. "Madison was under Doctor Nordstrum's care. He's always behind on paperwork and at this time of night, I'm sure he's gone home. The discharge papers probably aren't posted yet. I'll sign out for her." His voice was perfectly professional, mannerisms relaxed. He acted as though he worked here for years.

The clerk handed him a sheet on a clipboard. He filled it out and signed it, Dr. Seng. I had met Seng only once. He was a 'friend' of Nash and the leader of the Asian gang. Impersonating a doctor in front of two cops? Astounding. Seng gave a slight smile, handed the clipboard back to the clerk. "That should do it."

"Have a good evening, Mrs. Steuben. Take care of those dressings." He grabbed a candy and walked to the elevators. I wheeled Madison out as fast as I could.

The van roared to life. I glanced over at her. "Dr. Seng?"

"Nash arranged it. What perfect timing."

She leaned over and I met her halfway. Her kiss traveled to my toes. "I love you, Mrs. Steuben."

"Probably never Steuben, Willi. But I like the Mrs."

Even with her head bandaged, she seemed like her old self.

"Where to?" I asked.

"Midway airport. 4141."

"You know what that means?"

"Of course. Kim wrote you a note, didn't she?"

Shivers ran through my body. I told Madison about the ransacked apartment, the Rothman filters I found, but not the mysterious note written during the night.

"How did you know?"

"Kim left the same note for me. It's a locker number where Kim hid Reid's two original drawings for safekeeping. She wants me to have the two originals."

I shook my head. "That's why Reid returned to Kim's apartment. He found the note, figured the number was to a locker, dumped the drawer for the key."

"There were two keys, Willi. I had one. And you're right. Kim kept the other in that desk drawer. It's possible Reid won't connect the note to a locker at Midway Airport." It made sense, but the drawings were crucial to Reid's plans. He had murdered to get those drawings, and he would use police databases to search for that locker.

At Midway, I parked at arrivals. Madison waited in the van while I dashed in. The airport was almost empty at this time of night. When I finally located locker 4141, the door was partly open. The locker was empty. We were too late. I stood there like a confused tourist in a Tokyo subway station. Despite all Madison's abilities, the future remained untamable. Our actions fashioned unforeseen consequences.

Back in the van, I told Madison the bad news.

"It's gone," I said, catching my breath.

Exhausted, she laid her head back and pushed the seat back to full recline. "Let's go, Willi. We've got to get home." I threw a blanket over her. She smiled.

"You're sweet."

"I asked Josie Wallflower to come up to the house, keep an eye on things."

"Hope she brought some firepower. Reid's a maniac. You better call her."

By the time we made the tollway, Madison was asleep. I called Josie, but there was no answer. After three calls with the same result, I stepped on the gas.

I REACHED ROCKFORD IN ABOUT an hour. The van was practically flying. When the vehicle struck a pothole, Madison woke up.

"Willi! For God's sake, don't you see those flashing lights in your rearview?"

I hadn't noticed. I was doing eighty-five. The cop hung about fifty-feet back. When I slowed, he pulled three feet from my rear bumper.

"Shit!" I banged the steering wheel. The cop hugged the bumper. My stomach floated, and a strange sense came over me, not a fog but an unconscious missive. Thoughts turned into raindrops, the world turned dark and angry, the sky red. I banged the side of my head with my hand, as though I'd lost my senses. The cop pulled next to the van, lights flashing. The van didn't seem attached to the road, it floated as though skidding on ice. The cop motioned with his hand to pull over. I stepped on the gas.

"Willi!" Madison raised her seat to a sitting position. "What the hell are you doing?"

Her voice seemed echoed and distant. The cop turned on his side searchlight. The inside of the van lit up like a flashbulb going off. Madison screamed, "Pull over!" I wanted to scream too, but my mouth froze, foot glued to the gas pedal. My mind was coming apart. I rolled down my window, held out my hand, and pointed at the light. A vibration ran through my body, into my arm, and leapt out my fingertip. The searchlight exploded, plunging us into darkness. I slammed on the brakes to avoid hitting the car in front of me.

The cop turned on his siren, shattering my eardrums. Everything inside the van vibrated, loose change floated upward along with pencils and a water bottle from its holder on the console. With his top lights blazing, the trooper roared past us. Cars pulled over to let him by. Within a minute, he was a flashing dot in the distance. Change, water bottle and pencils crashed to the floor. My fingers stiffened on the steering wheel. Van tires glided back on the pavement. Gasping like a drowning person, I slowed.

"What the hell was that?" Drenched in sweat, I exited and pulled over on the shoulder. Clouds parted, revealing a moonlit sky. Wind from a passing truck shook the vehicle. My forehead touched the steering wheel, heart racing.

"Willi?" Madison whispered. "Don't fight it. Just let it be."

She took two mini-bottles of Jack from my pack, gave one to me. I broke the seal and slugged it down, body shaking like a wet dog. Madison sipped, eyeing me cautiously. Then she leaned over and kissed me. "You did good," she smiled and put her seat back.

"I don't know what happened. I think I went crazy."

"You're not crazy! It's real, very real. It's the unknown and your choices are acceptance or insanity."

I kept shaking my head or maybe trying to shake it out of my head.

"Welcome to the club, Willi."

"I should be in jail right now."

"But you're not. You're here, with me."

"Madison, I'm having a breakdown."

"Boy, does that sound familiar."

"Maybe we should stop and get a motel somewhere."

"No! We've got to get home." She pulled out her sketchbook and flipped through the pages. I turned on the dome light. Her reason for going home couldn't be clearer—a house in flames, not Graveno's hell hole, but our house, flames shooting out the windows.

"I didn't want to upset you. If it means what I think, we have to stop it."

"Oh my God! Josie Wallflower." Grabbing my cell, I dialed.

Only her phone machine answered.

CHAPTER 34

MURDER

ROCKFORD TO RIVER FALLS SHOULD have been five hours. I made it in four. Madison slept the whole way while I drove and worried if Josie was safe and whether there'd be a house when we arrived. I pulled off I-94 at exit three and headed south on Highway 65. Madison woke and rubbed her little lump, her name for the baby. We pulled into our long drive at 4:30 a.m. Walls of nocturnal darkness surrounded the van, pierced by headlights forming a tunnel through an ominous forest. I rolled down my window and slowed. The crunch of the tires against gravel announced our arrival. Wind in the pines sounded like ocean waves. The moon cast shadows over our front yard. The house was deathly dark, not one light inside. A single bulb glowed from the pole barn outlining Josie's pickup parked in front.

I pulled up and turned the motor off. Madison let out a long breath. "Something doesn't feel right."

"That's Josie's pickup." I rolled up the window. "No other vehicles, looks like we're alone. She's probably sleeping. I'll unlock the front door and turn on the hallway light. Come in when I wave."

"But I always leave that light on."

"Ya, well, you had a few things on your mind before you left." I got out of the van but didn't slam the door shut. The whirligig on top of the pole barn squeaked as a chilling breeze blew through the tall stand of red pines surrounding the property. Madison said if she saw anything suspicious, she'd call the police. But neither of us expected much from them. The blue wall of silence was as thick as ever when she accused Reid of harassment.

At the entrance, I reached under the mat, found the key, and inserted it in the lock. When I pushed, the door wouldn't open all the way. Something blocked it. With my cell flashlight on, I cracked the door open and, pushing a heavy object out of the way, squeezed in. A body lay in the front hallway, and a nasty odor filled the space. My heart almost exploded.

In the cell beam light, Josie Wallflower lay sprawled, trussed up like a chicken, duct tape over her mouth. Her eyes sprung open when I bent over her. Blood pooled from a nasty cut on her head. Scattered shards from a vase indicated a fight. The tape muffled her screams. Her head shook violently as I fumbled at ripping it off, then the sound of gasping when it came finally came off. I pulled out a pocketknife and began cutting the ropes.

"Willi," her voice in a pressurized whisper, "get the hell out of here!"

"Josie, what happened?"

"He soaked my shirt in acetone. Get the hell out!"

A sudden light in the hallway blinded me. A tall, dark figure towered over us—a pistol in one hand, in the other, a lighter. I dropped the knife and stood.

"Reid? What the hell...!"

"Welcome to the party, Willi. Tell Madison to come in or I'll barbeque your friend." He lit the lighter.

"Madison's still at the hospital in Chicago."

He pocketed the lighter, took two steps, and grabbed my neck. His vice-like grip choked my windpipe. "Let's take a walk and find out."

He dragged me out the door. His strength was herculean, handling me like a disobedient child. Gasping for air, I opened the driver's side door. The van was empty.

"See, I told you."

Reid placed the barrel against my head. "I'm counting to three, Madison..." he shouted, "come out or your boyfriend gets his brains splattered on the ground."

When there was no answer, Reid pointed the weapon into the air and fired. "The next shot is through his head."

A voice came from the direction of Josie's pickup.

"Don't shoot…" Madison walked out, hands over her head. The single light from the pole barn made her look like a phantom.

"Wise choice," he said.

He waved the gun, forcing us up the walk, past the tearful Buddha, and into the house, his hand still locked around my throat. In the entranceway, he threw me against the wall, grabbed Josie by the hair, dragged her down the hallway, and waved us into the kitchen. The ceiling light unveiled a macabre scene. Madison and I, faces drained of color, stood in front of the refrigerator. Reid's face distorted, mouth curved downward in a sickle-shaped line, surrounded by thick lips. His eyes sunk into his skull, finger on the trigger of a Smith and Wesson. Josie's hands bound behind her, rope stretching to her ankles, curving her body backwards like a bow, wrists bloody from struggling. Reid leaned against the island stove, pulled out a cigarette, and lit it.

"Oh yeah, no smoking next to flammable liquids." He blew smoke in our direction, flicked the match over Josie into the sink. "Now, let's see if I have this right. You fucked up the deal with Graveno, screwed up the assessment with Kim, and almost got away with all four drawings." He pointed the weapon at Madison.

I overcame the urge to lunge at Reid. I'd be dead in two steps. I glanced at Josie. My heart-stopped. Using my pocket knife, she slowly sawed through her ropes. I puffed, moving my gaze to Reid's eyes. He looked directly at Madison.

"Give me the two drawings. No one gets hurt. The DA has no motive for murder. The charges dropped. We all go home. It's simple."

A deathly silence fell over the kitchen. Josie froze. Madison's eyes turned to ice. "Fuck you, Reid."

Reid puffed out a laugh. "Defiant to the end, aren't you?" He pointed the weapon at me. "Maybe I need to show you how serious this is."

I shuffled backwards. "No point to prove, Reid. She'll give you the drawings."

"Willi no! As soon as he has those tubes, we're as good as dead."

"She's wrong, Willi. Maybe you can help. Get the drawings, and it's all over."

It almost sounded reasonable, as if it had come from the lips of a sane person.

"Don't believe him, Willi. He'll kill all of us and burn the house down as soon as he gets what he wants. Remember the drawing?"

"I don't know where they are, Reid. I thought they burned in the fire at Graveno's house."

"You're all such idiots. Tell you what. While you two argue over where the drawings are, I'll roast your friend." He snapped his lighter cover open. When he lit it, a figure appeared behind him. My mouth dropped open. "Kim?" I took a step forward.

"Another step, Willi, and you're dead."

"That's not going to happen, Reid." I lurched forward and raised my arm, palm straight up. The darkness in Reid's eyes revealed all humanity had left him.

Reid squeezed the trigger. The weapon roared. The steel tipped bullet cut through the air, leaving a turbulent shock wave behind it. Blood drops began raining from the ceiling, everything in slow motion. Madison's screams sounded like a foghorn. Another explosion, another bullet, one at my head, the other following a path toward my heart.

I stood without wavering, palm up, as though flesh and bone could stop a six hundred mile an hour projectile. Waves of energy distorted the room, stretching it like a rubber band. With a slight wave, like brushing off a mosquito, the first bullet went off course, drilling a large hole in the refrigerator. My head jerked around. The second bullet was already on the way to my heart. Kim's hand moved slightly, curving the bullet to the right. Hot metal buried itself into my shoulder. Blood spurted, body slammed backwards. Pain spread through every cell in my body. As if in a dance, Josie spun to her knees, stabbed Reid in the thigh up to the knife's hilt. Reid roared. The weapon discharged again. If the second bullet hadn't slammed me backward, the third would have gone through my head.

Before Reid could swing the pistol down, Josie jumped to her feet and caught his right wrist, smashing him with a full-force fist in the face. The big man staggered backwards against the stove. She smashed his nose, blood spattering into the air. Another blow to the forehead. His knees buckled. The gun spun out of his hand. A powerful uppercut shattered his chin. Reid crashed to the floor.

Madison caught me as I collapsed. Everything blurred. Pain exploded from my shoulder. The room tilted. She grabbed a dishtowel and packed it on the wound. With my head propped on her lap, deep turquoise eyes gazed into mine. "You were spectacular!"

I was dying. The thin thread of consciousness snapped. Markers that hold reality together shattered. Mind disassembled. Everything went dark.

CHAPTER 35

THE 2ND COMING OF ORLANDO ROCK

One Year Later

"HOW'S GENESIS?" WE DROVE HOME after a visit with Josie Wallflower, heading for the Iowa-Minnesota border. Madison held our swaddled baby girl in her arms. The road followed the Mississippi, a magnificent drive along rolling hills, fields of corn, broken down barns, and small towns. Like Madison's sculptures, the landscape fit together so perfectly with its odd shapes and dissonant colors. For the moment, everything seemed to make sense.

"Genesis knows how to latch on. My nipple is as big as a thumbnail… and sore. She's going to suck me dry."

"A hungry woman. Josie was so excited to meet her. Her gentleness with Genesis surprised me."

"Josie may be tough, Willi, but inside she's got a teddy-bear heart."

"Josie, tender?" I winced.

"We cried together about Kim."

"Do you think Josie still loved Kim?"

"Absolutely. Love remains involatile. A part of Kim will always remain within Josie. Just like a part of you, Willi, will always remain within me." She flashed a big smile and switched Genesis to her other breast. "Josie said she feels Kim's presence."

"Seems we all have ghosts in our lives."

"You're right. Josie's seen Kim."

"Josie's seen Kim?"

"She's seen her twice. Kim gave her a message."

"What message?"

"You wouldn't believe me even if I told you."

"Give it a try."

"Okay… death isn't real."

"Ha! You're right, I wouldn't believe it."

When I crested the hill, I slammed on my brakes, the vehicle shuddering, and swerved around a lumbering tractor that took up half the road. "It's real if we hit that tractor."

"Did I tell you? Cinderella is pregnant again."

"Um… no, Madison, you didn't tell me. That was fast."

"So happy for them."

"Why did you choose this route home?"

"You know, impulsive intuition. I wanted a scenic drive." Her eyes slid sideways, a mischievous smile on her face.

My eyebrows furled. "You were up every night at Josie's. Has the voice returned?"

She pressed her lips together. "After I drew that picture of Genesis before she was born, I thought everything would go back to normal. The DA had dropped all the murder charges. Reid went to jail." She glanced over at me. "Guess not."

"Normal doesn't exist in your life, Madison." I cracked the window to let in a little fresh air. "I still churn over that bullet missing me at point-blank range. And seeing Kim in the kitchen was shocking, but I wonder if it was real. Thinking about it gives me shivers."

Traffic in front of us slowed.

"Ouch!" Madison pulled Genesis away from her breast. "She bit me. Let's not talk about this, Willi. I think it upsets her." Madison wiped gurgling milk from the baby's mouth, swaddled Genesis, and shifted her position.

"Hmm… our scenic ride is turning into a traffic jam."

"Willi… what if I saw something that night you were shot? Something I should have told you about." She had a sheepish look on her face, lips pressed together.

"How unsurprising." I puffed out a laugh.

"I saw her too."

"What? You saw Kim and never said a word about it?"

"I know, I know."

"You were up during the night at Josie's. Was that about Kim or something else?" Traffic was now stop and go.

She laid Genesis in a baby carrier between the seats, pulled out her sketchbook, and flipped through a few pages. Her drawing of Kim standing behind Reid was shockingly like I remembered the scene, face illuminated by the kitchen light, the rest of her body in grey shadow.

"After I finished this, the voice told me the picture was incomplete. I added a medallion hanging between Kim's breasts."

I grabbed the coin from my pocket and held it between my fingers. "Did it look like this?"

She turned the page. The drawing of the hexagonal coin with a bird flying on one side matched mine. "Willi? Why didn't you show me this before? This is important."

"Important? Why didn't you tell me about Kim?"

"This is proof, Willi. We are a connection between…" She stopped herself mid-sentence.

"I don't think so, Madison. Why us, why Kim? Why now?"

"The right time to encounter the unknown is when it finds us." She reached over and touched my shoulder. "Never lose that coin." Traffic had come to a dead stop.

"So, when MOMA offered to buy those four pictures, knowing that you drew them but signed by Styles, for an unbelievable amount of money, that was the right time and place to sell? Even though two European museums wanted to bid more for them?"

"Exactly."

"The voice told you to sell?"

"Yes."

"But… was it the voice that told you to donate the money to charity?"

Madison looked down at Genesis, who slept in her small bed. "I won't deny it, Willi."

"Nine hundred thousand dollars was a lot of money."

"A lot of children will benefit from it. But something else is coming toward us."

"You mean like the Lily Foundation buying your giant Yoni sculpture?" I side-eyed Madison.

"Yeah, I think they will. I'm talking about a different something."

"What does that mean?"

"The universe is an enormous clock. But it doesn't measure time."

"Uh-oh, Madds. That's getting close to philosophical."

"Okay, you're right. I should shut up. But it's coming, Willi. Toward both of us."

"Why is living with you like riding a surfboard on a tidal wave?" With traffic at a dead stop, a man knocked on the driver-side window. I rolled it down. He wore a white shirt and tie, no coat, sleeves rolled up.

"A truck is blocking the road."

"What kind of truck?"

"I think it's a stalled cement mixer. Someone said it's going to be awhile."

"Ya, okay. Thanks." I rolled up the window.

"Willi, people are getting out of their cars. I don't have extra diapers with me and if Genesis poops, it's gonna get messy. Could you see what's going on?" The baby briefly opened her eyes. I shoved the medallion back into my pocket and got out. I needed a breather.

People milled about, asking questions about a traffic jam in the middle of nowhere. A quarter mile from our van, bridge construction had narrowed the road to one lane, but no one was moving. Cement mixers stood idle with their barrels rolling, their drivers gathered in groups smoking cigarettes, glancing at their watches nervously. Liquid cement doesn't have a long shelf life. When I arrived at the construction site, men wearing heavy overalls and steel-tipped boots ran past, coils of rope slung over their shoulders. A telescoping crane inched its way across the bridge. Workers lined a wooden railing, pointing down at rapids surging fifty feet below. A large concrete pouring bucket dangled from a crane's hook, the chain holding it had snapped. A broad-shouldered man, looking like a Viking warrior, walked lock step next to me. Compared to me, he was a giant. His long blond hair disheveled, blue eyes deep-set, lips thick and cracked. "Boss, where the hell have you been?"

I looked down at my shoes. They had changed to construction grade boots covered in grey mud. I wore dirty work overalls and a yellow hard hat. My body bulged with muscle, armpits sweating like a waterfall. A tag on my shirt read, Arthur Boss, Site Manager. I puffed out words that didn't seem to come from my throat.

"I had to piss. Why aren't those mixers unloading?"

"Listen, Boss, there's trouble. Tierney fell in the soup."

My feet moved mechanically up a double wide wooden plank onto the bed of the bridge. Rebar spread over its surface waited for its cement covering. A walkway extended along the side of the structure. Men pushed past, running with long poles in their hands. From a flimsy railing, laborers stared down at the rapids rushing around an unfinished piling framed by slotted sheet steel and three-quarters filled with cement. Men stood on the narrow catwalk attached to the metal structure, sinking long hooked pikes into the slushy mud. Their faces dripped sweat, distraught men hollered instructions from above, "More to the left, no… more! Deeper. Go deeper!" Fists pounded the railing.

A diesel generator growled behind me, and soot from the stack bellowed black clouds into the sky. The yelling became more frantic. Forty men roaring, their apprehension palpable.

"Shut up," I yelled. Everyone quieted. I climbed down a long wooden ladder onto the catwalk. The giant Swede followed.

"Explain!"

"Boss, when the chain broke, the bucket knocked Tierney into the soup. Five yards of cement took him under." He pointed at the dangling container above. "He fell about ten feet, sucked under instantly. We're trying to snag a piece of his clothing with these hooked pikes."

"Over here!" All heads turned. A worker had struck something. Men tugged the pike. A piece of Tierney's shirt brought curses from above. Workers smacked the flimsy safety rail. I looked into the giant steel lined hole filled with slushy grey mud.

"Shit! How long has Tierney been in there?"

"I don't know, maybe four or five minutes."

I walked the catwalk, letting out a long breath. "Pikes won't find him."

The Swede nodded. "I think you're right, Boss. It's like quicksand. He's probably twenty feet in."

"Get a rope tied onto that crane."

The Swede put his hand on my shoulder. "What's the plan?"

"We're not giving up. Lower that rope."

The crane's giant hook reeled down. The giant grabbed the heavy rope and pulled it over. I wrapped it under my arms and tied a knot.

"You're gonna jump into the soup? That's crazy, Boss."

"You got a better idea?" I looked into the boiling mass of liquid stone.

"Boss, what should we tell the drivers?" The Swede pointed to the road. "There're six mixers ready to unload. We can't let them stand there for long."

I looked up at the sky. Already the color had changed.

"Tell 'em it's not Tierney's day to die."

"Ya, but how about you?"

The Swede shoved pieces of tissue up my nose. "One breath, Boss, and you're dead. You realize that?" He tied safely goggles over my eyes.

With a pike in hand, I signaled the crane operator. The powerful diesel roared to life. As my feet left the ground, the Swede handed me a second pike. "God Bless, Boss."

The crane swung me over the piling. My feet dangled above a death pit. A spotter made eye contact with the driver and signaled to lower me in. The

Swede crossed his heart. Men stood silent. A thousand cubic yards of liquid muck below me, seventy-five feet deep. When my boots touched the surface, the world became still, the sky turned storm red. I took a breath. Two men took out stop watches. One cried out, "Three minutes and counting." My head disappeared under the surface.

Cold mud shocked my senses. I opened my eyes, but grey muck covered the goggles. Surrounded by darkness, the caustic liquid attacked my skin. Nothing could live for long here. The weight of steel pikes pulled me down. With a rod in each hand, I thrust them as far as I could into the depths. It was like searching for a light switch in a dark room. About twenty feet under, my pike hit something soft. I felt a tug and pulled. Something alive jerked the steel pole out of my hand. Covered in slippery slime, my body sank until I felt Tierney's hands grab my boot, then my leg. I clutched his arm and pulled him next to me, but he was a slippery worm, too slick to grasp firmly. Taking the rope off me required all my energy. Cold had penetrated to my core. Crucial seconds slipped away. I managed slipping the rope over his head and under his arms, then tugged. I could feel the suction as the rope tightened. The crane reeled us up. But Tierney was too slick to hold on to. I grabbed for his legs as he rose, but my fingers, too greasy and slimy, couldn't find a handhold. I sunk into blackness as Tierney ascended.

A thousand tons of cement pressed against me. Entombed in total darkness, I could see Madison weeping, holding Genesis in her arms. My body snapped right and left, my lungs burned, fighting to hold in breath, the urge to inhale insatiable. Arms flailed upward, legs thrust downward through cold soft mud, searching for something solid. I sank deeper until movement stopped. Reaching neutral buoyancy, I arrived at the place of my entombment. When something touched me, my eyes sprung open. Fingers wiped guck from my goggles. Not more than two inches from my nose, Kim's face glowed as if a burning ember, arms drawing me close. She pressed her mouth against mine, filling my lungs with precious oxygen. I was desperate and sucked in her breath. Her voice rang in my head. "Easy, Willi." With lips sealed against lips, lungs expanded and contracted as she pumped life back into me. A firm grip locked around my chin, and she dragged me upward. I rocketed into a different universe, past planets, into a star-studded galaxy, and far beyond my meager life. Kim laughed, "Willi, stop kicking! Don't be so difficult!" I reached up to touch her, but a larger, rougher hand grasped my wrist. The suction of the cement wanted me back, but the hand was firm and pulled. My head broke through the surface. The Swede roared like a beast, muscles bulging. Men hollered and whistled, screams filled the air. They acted like I was some hero, but I felt small in an incredibly large universe, lucky to be alive, glad to gulp sweet fresh air.

When I looked into the Swede's eyes, they were pure white, no irises, they glowed like spotlights, his laugher piercing. Clouds swirled in magnificent hues, the sky filled with crystal droplets as though heaven was made of kaleidoscopic colors.

"You did good, Willi," he said, as he tied a rope around my chest.

"Orlando?"

"I couldn't have done it better."

"I had help."

"Yeah, that's how it works."

I teared instantly.

A circular motion with his arm signaled the crane into action. My body felt like a cement block as it lifted, and they laid me on the catwalk next to Tierney. Water splashed over my face, and I blew cement covered plugs out my nose. I tore off my googles. All the while, yelling and screaming continued from the bridge above. I rolled over, looking for Tierney. He already had an oxygen mask over his face. The Swede, eyes deep blue and teary, knelt next to me.

"Welcome back, Boss." I tried to get on my knees, but he gently pushed me back.

"Orlando?"

"Whoa, Boss. Take it easy. It's me, Swede."

The multicolored sky turned to sunset orange. Men were still clapping and cheering.

"How's Tierney?"

"Tierney's breathing. We've got an ambulance coming. Maybe you should get yourself checked out."

"I'm fine," I said.

They lowered a platform and laid both of us on it. A flock of geese passed overhead, honking loudly, the sounds mixing with sirens of an ambulance wailing in the distance. When the pallet touched down on the bridge, the Swede helped me up, feet wobbling like a drunk. Men clapped as they peeled off my cement layered clothing and workers whistled, watching me sprayed down with cold river water. The big man toweled me dry. Someone brought fresh clothes.

"I gotta walk."

"Sure, Boss. Anything I can do?"

"Ya. See that long line of cement trucks… get those mixers unloaded!"

A roar of laughter spilled into the air and a wail of approval rose from the men's throats. Everyone scurried back to work. Tierney opened his eyes.

"Hey, Boss."

"Hey, Tierns. How're you doing?"

"Did you see her, Boss?"

"See who?"

"The woman. She held on to me until you got there."

Tears welled in my eyes, and I turned away so he couldn't see. "That's crazy."

"Life is crazy."

"Exactly right, Tierns."

"You saved my life, Boss."

"Ya, maybe. Maybe she saved both of us."

I headed down the walkway to the wooden planks connecting the bridge back to earth. A few steps from the bridge, my feet lightened, construction boots became my low-cut sneakers, workman's clothes melted away, and once again I wore my sweatshirt and jeans. When I looked back, grime covered workmen slapped Boss's back, showering him with adulation. My body shook and more tears streamed from my eyes.

Madison's deep sobs greeted me when I climbed into the van. My head bent against the steering wheel. Her hand reached for mine, warm fingers intertwining.

"You alright?" she sniffled.

"Ya. How about you?"

She wiped her nose. "I'm okay… What's under your fingernails?" she asked.

"Cement."

"You giving up clay for cement?"

"Seems so."

"She told me about it."

"Who?"

"Kim. She sat right there, in your seat."

I piped a laugh. "She gets around."

"I told her it was annoying the way she wiggles into your life."

"You what? Madison!"

"Kim told me to give you this." In her hand was my hexagonal coin. "She said you dropped it."

My throat constricted as I fingered the metal piece. "You know, I don't believe in any of this stuff."

Madison's eyes shifted, a smile formed on her lips. "Neither do I."

I puffed out a laugh. Madison joined in. Soon puffs transformed into hilarious laughter.

"Never happened," I squealed.

"Nope, never would, never could," she replied. We laughed until it hurt. We hooted like maniacs, like kids daring each other to eat worms. We laughed until tears streamed, until horns behind us blared as traffic moved once again. I was sure Genesis would wake, but she slept through our raucousness. Even as we edged toward the construction site, we passed laughter back and forth like a ping-pong ball… until I saw medics loading Tierney into the ambulance. Then the enormity of what happened fell upon me. The weight of cement pressing against my body, its roughness, its cold terror, dark and horrifying with no air, Tierney's desperate arms grasping me. I shook.

Madison touched my shoulder. "Kim said you saved Tierney's life."

"She saved both of us."

"You can't save yourself... by yourself. We need each other."

"Ha! They should put that on a sweatshirt."

Madison smiled. "That's the reason I wore that sweatshirt on the day I met you."

Traffic stalled briefly as we passed by. The ambulance doors slammed shut and the medics climbed into the cab, lights flashed and workers with bowed heads put their dirty hands on the vehicle, leaving cement smudged handprints. It wasn't just another worker inside, it was one of them. I looked over at Madison. Tears streamed down her cheek.

"Without you, Willi, he wouldn't be in there. He has a son and daughter. The daughter has a gift the world needs, but to get there, she needs her father. It's all connected." She wiped her eyes. "We all have a purpose."

I shook my head. "I met Orlando. I think it was for the last time."

"Orlando passed this one to you, Willi. The voice told me..."

"Told you what?"

"Something." That side-armed smile returned.

I fell into a deep silence. The universe was more miraculous than could be imagined. I was a small boat floating in a vast ocean and simultaneously that vast ocean was me. When I glanced at Madison, her deep turquoise eyes stared back.

We snaked by the construction site. The Swede looked over, and when our eyes met, he smiled, put a finger to his temple and saluted. I nodded back.

With sirens blazing, the ambulance carried Tierney away. The traffic mess cleared. Twenty minutes later, we followed roads twisting around endless fields of corn and beans. Genesis woke and fussed. Madison picked her up and rocked her until she went back to sleep.

A helicopter flew overhead.

"Willi?" Madison broke the silence.

"I'm here."

"What if there was something else…" she looked over at me, "something I should have told you a long time ago?"

"Something important?"

"Um… I think it is." She placed the sleeping Genesis back in her bed.

I laughed. "So unsurprising. And what would that something be?" The helicopter flew low over the cornfields, making a horrendous thumping sound.

"What if you saw a light, a distant light, but that light turned out to be a fire, an enormous fire coming from across the universe?"

"That's vague, Madison."

Her forehead wrinkled. "I… I've been drawing things I don't understand. Pictures of intricate puzzles, a giant wedge shaped form, strange mechanical forms that seem to fit together, but I don't know how."

"Are you saying you've drawn a machine?"

"Exactly. I've got pages full of… I don't know what. Perhaps some kind of… of atom smasher or a weapon system, or maybe it's a spaceship."

It was so incredulous I puffed out a breath. "Spaceship?"

"I don't know. I'm just saying."

She pulled a new sketch pad from her bag and flipped through pages of drawings. Masses of zigzag lines connecting to strange mushroom-like forms wound together like spaghetti, some of them in parabolic shapes.

"Have you shown these to anyone?"

"An engineering professor in one of my drawing classes took an interest in them."

Lines creased my forehead. "An engineering professor?"

"I think he said nuclear physics. He wanted to show them to someone."

Rounding a sharp curve, I slammed on the brakes. The helicopter had landed in the middle of the road. Madison paid no attention. Her pencil moved furiously across a blank page.

"Madison! For God's sake, what's going on?"

Six men, all wearing FBI flak jackets, swung out of the helicopter. Two stood by the aircraft holding rifles, the other four swiftly covered the ground between us, holstered weapons strapped across their chests. Madison folded the note, then reached under her shirt and snapped the chain holding the key around her waist.

"There's four bottles of milk pumped for Genesis in the cooler. A number for a wet nurse if you need one. She should be fine."

"Fine? This isn't close to fine!" I panted. The officers surrounded the van. One of them knocked on the passenger side window. Madison rolled it down.

"Madison Ayana?"

"Yes, sir. That's me."

"Agent Jeffrey Sanders. FBI." He flashed an official looking badge. "Ma'am, the Director of NASA's Division of Planetary Defense wishes to meet you."

Madison leaned over, her eyes like jewels. "You gonna be okay?"

I could only smile. "We'll be fine."

"I love you Willi Steuben." She stuck the folded paper in my pocket. A relaxed smile crossed her face. "Don't read it till you get home." She kissed me, then swung out of the van with the notebook in her hand.

When I attempted to get out, one officer leaned against the door and shook his finger. He blocked the door until Madison stepped into the aircraft. In a swirl of dust and heart-penetrating thumping, the helicopter lifted off. I sat watching it become a speck of dust in the distant sky. Genesis barely stirred. I pushed out of the driver's seat and stood in the middle of the road surrounded by miles of sweet corn stretching to the horizon, the sky as blue as a turquoise marble. From the north, a flock of honking geese flew in a V formation over the tasseled corn, following their invisible ancient path. I took the note out of my pocket and unfolded it.

The key that had been around her waist for as long as I knew fell into my hands. The note read: 'Remember the metal box I took from Styles' house? It's time to open it. It's buried off the NW corner of the studio. The contents will save my life. Meet me, Lake of Isles, Thursday, 4:00 p.m. Bring Genesis, metal box, and a bottle of Redblend. The geese are flying south, Willi. I love you so much. Madison.'

P.S. When you write it, the first chapter will begin—*They Fly South to Fall in Love.*

I had no idea what she meant.

T H E   E N D

AUTHOR'S BIO

AFTER HIS RETURN FROM A two-year pottery apprenticeship in Japan, Bill met and married Cynthia Mosedale, also a ceramic artist. The duo created Linden Hills Pottery, (www.lindenhillspottery.com) and made it an award-winning ceramic studio. They both taught in multiple venues, and sold at art fairs throughout the United States. Their children, now grown, still help in the pottery and at art shows.

Bill took writing courses at the University of Wisconsin River Falls and at the Literary Loft in Minneapolis. His first short story, The Bruised Peach, was published in Pulp Literary Fiction Magazine as a Hummingbird editor's choice winner. *The 2nd Coming of Orlando Rock* was his first novel that he shelved for almost 10 years. His second novel, *The Change*, won an SDSU merit award and *Killing Bodhi*, his third novel, was a Page Turner Award Finalist.

When Bill rediscovered Orlando Rock, he found the characters' voices vibrant once again, but the story they told differed from the one he wrote ten years before. A forceful evolution of the original version took shape.

The setting leans on Bill's experiences at art shows and as a studio artist. The story reflects his experiences into 'other' worldliness after recovering from a near death experience.

He still makes pots, writes every day and enjoys the winding Willow River just off his back porch in Hudson, Wisconsin.

CPSIA information can be obtained
at www.ICGtesting.com
Printed in the USA
LVHW110251030822
725080LV00012B/173